Taming
the Moon

Taming the Moon

SHERRILL QUINN

BRAVA

KENSINGTON PUBLISHING CORP.

www.kensingtonbooks.com

BRAVA BOOKS are published by

Kensington Publishing Corp.
119 West 40th Street
New York, NY 10018

ISBN-13: 978-0-7582-3191-8
ISBN-10: 0-7582-3191-1

First Kensington Trade Paperback Printing: March 2010

10 9 8 7 6 5 4 3 2 1

Printed in the United States of America

Prologue

O livia Felan held her daughter close, breathing in the sweet scent of little girl and bubblegum, and tried not to cry. She wouldn't give *him* the satisfaction of seeing her tears.

Through the open window she could hear the sounds of New York—horns blaring, tires screeching, sirens. Cool April wind blew into the room.

A shiver rolled down her spine, but it wasn't the coldness of the air that made her shudder. Thanks to her werewolf metabolism, her internal thermostat ran hot. No, what made her shiver was the thought that she could lose her daughter, that he would take the little girl from her forever. Fear coiled deep in her belly. The sounds of the City That Never Sleeps faded as she let the feel of Zoe in her arms soothe her.

"All right. That's enough." Brawny hands pulled Zoe out of her arms, though not roughly. "I need to talk to your mother, sweetheart." Dark eyes glanced at Olivia, promising retribution. As he looked down at the six-year-old, stroking gentle fingers over the top of the little girl's head, there was nothing but tenderness in his expression.

His voice soft, he suggested, "Why don't you go into your room and play with your dolls?"

That sweet little head with its long, dark curls bobbed. "Okay, Uncle Eddy." Zoe looked at Olivia with a bow-lipped smile. "You'll read me a story before you go, won't you, Mommy?"

Olivia nodded and smiled, relieved when her lips didn't wobble with the fear crushing her from the inside. She didn't want Zoe to realize what a precarious position she was in—they *both* were in. "You bet, baby."

Zoe smiled again.

Eddy bent and pressed a kiss to the top of her head, his face softening as he watched her walk down the hallway. "You know I love her as if she were my own. I would hate it if I were forced to carry through on my threat."

But he would, Olivia knew. For the Alpha of the pack to voice an empty threat was full-on stupidity and the surest way to invite a challenge. Eddy was anything but stupid. He might say he loved Zoe, but he'd kill her in a heartbeat.

Olivia had no guarantee that he wouldn't even if she did manage to do what he wanted.

"I love it when she calls me 'Uncle Eddy.'" His voice was indulgent, just like that of a loveable, doting uncle. Of which he was none—neither loveable, doting, *nor* any relation whatsoever to Zoe.

Olivia waited until the bedroom door had closed behind Zoe before she turned to *Uncle Eddy*. "I don't want her calling you that."

His eyes narrowed. "Do I have to teach you—again—that what you want doesn't matter?" His voice had taken on that raspy quality she could only equate to a snarl. "You're nothing, Livvie. Nothing, unless I say you're something. And unless you obey me in this, you'll forever be nothing."

She forced back the overwhelming urge to attack him, to do something physical to protect her child. But she knew the only way she could protect Zoe—for now—was to accede to Eddy's wishes.

Someday, though . . .

"No, you don't have to teach me anything." Olivia dropped her gaze in a submissive pose. She was, after all, the Omega of the pack. The whipping dog. The bitch that took whatever the pack wanted to dish out.

It didn't make her feel any better to be told she was an integral part of the pack, that she was the one who allowed them to let out their aggression so they could maintain their façade of civility among humans. It was against her nature to roll over and show her belly to anyone. But unless she wanted her throat ripped out, for now she had to submit.

But one day she'd be in a position to assert herself. Just . . . Not today.

"Good." Eddy sauntered toward her, his thick fingers rubbing against one eyebrow. "Now, what was this you told me over the phone? That Sullivan isn't dead?"

Olivia drew in a calming breath. "No. I was interrupted. That wouldn't have happened if John hadn't played with his food five months ago. *His* target would be dead, and I'd have had a clear shot at Sullivan."

Eddy's eyes narrowed. Clearly he was displeased with her tone. Or her excuse. Or both.

She hurriedly switched tactics. "But I know where Sully—Sullivan—is. Or, rather, where he'll be. He's gone back to work." She put as much conviction behind her next words as she could. "I can finish the job. I can! I just needed to see Zoe."

God, she despised the wheedling tone of her voice. Three years as the pack's Omega, and she certainly sounded the part. Damn it.

Eddy began humming a children's song, and the words to it flitted through her mind. *Ring around the rosie, pockets full of posies. Ashes, ashes, we all fall down.*

God. He'd hummed that right before he'd exacted "payment" by killing the family of the last werewolf who'd defied him. It was Eddy's "tell"—the thing that signaled he was about to become very violent.

She didn't think he was even aware of it. Just the same, it sent ice down her spine.

"So, now you've seen her." Quicker than her eye could follow, he wrapped his hand around her throat and shoved her against the wall.

The back of her head smacked against the hard surface, and she winced. Stars danced briefly before her eyes but quickly faded. It took more than a bang on the head to take down a werewolf.

He brought his face close to hers. The stale smell of cigarette smoke couldn't be covered up by all the mints he ate. "This is the last time you disobey me without repercussion, Livvie."

She focused on keeping her eyes downcast but otherwise not showing any fear. To show fear showed weakness, and she wasn't weak. Submissive, yes, but only because she had to be.

Never weak. One day she hoped she could prove that to Eddy with a finality that would take his breath away.

And she'd give him an extra bite just for him calling her Livvie all these years. She hated it.

She hated him.

"I didn't—"

"Didn't I tell you not to return to New York until the job was done?" His fingers tightened around her throat. When she started to speak, he gave a low snarl. "Don't talk. Nod."

She nodded.

"And is the job done?"

She shook her head. Good thing she wasn't meeting his eyes, or he might see the truth there.

Not only was the job not done, but she'd royally fucked it up by turning her mark into a werewolf.

Good going, Liv. Could you have possibly made it any harder?

"I—"

Fingers tightened further around her throat, and he slammed her head against the wall again. Hard enough that she couldn't hide another wince as she shot a quick glance at him. His face darkened. "I. Said. Don't. Talk." He scowled. "Fucking-A. I don't know why I put up with you sometimes."

Because he had serious inadequacies that he covered by demonstrating his power.

Because he was a psychopath who liked to hurt people.

Because throwing his weight around made him feel like a man.

Take your pick. How he'd managed to remain as pack leader for as long as he had was beyond her. Those who didn't outright hate or fear him seemed to be merely biding their time until they could do something about him.

When that would happen was anyone's guess. Certainly as the Omega of the pack Olivia would be the last to know. For now, Eddy *was* the leader, and that was what mattered. It was the hand she'd been dealt and had to play as best she could.

So she stood still and waited.

Like a good little wolf.

Her pulse fluttered in her throat. Spots started to dance behind her eyelids. If he didn't let up soon, she'd pass out.

She knew that from experience, because it had happened before. It was another way he had of exerting his control over her. Choke her into unconsciousness and, many times, she'd come to while he raped her—one of the many ways he had of showing her just how little she really meant to him and how easily he could do anything he wanted to her with impunity. How completely he held her life in his hands.

Literally.

"Look at me."

She raised heavy lids and stared into dark eyes glinting with the knowledge that she'd gotten the message. He dropped his hand and strutted away from her, confident that she'd stay put.

She watched him, loathing him with each shaky breath she drew. When the bastard had moved in next door, fate had dealt her a dead man's hand. He'd seen her, had wanted her, so he'd taken her, turning her into a monster. Six weeks ago he'd told her he had a special job for her, a job that could elevate her from Omega to something . . . well, something more than the bottom of the pack.

She'd perked up, as he'd known she would. But when he'd told her the job was to murder someone, she'd refused. She was a middle school phys ed teacher, for crying out loud. Not an assassin.

But then he'd taken Zoe, threatened to kill her if Olivia didn't do as she was told. She'd seen him act with swift ruthlessness where disobedience and defiance were concerned. Just a few months ago he'd broken the neck of another pack member's son as casually as if he were flicking lint off his sleeve. So she had no doubt that, even though he might love Zoe in his own twisted way, he *would* carry through on the threat. So this time when he'd told her to go, she'd gone. Thankfully she had enough tenure and foresight to ask for a leave of absence from work.

Eddy turned to face her. "Go kill Sullivan. You have one week."

She opened her mouth, then closed it. He'd not given her permission to speak yet.

A slight smile tilted one edge of his mouth. "Very good, pet." He gave an approving nod. "You may respond."

"A week?"

He lifted his brows. "I've given you six weeks already, two of which you squandered by being stubborn. I hardly think you need more than another week."

She clamped her lips together and gave an abrupt nod. Arguing with him would accomplish nothing except to have him shorten the deadline even further.

He sighed and shoved his hands into the pockets of his trousers. "I'm not such a bad guy, Livvie." He shrugged. "I just know what I want, and I'm willing to do whatever it takes to get it—and that includes killing everyone who gets in my way. Some women find that kind of confidence appealing. Attractive, even."

What kind of women? The ones with a death wish?

She licked her lips. "May I ask what it is you want? Why is it so important that Rory Sullivan be killed? What did he do to you?"

Olivia thought for a moment he wasn't going to answer her, feared that she may have gone too far when his face darkened. But it was remembered rage that colored his features, not anger directed toward her.

"Let's just say there's a man I want to destroy, and I'm beginning by removing everyone who's important to him. Starting with his friends." His lips parted in a grin. "I hear he's fallen in love, so very soon I'll be ready to take that away from him, too. Although"—he tapped his chin—"if she's fetching enough, I may have to use her before I kill her."

"*You'll* kill her?" The words left her mouth before she could stop them. She bit her lip, preparing to be smacked because of the incredulity in her tone.

The smile faded from his face, and his eyes narrowed, though he didn't lift his hand to her. "Yes. The male friends are peripheral, not enough for me to bother with personally. But a wife?" The grin returned, this time so full of malicious glee it wrapped ice around her gut. "To watch his face, the agony in his eyes as I fuck her and then kill her, with him powerless to stop me?" He nodded. "That is something I must do myself."

Well, if he was going to use Olivia to do some of the dirty work, she damn well deserved to know why. "Who is this man? Why do you hate him so much?"

Eddy turned away from her. "Merr . . ." He broke off and shook his head. "He had everything—a loving family, wealth, power, and the poor sod couldn't stand that he wasn't normal." With his heightened emotions, Eddy's New York accent slipped a bit and took on a British flavor. He shook his head again. "It should have all been mine. If his father had just done what I'd asked—*begged!*—things might have been different."

He trailed off, seeming to be lost in his thoughts. After a moment he shrugged. "Never mind. It's not something you need to know." He glanced over his shoulder at her, eyes hard. "All you need to know is that for your daughter to remain safe you have a job to do."

Eyeing the distance between them, Olivia wondered if she could catch him off guard long enough to kill him. She could morph her fingers into claws now, just like he did. She might be able to do it.

It would only take one quick slash across the throat.

But then what about Zoe? There was at least one bodyguard standing outside her door, his bulk casting a shadow onto the floor of the hallway.

Olivia briefly closed her eyes. She'd never be able to do it. She couldn't kill Eddy and go for the bodyguard before he could get to Zoe.

She had no other choice. She must finish the job she'd been given.

Thinking back over the last few days, she remembered her first impression of Rory Sullivan. Tall, dark, and dangerous.

An earnest protector.

Sexy as hell. But . . .

He had to die.

Chapter 1

Detective Chief Inspector Rory Sullivan chased the rape suspect down the paved pathway in London's Battersea Park, a sense of euphoria he'd never before experienced lending strength and speed to his strides. He had never run this fast, never felt like he could keep running without tiring.

On one level Sully realized it was his new werewolf metabolism that enhanced his abilities. And even as he appreciated that aspect of his . . . condition, the fact that he also felt a nearly overwhelming urge to sink his teeth into the man, to feel his hot, rich blood course down his throat didn't escape him.

He hated himself for it. He hated his erstwhile friend Declan O'Connell for getting him into this mess in the first place.

And he hated the one who had turned him. If he ever found out who it was, if he ever had an opportunity to kill the bastard, he'd take it.

He didn't know anything about being a werewolf, but one thing his instincts told him: werewolf justice was swift. And final. He couldn't wait to exact his own on his maker.

He increased his speed, his heightened sense of hearing picking up the sound of the suspect's labored breathing, the thud of shoes on the paved walkway, the shouts of the other officers giving chase.

A snarl worked its way free of his throat. The team couldn't have the creep. The sodding lowlife was *his*.

Sully launched himself through the air and brought the man down onto the pavement. He flipped him over, taking care to keep the man's lower body under control so the bastard wouldn't get a chance to knee him in the nuts.

Though the son of a bitch tried anyway.

Rage exploded through Sully's skull, making his eyes burn, his teeth ache. A pulse pounded in his throat. Through a haze of crimson he saw the rape suspect's eyes widen, the pupils dilating with fear.

Ah. Fear.

Sully drew in a deep breath and held it, savoring the ethereal essence of that tangy emotion.

"What are you, man?" The rapist struggled beneath him, hands and feet scrabbling for traction on the rough pavement. Blood seeped from scrapes on his cheek and chin, drawing Sully's gaze there.

His nostrils flared with his indrawn breath. Beneath the stench of marijuana and fear was something else. Something good.

God, this guy smelled . . .

Like food.

And this puppy was hungry.

Sully brought his gaze back to the suspect's and leaned closer.

Wide eyes focused on Sully's face. "Your eyes . . ." His gaze drifted down to Sully's mouth.

Sully grinned and ran his tongue over the tip of elongated canines. He'd never been one to play with his food before he'd become a werewolf, but now he was finding it could be fun.

"What the fuck are you?" The suspect's voice choked to silence as Sully tightened his hands around the man's throat.

From a distance Sully heard someone call his name, then again. "Sully?" Footsteps crunched along the pathway, gaining speed. "DCI Sullivan!"

The horrified alarm in the newcomer's voice drew Sully away from the wolf and back to himself. He drew in another breath, this time a calming one, and pushed the beast back. He couldn't help giving one last squeeze of his fingers around the rapist's throat, then pushed away from him and stood. He walked a few paces away, his back to the group of uniformed officers who swarmed over the babbling suspect.

He scrubbed shaking hands over his face. Now that the euphoria of the adrenaline rush was fading, he was appalled at his loss of control. One minute he'd been chasing the suspect on foot, the next he'd tackled him to the ground and had been ready—with incredible eagerness—to tear into the man's throat.

One thing he had always prided himself on was his ability to not let criminals get under his skin, not allow them to prod a response from him. Calm and cool, that was DCI Sullivan.

Not anymore.

God. What kind of hell had Declan brought him into?

From behind him he heard the slide of restraints being

fastened around the suspect's wrists, the scuffle of feet as the man was led away.

"What the hell was that all about?" Detective Constable Aubrey Lindstrom moved in front of Sully. "You return from holiday and start attacking suspects?"

Sully closed his eyes until the burning stopped. Once they felt normal again—once *he* felt normal again, or as close to normal as possible—he opened them to see Lindstrom standing there, a muscle twitching in his jaw, waiting for a response.

"It's nothing."

"Nothing?" Lindstrom glanced over Sully's shoulder, then pointed toward the departing police cars. "That bloke is going to tell everyone who will listen that you tried to kill him." His pale blue eyes held a mixture of confusion and frustration. "This is me you're talking to, Sully. Remember? The guy who sees through bullshit?"

DC Lindstrom had a knack for ascertaining when someone was lying—whether it was a suspect or a man he'd worked with for nearly ten years. But Sully couldn't very well tell him what had happened to him on holiday. For one, he wouldn't believe it.

For another thing, it meant potentially exposing his friends as well, which he wouldn't do.

Even if he wanted to break every bone in Declan's body, it wouldn't change anything. Something told him this was a secret better kept than exposed.

If humans found out that werewolves really did exist, he and his friends—and every other werewolf out there—would be in danger.

He shouldn't give a rat's ass, but he did. The fact that he no longer thought of himself as human started the rage building again.

He used to be human. Now he was something . . .

More.

Or perhaps something less.

Maybe a little of both.

"Look, I . . ." Sully broke off with a sigh and rubbed the back of his neck. He loosened his tie. Pushing his suit jacket back, he thrust his hands into his front pockets. "I can't go into details, all right? I'm just a bit tired."

With a slight lift of his eyebrows, Lindstrom gave a nod telling Sully clearer than words could that he wasn't buying that, either. "Well, you can expect a call to the Chief's office. You know that, right?"

Sully pursed his lips. Frustration burned in his gut, tempting the wolf to come out and take care of things. With a growing sense of panic, he pushed the beast down again and turned toward the park exit. "He can do whatever he wants," he said with a barely restrained growl.

"Yes, he bloody well can." Lindstrom put one hand on Sully's arm and pulled him to a stop. "And if you go in with an attitude like that, mate, he'll slap you with a suspension so fast your head will spin."

Sully jerked away from the detective. The entire situation was a sodding mess, and the only ones who could help him were the two people he didn't want to see. If his so-called friends had been up front with him from the beginning, his life might not have been plunged into this hell. He trapped a howl of fury in his throat. "You let me worry about that," he rasped and stalked to his car.

"Yeah. I'll do just that," he heard Lindstrom mutter.

Sully unlocked his unmarked sedan with the remote key fob and opened the door. He sighed and looked at Lindstrom over the roof of the car. "Thanks."

"For what?"

Sully jerked his head toward the park. "For back there. For . . . bringing me to my senses."

The detective shrugged. "You'd do the same for me."

Sully gave a nod. He would. They had each others' backs. "See you back at the Yard."

A scant half hour later, Sully stood in front of his superior's desk, receiving the dressing-down of his life.

"Just what the hell were you thinking, Sullivan?" George Glace's voice climbed a full octave.

Sully hid a wince. The Chief Superintendent was in rare form. Rightly so, he supposed, but it didn't mean he liked being taken to task like a boy still in knee britches.

"Tackling a fleeing suspect is one thing, but wrapping your hands around his throat is unacceptable. And, I might add, bordering on illegal as it would imply excessive force. Not to mention it's highly irregular."

Sully turned his face to one side to hide a smirk. Everything with Glace was "highly irregular," from a hangnail to one of his best DCIs nearly choking a suspect to death.

Though what he'd wanted to do was feast.

That thought erased the smirk.

"You'd better *not* be smiling." The Chief Superintendent stalked around the corner of his desk, his tall, lanky frame as stiff as a two-by-four. "The only possible saving grace for you in all of this is that the suspect seems to be quite mad. He's been raving on about your eyes changing color and your teeth being sharp like an animal's." He shook his head. "I won't be surprised if the tox screen comes back showing he's high on something."

Sully remained silent. He could guarantee forensics would show the suspect was high. Sully had smelled it on him. The Chief was right in one thing. It definitely worked in his favor if people thought the rapist was a strung-out lunatic.

Because everyone knew that werewolves weren't real.

He clenched his jaw so hard it cracked.

"What's gotten into you?" Glace crossed his arms, drumming the fingers of one hand against the opposite elbow. "You've been back from your holiday for two days, acting like a lion with a thorn in its paw."

Make that a wolf, and he'd be half right—though the thorn wasn't in his paw.

Which was why he was so surly.

"Sir—"

"Save it." Glace walked around his desk and sat down, tipping his chair back. The slight squeak as he rocked back and forth grated on Sully's already tightly drawn nerves. The Chief sat forward and rested his elbows on the desk, steepling his fingers. His graying eyebrows beetled. "At this moment, Detective Chief Inspector Sullivan, you are on an extended personal leave of absence."

"Leave of absence!" Sully scowled. "I don't need a bloody leave—"

"Yes. You do." Glace eyed Sully. "I could make it something of a more official nature, though I'd prefer not to have that sort of thing on your record." He watched Sully, and when he didn't respond, Glace went on. "Turn in your badge and car keys. You're to conduct no official police business during your leave. You may keep your weapon." He put the tip of his index finger on his desk blotter, pointing to the spot where the badge was to be placed.

Sully ground his jaw but did as directed. He yanked his badge off his belt and tossed it onto the blotter. Taking the car keys from his pocket, he plunked them onto the desk as well.

"Whatever's eating at you, Sullivan, I suggest you deal with it while an investigation into this"—Glace waved one long-fingered hand—"distasteful situation is conducted. And hope that, because of the suspect's unhinged behavior, police brutality charges aren't brought against you."

Sully repressed the urge to snarl. "Maybe I'll go on another holiday."

The Chief opened the top drawer of his desk and scooped Sully's life into it. "Good idea. You do that. And get your head screwed on straight while you're at it." He closed the drawer and leaned back in his chair with a sigh. "You're a good policeman, Sullivan. A good *man*. I'd hate to see your career go arse over elbow."

Sully nodded, the only thing he could manage at the moment. When Glace gave a wave of dismissal, Sully turned and strode out of the office.

By the time he got to his desk the rage had returned. He wanted to hit something. Someone. He wanted to run until he couldn't run anymore.

What he didn't want to do was talk to Declan, the sodding prat who'd gotten him into this mess. That Irish devil was a bastard of the first degree. Declan was a dirty, rotten son of a bitch who'd let him get involved in something dark and dangerous without giving him all the facts. As far as Sully was concerned, it was Declan's fault he would turn furry once a month, starting . . .

He glanced at his desk calendar. Starting in two fucking weeks. Though he'd felt an urge to shift a couple of times already, he'd have no choice of it during the full moon.

Damn Declan. He was . . .

Sully scrubbed his hand against the back of his neck. Damn it. Whatever else he was, Declan was his friend. And one of two people who could help him through this.

"So?" Lindstrom leaned forward in his chair at the desk next to Sully's. "What did the old man have to say?"

Sully brushed the edge of his suit coat aside to show where his badge would normally be clipped to his belt.

"Damn." Lindstrom's pale gaze met his. "I really was hoping he wouldn't go that route."

Sully sighed and sat down in his chair. Lindstrom was not only a good cop, he was a good friend. A good partner. "He really had no other choice, did he?" Sully stared at the top of his desk for a moment, gut churning with regret, frustration, and restrained rage. Biting back a curse, he pushed to his feet with enough force to send his chair rolling back to thud against the desk behind him.

"Oi!" The detective behind the desk looked up with a frown. "Watch what you're about, Sully."

"Sorry," Sully muttered. He shoved his right hand into the front pocket of his trousers. He looked at Lindstrom. "I have to get out of here." He couldn't stand the thought of heading back to his terrace house or, God forbid, home to the family estate in Suffolk—it would send him 'round the bend if he had to go stare at four walls or pretend to his mother that he was fine.

He was far from fine. He'd never been further from being fine. He was about as fucked up as a man could get.

And, as much as he hated to admit it, he needed Declan's help.

"I'll probably be headed to the States for a bit." He straightened a stack of folders on his desk and then met Lindstrom's gaze. "Sorry to do this to you."

Their caseload was horrendous, and the last thing the detective constable needed was to have to take the load by himself. But there was nothing Sully could do about that. He needed to get his head on straight and come to terms with this new twist in his reality.

"Don't worry about it, mate. We'll manage." Lindstrom gave a slight smile. "You take care of yourself."

Sully nodded. He said his good-byes and left the building, stopping for a moment on the pavement to stare at the New Scotland Yard sign. This was his job, his *life*, and he was damn well going to fight to keep it. Up to this point his record was impeccable, so he didn't think the review would cause him to lose his job, though the timing of his next promotion would probably be affected.

To sit at home and wallow wasn't in his nature. There was something he could do, as much as he might be reluctant to ask for help. Scowling, he yanked his mobile phone from its holder on his belt and punched in Declan's number. As soon as Declan's sleepy voice came on the line, Sully muttered, "I need your help, you son of a bitch."

"Do you have any concept of time zones at all, boyo?"

Over the phone line Sully could hear the rustle of bed linens and pictured Declan rolling over to look at the clock. He glanced at his wristwatch and did the math. It was only three in the morning in Arizona where Declan was. Tough shit.

"I nearly bit the head off a suspect today. Literally." Sully hailed a cab. As he climbed into the backseat of the black Austin, he switched the phone to his left ear and pulled the door shut. "Lyall Mews, Belgravia," he said to the cabbie. The car pulled away from the curb, and Sully turned his attention back to the phone. "I've just returned from holiday only to be this close"—he measured a small space between thumb and forefinger—"to being suspended, you bastard." He settled back against the car seat cushions.

"How exactly is that my fault?" Declan's voice was heavy with sleepy irritation, which thickened his Irish brogue. Sully heard a feminine voice murmur in the background, and Declan's tone immediately softened. "It's just Sully, love. Go back to sleep."

"Is he all right?" Sully heard her ask. Pelicia Cobb, Declan's fiancée—the woman Declan had asked Sully to help him protect. The woman in whose home Sully had been attacked by a werewolf, his life forever changed.

Forever fucked up.

Royally.

"He's fine. Go back to sleep."

Sully heard the soft smack of lips meeting lips, and Pelicia's sleepy sigh. Then Declan said, "I told you that you should've come to the States with us from the get-go."

"I didn't call to hear you say 'I told you so,' " Sully interrupted. "Just . . ." He heaved a sigh and ran his fingers through his hair. "Just tell me the offer to come stay with you and learn how to control this . . ." He met the gaze of the cabbie in the rearview mirror and changed what he'd been about to say. "Tell me the offer is still on the table."

"The offer's still on the table."

The cab pulled up in front of his four-storied terrace house, and the cabbie told him the amount of the fare. Sully muttered, "Hold on," into the phone. He pulled out his wallet and extracted several five-pound notes and handed them to the man. "Thanks."

"Right. 'Ave a nice day, guv."

Sully got out of the cab, pausing on the walkway in front of the house and watched the car pull away. A few doors down, a woman climbed out of another taxi. He couldn't see her face, but long, dark hair streamed over her shoulders and caught the sunlight with strands of red and gold.

His fingers curled with the desire to stroke through those tresses, to feel their silken strands against his skin.

He drew a breath and smelled a light, orangey perfume and, underlying that, a sexy, musky all-woman scent that made his cock jerk against his thigh. He stared at her, his gaze zeroing in on the flare of her buttocks in tight blue jeans. His gut tightened with something that went beyond lust. It was . . .

Primal.

More than mere want. It was need.

Deeper than he'd ever felt before.

Sully was five paces down the pavement after her before he realized he'd moved. There was something vaguely familiar about her, something that drew him like an unaware fly to the spider's web. Just as he decided to keep following her, to find out who she was, Declan's voice sounded in his ear.

"Hey! You still there?"

Sully stopped. He watched the woman who, without a glance in his direction, started up the short front walk of a redbrick terrace house three doors down. Her head was turned, so he still couldn't get a look at her face.

For all he knew, she could be butt-ugly. But with an ass like that, somehow he doubted it.

He huffed a sigh. Turning back toward his own house, he shoved his right hand into his pocket. Jingling his keys as he walked, he told Declan, "I'll make travel arrangements and be in Tucson tomorrow." He went up the pavement to his front door and drew his keys from his pocket. "My passport's up-to-date, so it's just a matter of booking a flight." He unlocked the door and went inside, closing the door behind him with one heel. "Fuck. I hate this. I really, really hate this."

"It's not that bad." Declan was beginning to sound more alert. "You'll find there are a lot of things you can do now that you couldn't do before. You'll have lots more stamina, for one thing. In all areas," he added with a low chuckle.

Sully ignored the innuendo. Since he had no sex life at the moment to speak of, whether or not he had more stamina wasn't an issue. "Yes, and I can run faster, see clearer, hear things from greater distances." He gave a growl of frustration. "I also nearly killed a man today. If my DC hadn't caught up to us when he did—"

"But he obviously did, otherwise you'd be sittin' in a jail cell and not talkin' to me on the phone." Declan heaved a sigh. "Look, call me when you have your travel itinerary, and we'll pick you up at the airport, okay? Until then . . . buck up. It'll be all right."

"Hmm. Maybe." Sully said good-bye, not waiting for Declan to respond, and closed his phone, disconnecting the call. He loosened and then pulled off his tie, tossing it onto a decorative table in the narrow entry hallway. Then he went upstairs to pack and try to begin coming to terms with his new life.

Chapter 2

Olivia prowled around the back yard of the swanky town house, taking particular care to be quiet so the werewolf inside wouldn't hear her. She tried to find a way in and cursed under her breath at being thwarted. Damn. Cops were the same world-over. This guy's place was buttoned up tighter than the White House.

Or, since she was in London, maybe Buckingham Palace was a more appropriate analogy.

She'd already lost almost twenty-four hours of her seven-day reprieve getting from New York to London and waiting outside New Scotland Yard for a glimpse of DCI Sullivan and the chance to follow him home. He'd finally come out, looking as pissed as hell and, interestingly enough, flagged down a taxi instead of driving off in an unmarked police car as she'd thought he'd do.

She'd grabbed a taxi of her own and followed him, having the driver pull over a few houses up from where Sully got out. Thankfully Sully was so preoccupied with his current . . . predicament that he hadn't noticed he'd been followed.

When she had first gotten out of the taxi she'd seen him

glance her way. She'd quickly turned so he wouldn't see her face, her heart beating fast. Her citrus-based perfume would mask her scent, so he wouldn't be able to smell her as another werewolf.

She had to act like she belonged in the neighborhood, so she'd walked down the short sidewalk to a nearby town house as if it was hers—thankful no one poked their head out asking what she was about, loitering around their front door.

While they were both outside, her enhanced werewolf hearing had allowed her to listen in on his phone conversation, even from three doors down. As soon as she'd heard him making plans to leave the country, she knew she had to act.

If she didn't get him now, she'd lose at least another day or two waiting to get him once he got to Arizona. She paused, peering into a downstairs window.

It looked like some sort of home office. A big mahogany desk took up one side of the room, a comfy sofa on the wall facing it, and book-lined shelves made of the same dark-hued wood. She didn't know much about Rory Sullivan, but she recognized that he had money.

Hell, the fact that he lived in one of those old town houses made her think he had oodles of money. Probably old money, but who knew? There were a lot of nouveaux riches in the world these days, even with the uncertainties in the stock markets in the last couple years.

God, what would her life have been like had she had this kind of money? Instead of living in a modest apartment in the Bronx, she and Zoe might have been living large in the East Village or Gramercy. At the very least, she probably wouldn't have been turned into a werewolf, so anything different would be an improvement.

Now's not the time, Liv. She pushed away the feeling of despair at her current situation, remorse at what she was being forced to do—and, yes, jealousy at Sully's good fortune—and focused once again on a way to get to him.

Thirty minutes later she heaved a sigh of defeat. She could break in, but he'd hear her and be prepared for a fight. Before, when he was human, she would have been twice as strong as him. If she hadn't been interrupted by O'Connell, the job would have been finished in the Isles of Scilly. Without the element of surprise on her side, she had a slim-to-none chance of defeating him.

Now that he was a werewolf he was stronger and faster than her, so it would be better if she could avoid a fight. She couldn't afford to be wounded—or worse. Zoe's life depended on her mother murdering this man.

An innocent man. A good man.

Someone Olivia might have liked to have called "friend."

A light flicked on inside the study. Sully walked in, head down, brow furrowed. She caught her breath and moved to one side of the window, slowly so as to not draw his attention.

My God, but he's handsome. She swallowed and tried to control the primeval reaction of her body to the superior specimen of male. Over six feet of lean muscle, symmetrical features, and glittering green eyes took her breath away.

She'd never been introduced to him, but she'd observed him while he was staying at that little bed and breakfast on the island of St. Mary's.

And she'd tasted his blood. His flesh.

So on some level she felt she knew him.

He was more than just his looks. He was a staunch defender of the innocent, and a man who saw things in black and white.

She bit her lip. Wasn't he going to be surprised at just how gray things in his life had gotten? Looking at the expression on his face, at the dispirited look in his eyes, she thought perhaps not. It seemed as though he may have already had a lesson or two.

She could only hope he hadn't yet mastered control of the wolf, for it was on his lack of control she had to pin her hopes of destroying him.

Olivia blinked back tears. God in heaven, how had she gotten to a point where she was willing to take someone's life?

The answer was simple. It was all about Zoe.

Olivia would do anything—*anything*—to protect her little girl. Even if it meant going against everything she believed in.

But she had to do it smart. That meant not attacking him where he was comfortable, where the advantage was his. That meant getting him off on his own someplace where the chances of being interrupted again were slim.

That meant she had to keep her focus on the task at hand and not on his body. Or his face. Or those big hands that, at the moment, were clenched at his sides.

Big hands that she wouldn't mind feeling on her skin.

Stop it! She tried to ignore the frisson of arousal that tightened her core, made her clit throb with insistent heat. There was no future for them, of any sort. Because in under six days' time, one way or another, he'd be dead.

Or she would be. But then what would happen to Zoe?

No, she couldn't fail. It had to be Sullivan.

So, what was she going to do? Sit in his back yard like a dog, or hop a plane and beat him back to the States?

There was only one thing she could do. Wherever Rory Sullivan went, she would go, too.

She began plotting her next moves. She would do a search on the Internet for Declan O'Connell's address and get to Arizona before Sully did. Hell, if she couldn't locate O'Connell, she'd camp out at the airport and wait for Sully to show up. She could follow him and at the first opportunity take him out in the relative isolation of the desert. Whatever it took to make it happen, she would do it.

"Tucson, here I come," she whispered and quietly made her way around the house to the front. Once she was far enough away that she was sure he wouldn't hear her, she broke into a run to the closest main street and flagged down a taxi.

The next evening, Sully watched the passing scenery from the backseat of Declan's Mustang as they made their way from the airport. They'd already been on the road for thirty minutes. "I'd no idea you lived so far from town," he commented.

"We haven't technically left the city." Declan brought the car to a stop at a traffic light. "This is still part of Tucson."

The mountains to the north were closer, and Sully found himself envying Declan—however briefly—for the chance to live with such raw beauty all around him. The bright blue sky contrasted with the craggy slag heaps, and the desert floor held cacti and other plants flowering in yellows, purples, and oranges.

Still, he'd called London home for over twenty years. This place, while beautiful, was too quiet. Too untamed.

As if to prove his point, a scrawny-looking dog crossed the road to his right.

"Coyote." Pelicia twisted in the passenger seat. She

glanced back at Declan. "Right?" At his nod she looked at Sully. "They're all over the place out here, Declan says. That and javelina—they're somewhat like pigs—bobcats . . . oh, and let's not forget the rattlesnakes and scorpions," she added with a sidelong glance at Declan. "Declan showed me my first rattlesnake yesterday while we were out for a walk."

"What did he do, point to himself in a mirror?" Sully muttered.

"For God's sake, boyo, let it go." Declan shot him a dark glance over his shoulder. As he turned forward again the light turned green. He drove through the intersection. "What's done is done. You need to deal with it. Besides," he went on in a blithe tone, "no snakes have gotten into the house, and the scorpions are usually dead by the time we find them." He laughed at Pelicia's little roll of her eyes and cupped his right hand behind her head, beneath the single plait of blond hair that rested against her back.

Sully saw his fingers stroke behind her ear, and the two shared a look that made envy curl around his gut.

The image of a woman with long, dark hair and a sexy ass flitted into his mind. Along with it came the remembered scent he associated with her—light citrus mixed with warm woman. Damn. He should've followed that woman by his terrace house in London, at least gotten her phone number.

So you could . . . what? Have her over for dinner some night à la Hannibal Lecter?

He scowled and folded his arms over his chest.

Declan met his gaze in the rearview mirror. "Anyway, you might find there are some advantages now when it comes to doin' your job."

"Advantages on the job, you say?" Sully shifted in his

seat and raised his eyebrows. "You mean, like I can run faster?"

"Aye."

"And see more clearly and at farther distances?" He kept his tone even with an effort.

Declan nodded.

"And that my senses of smell and hearing are better?"

Declan glanced around with a slight frown as if Sully's too-sedate tone was finally getting through to him. "Aye," he drawled slowly.

"And try to rip out the throat of my suspect and so perhaps lose said job?" Sully clamped his jaws together against the howl of rage threatening to break free. Regardless that the Chief had sent him on a personal leave rather than an administrative one, the outcome could still be the same.

He could be sacked.

If he couldn't be a cop . . . He drew in a breath. Serving at the Yard was all he knew. If he couldn't be a cop, he didn't know what else to do. Going home to his family's estate was out of the question, though he knew his mother would love for him to come home. But living the life of a rich, pampered sot wasn't for him.

Making a difference in people's lives by getting bad guys off the street—*that* was what he was all about.

"That happened because you haven't yet learned how to control the wolf." Declan didn't bother to hide the irritated growl in his deep voice. "If you'd listened to me in the first place—"

"It was *because* I listened to you in the first place"— Sully leaned forward—"that I'm in this fucking mess." He slumped in his seat. "Never mind," he muttered, interrupting Declan's retort and avoiding Pelicia's gaze. He didn't want to make her feel any guiltier over what had happened to him than she already did. "Just"—he met Declan's gaze in the rearview mirror—"tell me that when I go home in six weeks I won't be trying to eat my suspects."

"You won't be tryin' to eat your suspects."

Pelicia twisted again in her seat, her gaze bright with compassion mingled with lingering remorse. She said in a quiet voice, "This is something you *can* learn to live with, Sully. Once you've learned how to control your emotions, you'll see a marked difference in your reaction to things."

Sully gave a nod. *That* he'd have to wait and see about.

"Here we are." Declan turned the car onto a gravel driveway, winding between tall green cacti with arms and smaller purple cacti with flat, circular appendages. "I've put you in the guesthouse—reckoned you'd want some time alone, and some space—but you're more than welcome to stay with us in the main house if you'd prefer."

"The guesthouse is fine." Preferable, truth be told. With a sense of wonder Sully took in the sprawling adobe house with its southwestern architecture. So very alien compared to what he was used to in London. "This is . . . different."

Pelicia grinned and opened the door. As she got out of the car she said, "Yes, we don't see much of this style of house in England, do we?" She pulled the lever to move the seat forward so Sully could climb out of the back.

"No, we don't." Arms above his head, Sully stretched, working kinks out of his muscles brought on by the nearly forty-five minute ride. So many new smells—predominantly one of citrus. He glanced around and saw two lemon trees at one side of the house.

"So?" Declan walked around to the boot of the car and popped the lid. "What do you think? I mean, I realize it's not the same as the stately old manor house you grew up in, but—"

"Shut it." Sully took the big suitcase Declan handed to him. Looking at the gravel, he realized he'd be better off carrying the thing rather than trying to wheel it over the uneven surface.

"The guesthouse is this way." Pelicia took his small overnight case from the boot and started around one side of the house.

Sully obediently fell in line behind her, aware of Declan bringing up the rear with a third suitcase, smaller than the one Sully carried.

"You brought more luggage than a woman," Declan muttered.

"Shut it." Sully wasn't in the mood to listen to the Irish version of the Mad Hatter. "I brought what I needed."

"Even Pelicia didn't bring this much crap with her, and she's stayin' three months before she has to get back to Scilly and wrap things up there."

Before Sully could tell him to shut up for a third time, Pelicia looked over her shoulder. "Declan, stop it."

"Stop what?" His voice was all innocence.

"You know very well what. You're trying to rile Sully, so just stop it. Let the man rest from his journey before you throw him headlong into a training session." Her pretty lips bowed down, and she shook her head in an age-old feminine gesture of irritation. Without waiting for either man to respond, she said, "Here we are." She took a key from her pocket and unlocked the red door of the small guesthouse.

Sully followed her inside. Setting down the suitcase, he gazed around the room. The front door opened directly into a living room with a plump leather sofa sitting in front of a beehive fireplace, a large flat-screen TV, and various pieces of Native American pottery on the built-in bookshelf beside it.

The room was decorated in warm beiges and dark reds, giving it a calming effect and making him feel like he was home. The stress of travel—the endless tension of being surrounded by humanity first in busy airports and then on crowded flights—began to fade. All he needed was a few hours to himself and then he'd feel . . .

He stifled a snort of disgust. He would never feel like himself again, not with this *thing* now a part of him, this beast that roared with fury and hunger.

He turned his attention to the other side of the fireplace, where a set of French doors let in the early evening sunlight. He wandered over and looked through the glass. A cobbled patio with a table and chairs and, beyond that, a small flower garden enclosed on all sides by bushes covered in white and dark pink blooms.

"Oleanders," Pelicia murmured at his side. When he glanced at her, she made a gesture toward the outdoors and explained, "The bushes that line the yard are oleanders. Declan told me they're poisonous, so don't try to eat them."

He raised one brow. "Don't eat the bushes. I'll try to remember that. Thanks."

She smacked him lightly on the arm. "You and Declan are both a couple of smartasses. No wonder you get on so well together."

"Hmm." Sully wasn't so sure about that anymore.

"You do." Pelicia put her hand on his arm. Her blue eyes earnest, she said in a soft voice, "For what it's worth, if you hadn't been there, that wolf might have attacked me. You saved my life."

He grimaced. "So . . . all I did was get in the way, is that what you're saying? It wasn't anything I did on purpose."

"No, I'm not saying that at all."

Unable to maintain a serious expression, he grinned.

She smacked him on the arm again. "See? A smartass, just like O'Connell."

"Hey. And here I was thinkin' you liked my ass." Declan walked over to them.

She just rolled her eyes again. Turning around to face the living room, she pointed at a doorway on the right. "The bedroom and *en suite* bathroom are through there, and there's a small kitchen on the other side of that wall." She motioned toward an opening on the left of the living room. "Though we do insist you take your meals with us."

"Of course." Sully picked up the largest of the suitcases and started toward the bedroom. He paused in the doorway and looked back at his friends. "I think I'll have a short lie down, if that's all right."

"That's fine." Pelicia's voice was soothing. "We'll have a late dinner at eight p.m." She grinned. "Well, that's a normal time for me, but late for Americans. That gives you"—she glanced at her wristwatch—"three hours to get situated. It'll be dark in about an hour and a half or so, but the walkway is lighted."

"Ah, he won't need lights, darlin'." Declan wrapped an arm around her shoulders and pulled her tight against him. "Remember?"

A light blush moved under the fair skin of her cheeks. "Oh. Right." She looked at Sully with apology reflected in her eyes. "Sorry."

He shook his head. "Don't start with that again. It wasn't your fault." When she opened her mouth, he forestalled her by raising one hand. "I'm fine. I ate at the airport during my layover, so dinner at eight is fine, too."

God, three hours to be by himself. He didn't know if he should be happy or panic at the idea of being alone again with his thoughts.

"Okay, then." Declan walked over to him and put one hand on his shoulder, giving a slight squeeze. "It'll be all right, mate. Trust me."

Sully lifted his chin in acknowledgment but didn't say anything.

Declan gave another squeeze, then he and Pelicia left the guesthouse, closing the door softly behind them.

"He seems so . . . bereft," Sully heard Pelicia say, her sweet voice holding a wealth of worry.

"He'll be fine." Declan's voice held no doubt.

Sully wished he could be as sure.

He stood there in the doorway of the bedroom, holding onto his suitcase like some bloody befuddled bellman. With an oath he dropped it in the doorway and flopped onto the bed, legs hanging over the edge, feet flat on the floor. He closed his eyes but couldn't slow his swirling mind.

The need to move, to try to escape his thoughts, rushed through him. His skin prickled, the hairs standing straight up on his arms and the back of his neck. His jaws began to ache, his eyes burned.

Deep, deep inside the wolf howled to be set free.

Sully surged up off the bed, toed off his shoes, and yanked off his socks. He tossed aside his clothing with an urgency that made his hands shake.

Even though the next full moon was still two weeks away, he felt the pull as surely as if it were bright in the sky. Declan had said that could happen, but Sully hadn't wanted to acknowledge it. He was still human, still a *man*. He wasn't ruled by his beast—he would be able to control any desire to set the wolf free.

But, at that moment, he couldn't fight it.

He didn't *want* to fight it.

He wanted—*needed*—to be as wild as he felt.

Bones began to shift. Some lengthened, others shortened, all drawing muscles, cartilage, and ligaments into their new forms. Sully fell to his hands and knees, agony screaming through every cell, his breath rasping in his throat as, against his primeval instincts, the part of him still human fought against the change.

In the span of a heartbeat, fur sprouted over his skin. One more and his shuddering transformation to wolf was complete.

After a few seconds, waiting for the pain to fade, he lifted his head. So much clearer now.

Smells, stronger. One in particular. His nose twitched. What was that? He bent and sniffed at one leg. Whatever the smell was—kind of woodsy with underlying scents of pine and citrus—it emanated from him.

He lifted his head and padded into the living room. Stopping in front of the patio doors, he stared through the glass. A hummingbird fluttered near the bushes. Sully could see the edge of every tiny feather, the flutter of its wings.

He had to get out there, outside, now.

He lifted one paw and pressed down on the door latch. As the handle moved, his paw slid off it and the gold latch went back into its original position. He growled in aggravation and tried again, slightly curling his paw over the handle.

The door popped open. Sully nudged it open farther with his nose, then slipped through the doorway and into . . .

Freedom.

Ignoring the hummingbird and a small lizard that skittered across the concrete patio, he shoved his way through the oleanders. On the other side of the bushes was a small gulley—a wash, he remembered hearing them called.

He trotted down the wash on all fours, nose twitching as he took in the new smells of this foreign place. The flap of large wings caught his attention, and he stopped, head up, and watched a hawk circle overhead.

Free.

Run.

With a low grunt, he dug his paws into the sand and took off. As he found his footing, he increased his speed, running full out for several minutes until his lungs felt like they would burst. He settled into an easy lope. A jackrabbit, startled from its cover beneath a large bush, darted out in front of him.

Its heart raced and big feet threw sand behind it as it ran. Sully gave chase, scrabbling in loose dirt, trying to keep up as the smaller animal twisted this way and that with incredible speed. Just as he was about to close his jaws around it, something else caught his attention.

The jackrabbit skittered off while Sully lifted his nose to the wind for a better sniff.

There was that scent again—the one something like pine and citrus. Like him, yet different. This one smelled . . .

Female.

Chapter 3

Olivia sighed and wiggled on the driver's seat of her rental car, trying to get comfortable. Mid-April, and it was already well over ninety degrees in the Sonoran Desert. She didn't want to keep the car running—more because she didn't want to draw any attention to herself and less because of environmental concerns—so without any air-conditioning her T-shirt stuck to her back and sweat trickled down her cleavage.

Hell, she was getting ready to kill a man. She didn't have the luxury—or the energy—to worry about things like comfort and car emissions.

She sighed again. At one point, on the airplane from London to New York to Phoenix, she'd rethought her plan. She wasn't stupid. There was no guarantee, even if she did kill Sully, that Eddy would let Zoe go. And if he did, the little girl and Olivia would still be in danger from him—

For the rest of their lives unless she could find a way to escape.

That way could be Sully and his friend O'Connell. But only if Eddy wasn't surrounded by his pack. No way could three werewolves take on an entire pack.

And Eddy was never away from his pack. Ever. So she was full circle back to the original plan.

Kill Rory Sullivan.

She'd found out where Sully's friend Declan O'Connell lived—easy as pie to do an Internet search on the man—and had the car parked on a little dirt road off the larger street where O'Connell lived.

Far enough away to not draw attention, but still close enough that she could keep an eye on things with her enhanced werewolf vision.

She'd seen the three drive up in a low-slung Mustang almost half an hour ago. Using her citrus-based perfume liberally in order to mask her scent, she'd already scoped out O'Connell's place and knew the best options for a quick entry and exit. The last thing she needed was for them to be on the lookout for a strange werewolf that had been on the property.

She figured she'd wait until closer to midnight, when they should all be asleep, and then she'd go after Sully.

This was something she had to do. For Zoe. Olivia pushed aside the guilt that insisted on tapping her on the shoulder. Perhaps if she'd been able to establish some alliances within the pack she could have gone to someone for help. As it was, everyone took out their bad moods on her. She highly doubted if any of them were willing to help her, though she figured that sooner or later someone would try to seize power from Eddy.

Whoever took over—it would be a bloody battle for dominance—could be even worse than the Alpha they already had, although she was hard-pressed to imagine how.

Eddy had turned her into a werewolf, made her the Omega of the pack regardless of her natural assertiveness, and threatened the life of her daughter. As far as Olivia was concerned, it couldn't get any worse.

Or, at least, she couldn't *let* it get any worse.

Giving up on comfort, she opened the door and climbed out of the car. After carefully and quietly closing the door, she stretched, hands on hips, shoulders back. That didn't help. She felt . . . antsy. Like thousands of the little critters were crawling across her skin.

She needed to run. As much as she sometimes hated being a werewolf, one thing she did enjoy was running as a wolf. There was such freedom, such exhilaration in being alive. When she went the way of the wolf, there were no worries. No fears. Just instinct.

She went around to the passenger side of the car and, after checking to make sure no other vehicles were coming down the dusty, barely there road, she took off her shoes and socks, tucked her socks inside one shoe, and tossed the shoes onto the floor mat in the back. She unfastened her watch, checking the time—five-thirty, which meant it would be dark in just over an hour. Then she quickly took off her clothes, folded them haphazardly, and tossed them onto the backseat. Closing her eyes, she pictured her wolf form in her mind.

Deep breaths helped her control the pain as she went through the transformation. Eventually, as she got used to it—or so she'd been told—the pain would manifest itself as mere discomfort. But, as she panted through the last shift of muscle and bone, it hurt like hell.

She opened her eyes and saw the world differently. Shades of gray, black, and white, with some smatterings of blue and yellow, met her gaze. Turning, she darted into the desert and, as she picked up speed, dodged various cacti and thorny bushes.

Does everything out here have prickers?

She'd been running at full tilt for only a few minutes, the wildness on the inside churning with each step, when she skidded to a stop, halted by a strange yet vaguely familiar scent.

Lifting her muzzle, she sniffed the air, turning her head toward the direction from which the tantalizing aroma—one that smelled much like sage—wafted.

She inhaled again. Her ears swiveled toward the sound of paws padding closer.

Another *werewolf.*

Male.

The wildness inside her churned in a different direction, heightening her carnal senses. Sex now would be good.

Very good.

Sex would let her escape reality, however briefly, much more than going wolf did.

Werewolves were territorial, and though O'Connell hadn't been home very long, he would have realized if another wolf was close by and would have driven him off. Or been driven off.

Since he still lived there, that obviously hadn't happened. So the wolf was either him or Sully.

The wolf moved closer, and she recognized the scent.

Sully.

Then he was there, pushing his way between two scruffy bushes, and he was magnificent. Almost completely black with a hint of brown in his undercoat peeking through as his fur shifted with the breeze. Broad chest and large paws, and an alert stance that clearly indicated he was alpha. Amber eyes stared at her with intelligence and a hint of wariness in their depths.

That was unusual—an alpha unsure of himself. Or perhaps it was that he was so newly turned and *that* was where the uncertainty lay. And, she saw as she looked more closely, more than a hint of self-loathing darkened those amber eyes.

She walked forward with measured steps, taking care not to make any sudden moves that would startle him or, worse, move him to aggression. She got quite enough of that from her pack.

When she reached him she paused. *Strike now*. He wouldn't be expecting it.

She hesitated. That damned vulnerable look in his eyes cut her to the core. It was her fault he was in this predicament. Her fault he held loathing for himself.

And he'd hate her, the one who'd created him.

After all, she hated her creator, too.

Strike now.

She brought her head forward and gave a delicate lick to the side of his muzzle.

A quick kiss "hello." A gesture meant to put him at ease.

He responded with a low grumbling growl, not one of irritation but rather one of interest. She gave him another lick and, before he could anticipate her plan through her stance or expression, she lunged and fastened her teeth in his throat.

Sully reared back under the unexpected attack. The she-wolf's change in demeanor shocked him, as he suspected it had been meant to.

Damn. Bitches were bitches the world over, no matter what form they took.

Instinct—both that of his wolf and of his hand-to-hand combat training from the Yard—took over. Instead of fighting her, he relaxed. It threw the she-wolf off balance, and she stumbled backward, loosening her grip on his throat.

It was enough. Sully shook himself free, ignoring the white-hot agony searing through him as fur and flesh were left in her mouth. He pushed through the pain and launched his own attack.

She managed to dodge his first strike, but after feinting to the left, he ducked past her flank and bit down across the back of her neck. Using his greater bulk and strength he forced her to the ground.

He swallowed the blood filling his mouth, never loosening his grip on her, fighting the primal urge to finish her. He didn't want this strange wolf dead. He wanted answers.

Beneath him she shuddered with the large breaths she took, though she growled at him instead of whimpering in surrender.

She was beaten but refused to accept it.

He admired her tenacity even as it rankled.

The she-wolf bucked against him, trying to dislodge him, and he held firm. He knew his bite hurt, but it wasn't a fatal one. Merely one to keep her down until she acquiesced.

With one last shudder she lay still. He felt muscles moving beneath him, felt fur receding. He let go of her and stepped away a foot or so as she continued to metamorphose back into her human form. Not wanting to give her an opportunity to get away but knowing he needed to be human in order to get any answers from her, Sully focused on changing back to his human form.

He rode through the agony of muscles and bones sliding into another shape, his body quaking. When the shift was finished, he rose to his feet, still shuddering from the pain. His cock rose like an iron rod. He had the fleeting memory of Declan telling him that he would be aroused after shifting from wolf to man, but in his anger he hadn't paid much attention. In his first time shifting from wolf to man, he gritted his teeth against an agony completely carnal in nature.

The other werewolf, also in human form, knelt in the sand, her head bowed, long, dark hair obscuring her face. Beaten.

Submissive.

The taste of her blood lingered on his tongue. His heart racing from the heat of the life-and-death struggle, Sully realized that, for the first time in years, he felt alive. Finally felt more than just going through the motions of life. More than just putting one foot in front of the other; getting through each day on a job that, while he loved it with his entire being, held more cynicism than hope.

And that *more* was something rich and dark. Primal.

He looked at the woman with one thought—*his*. He'd fought her and won. She was his.

"Who are you?" he asked, his voice rough with anger and arousal.

She didn't respond.

With a muttered oath, Sully strode forward. Bending, he grasped her by the upper arms and hauled her to her feet. He gave her a little shake. "Who the hell are you?"

"I'm nobody." Her voice was low, throaty. Sexy as hell.

He licked across suddenly dry lips. Crooking his fingers under her chin, he lifted her face to him. Clear blue eyes dark with pain met his. He caught his breath at the emotion reflected in her gaze. It was from more than the physical pain, he knew. Declan had told him enough so that he understood a shift from one form to the other brought about accelerated healing.

After all, his throat was fine.

No, the pain he saw in her eyes went soul deep.

Even as it made him wonder, his aggression still rode high.

She gazed down his body and stopped at his cock. Her nostrils flared.

Amid the scents of anger, fear, and defeat, another smell arose.

Lust.

His erection engorged even further.

She reached out toward him, and he knocked her hand away. She'd just tried to kill him. As much as he'd like to feel her hands and mouth on him, no way in hell was he letting her anywhere near such an integral piece of his anatomy.

"I don't think so, sweetheart." When she made to move away from him he tightened his grip on her arm. "Tell me who you are."

She looked at him again. He saw something shift in her eyes, courses of action considered and discarded until she made a decision. "You can call me Marie."

Marie. Probably not her real name, but it was better than *Oi, you!* "Marie it is." He studied her a moment. "Mind telling me why you just tried to kill me?"

She sighed. "It was a mistake. I'm sorry."

Hmm. Sorry she made a mistake—which he wasn't so sure he bought—or sorry she hadn't been successful?

She shifted her stance, widening her legs, and a fresh wave of the scent of her tangy arousal wafted to his nostrils. She put her hands on her hips and moved her shoulders back, thrusting out her breasts. "Well? Am I forgiven? Or do I need to . . . make it up to you?"

God. She wanted it as much as he did. Didn't have to ask him twice. And as long as he kept her facing away from him, she wouldn't have another chance to try to kill him again.

His cock pointed toward his belly, the tip ruddy with arousal and already dripping with pre-cum.

This stranger, her silky skin beckoning him, was just as lust-ridden as he. Sully wanted to pound into her like the animal he was.

Which was just what his wolf wanted. *Needed.* A fast, hard fuck.

The woman slowly turned her back to him and knelt, then dropped forward onto her hands and knees. Arching her back, she thrust her shapely ass toward him, letting him see the slick folds of her sex.

Thank God. She was wet and ready.

So was he.

Sully went to his knees behind her. Grasping her hips, he held her while he rubbed his cock through her cream.

"God!" Her voice was throaty, low. "Get on with it already."

The musky scent of her arousal—mixed with a citrus aroma—wound around his senses, tightening around him with silk-like threads. Sully brought one hand down and guided the tip of his cock into her pussy. Dear God, but he felt like he'd die if he didn't feel her around him now.

Lust, sharp and raw, surged inside him. With a growl he began pushing his way past slick, tight muscles until he was snug against her, his tight balls resting against her swollen sex.

She mewled and pushed her hips back, pressing against him, her inner muscles fluttering around his cock like tiny fingers. She lowered her torso, supporting herself on her forearms.

The movement inched her off his cock. Sully snarled and yanked her hips back, shoving his cock as deep as he could get it. Unable to stop the instinctive motion of his hips, he began thrusting inside her. Deep, hard.

Fast.

The drag of his cock through the tight clasp of her cunt had him howling inside. He needed . . . more. Something . . .

Following his instinct, he yanked her up onto her knees and leaned forward, fastening his teeth to the meaty part of her shoulder, as much to mark her as his as to hold her in place. Hot, coppery blood seeped into his mouth. Renewed heat surged through his body.

She moaned and thrust her hips against him, taking him as surely as he took her. Tendrils of hair stuck to the sweat on her neck.

His balls drew tight against the base of his shaft, and a shivery sensation along his spine signaled his impending climax. Wanting her to come with him, he slid one hand across her belly, fingers scissoring around her swollen clit.

She groaned. She undulated her hips and slid her hands to her breasts, and he knew she was fingering her nipples.

He wished he could do that for her. God, he wanted his hands everywhere on her body. Later. He'd touch her everywhere later.

And maybe even find out what her real name was.

And exactly what her game was.

Later. He'd find that all out later. Now was for . . . *this.* He surged into her again and again. Determined to feel her cunt milking him, Sully tugged and rubbed her clit harder. Lifting his mouth from her shoulder, he muttered, "Come with me!"

His voice sounded guttural, hardly human.

The woman writhed against him, slamming her hips

backward to meet every hard thrust of his cock. The slap of flesh against flesh, the smell of their arousal spiked his passion even higher.

The walls of her pussy clamped down around his cock. She let out a long wail and quaked beneath him.

One final plunge. Sully threw his head back and shouted his release, hips jerking as he jetted into her, gasping as the strong muscles of her cunt milked him of every last drop.

He collapsed onto her, pressing her against the sandy ground, satiated and relaxed for the first time in what felt like months. He kept his cock inside her, enjoying the feel of her pussy fluttering around him in little aftershocks of pleasure.

After a couple minutes, he roused enough to slide off to one side. His softened cock slipped out of her. He pressed a kiss to her shoulder, just underneath the ragged marks left by his teeth—marks that, he noticed, were already beginning to heal.

She lay relaxed against him for only a couple seconds before she stiffened. "Someone's coming."

Shit. He'd been so wrapped up in fucking her, in the sight and sound and smell of sex, he hadn't paid much attention to his surroundings. She was right. A new scent invaded the air. A scent he recognized.

Declan.

"It's all right," he muttered, getting to his feet and helping her up. "It's just my friend Declan. Stay behind me," he added, thinking to preserve her modesty. He turned toward the sound of Declan's footsteps in the gravelly sand.

From behind him he heard a noise and twisted to see the tail end of a wolf disappearing between two bushes. Marie was gone.

"Son of a bitch!" She was fast. Sully debated a moment

about going after her, but if she could shift into her wolf form and be on the move that quickly . . . he'd never catch up with her.

Declan came up over a small incline, one dark brow rising upon seeing Sully. He drew in a breath and glanced around.

"She's gone. Long gone." Sully walked forward, wincing when his foot came down on a sharp stone. He frowned and walked past Declan. "You know, this is pretty inconvenient, being starkers when you turn back into your human form."

"Tell me about it." Declan chuckled. "Although in the right place at the right time with the right woman, it's pretty damn *con*venient."

Sully thought of Marie. His cock perked up in interest. "Down, boy," he muttered.

"What's that?" Declan asked, taking a few jogging steps to catch up to him. Sully knew his friend had heard his comment, since his hearing was as enhanced as Sully's.

"You heard me. I can see where *this* could be rather inconvenient, too."

"Not if you're in the right place at the right time with the right woman."

"Oh, shut it." Sully walked carefully between two tall cacti, ducking his head to avoid one of their massive arms. "What's this called again?"

"Saguaro," Declan said, giving it a Spanish inflection so that the *g* sounded like an *h*. "This is a cool place, isn't it? Nowhere else like it on Earth."

Sully gave a noncommittal grunt. "A ski weekend in Switzerland is cool. Safari in Africa is cool. Trudging past cacti twice as tall as me with sand in places I've not had sand before is not cool."

He picked his way across the gravel driveway of Declan's property, heading toward the guest *casita*.

"Well, I came to find you to tell you that dinner's ready." Declan stopped near the front door of the main house.

Sully glanced back at him. "Give me a few minutes to get cleaned up."

Declan nodded. "Just go 'round to the back door and come on in. We're being informal tonight and eating in the kitchen. It's only family, after all." He grinned and went into the house, closing the door softly behind him.

It's only family.

Sully snorted. Yeah, just one big happy werewolf family. He curled his fist against the urge to slam it into something. Like Declan's smarmy face.

He glanced back toward the desert. He didn't know who Marie was or why she'd run from him—or why she'd tried to kill him and then let him fuck her—but he was sure as hell going to find out.

Chapter 4

Oh, God. Oh, *God*. OhGodohGodoh*God*.

Olivia skidded to a stop beside her car and shifted back to human, suffering through the pain in panicked silence. When she was human again, she grabbed her clothes off the backseat and dressed as fast as she could. Her heart thudded behind her ribs, less because of exertion from the mile or so she'd just run and more due to fear.

Leaving her shoes and socks on the back floorboard, she slammed the door shut and ran around to the driver's side. She opened the door and retrieved her keys from beneath the seat, then got into the car and started it up.

Olivia pulled the door shut and put the car in gear, spitting sand and gravel beneath her rear tires as she pulled away from the side of the road.

She didn't think he'd followed her, but she didn't want to take any chances.

God. She'd just had sex with Rory Sullivan. The man she'd gone there to kill.

Talk about fucking things up.

But, as usual after transitioning from wolf to human, she'd been so aroused she probably would've humped the first man that came along. That it was Sully threw a huge kink in the works.

"Can you possibly make things any worse now, Liv?" She glanced in the rearview mirror and breathed a small sigh at the clear road behind her. Turning her gaze back to the roadway ahead, she concentrated on driving to the hotel. If O'Connell hadn't come when he did, she could have taken advantage of Sully's . . . relaxed state and tried for another kill.

But all her mind could focus on was how sated she felt and how hot the sex had been and what a great body he had and . . .

Not on how she could go about ending his life.

By the time she reached the hotel a few miles away she'd managed to work it around in her mind to the point that what she'd initially thought of as a mistake might very well be turned to her advantage.

He'd be curious. And still angry that she'd attacked him. She could use that as a way in.

She just needed to run into Sully again. She'd get up early in the morning, shower, use her citrus perfume, and park downwind of O'Connell's. Then if they went any-where, she could follow and let him find her.

Over dinner, Sully tried to ignore the way Declan kept eyeing him, but by the time Pelicia went to the kitchen to fetch dessert he'd had enough. "What?" He glared at the Irishman.

"You can blame me all you want for this"—Declan leaned forward, bracing his elbows on the table, clasping his hands loosely—"but it won't change what's happened. And if I had to do it over again, I would." His jaw tight-ened. "I'd do anything to keep Pel safe."

Sully drew in a deep breath. Like him, Declan was a natural protector, and would let nothing stand in the way of keeping his woman safe. Sully understood that. Hell, he even appreciated the depth of Declan's love for Pelicia. It didn't mean, though, that he appreciated being the "nothing" that had stood between Pelicia and a werewolf.

But what was done was done. Declan was right about that. He needed to move on and deal with the changes occurring in his life.

Pelicia walked back in with a lemon meringue pie and a carafe. She set the carafe down, saying to Declan, "Would you pour the coffee, please?"

Declan did as he was asked. As she set the pie on the table, he leaned forward and swiped the tip of his finger through the meringue.

She swatted at his hand, the frown tugging at her mouth not matching the twinkle of good humor in her eyes. "I swear, you're worse than a two-year-old."

"Just don't believe in waitin' when I see a good thing." He grinned and leaned back in his chair.

"Well, you need to wait. Sully's our guest. He gets served first."

"I thought he was family." Declan lifted an eyebrow and folded his arms over his chest. "See how you rate?"

"Higher than you, of course." He ignored Declan's scowl, which he knew was just for show, and accepted the small plate Pelicia handed him. Picking up the dessert fork, he cut into the tip of the pie and lifted the piece to his mouth. Sweet and tart exploded on his taste buds. "This is good," he said around the mouthful of pie.

"The local grocery store's bakery does a wonderful job with pies and cakes. While I enjoy cooking, I don't do as much baking, so it's nice to be able to just run down to the corner and pick something up." Pelicia gave Declan a plate that held a piece that was easily a quarter of the pie. "You let me know if you want more, Sully. With your metabolism, you'll burn through those calories in no time."

He gave a nod and took another bite.

Pelicia picked up her coffee cup and turned, and Sully realized she was leaving the room.

"Aren't you havin' any pie, darlin'?" Declan reached out and touched her hip.

She shook her head. "I'm too full from dinner. I'll just put a little extra sugar in my coffee." She grinned. With a glance at Sully she said, "Besides, I think you blokes need to talk. Or throw a few punches. Whatever." She left the room, humming under her breath.

"That sounded rather like the theme from *Jaws*." Sully forked up his last bite of pie and leaned back in his chair.

"Well, we've the sharp teeth at any rate." Declan stood and stretched, bones cracking loudly enough that Sully heard them. Then he realized that it wouldn't have to be all that loud for him to hear.

While he saw the advantages of that, he still wasn't so sure he liked it.

He pushed away from the table and got to his feet. "I've lost my desire to plant my fist in your face. Though, knowing you, you'll give me reason enough in the not too distant future."

"An' aren't you just the comedian?" Declan shook his head and wandered into the living room. "So . . . you want to talk about your new friend?"

Sully shot him a look. "Not particularly." He walked over and stared through the patio doors. It was dark now; the living room behind him was reflected in the glass. But if he focused hard enough he could see the desert beyond the reflection. The tall silhouettes of the saguaro against the darker night, stars twinkling in the inky sky.

Movement caught his eye, and he watched a lone coyote wander along the edge of the yard on the other side of the oleanders. It paused and looked toward the house as if sensing it was being watched. Then it started on its way again, at a faster clip than before.

"Don't you think it's strange that you just ran into another werewolf—and a female one at that—by accident?" Declan's voice held a sardonic note that wasn't lost on Sully.

"What part of me saying 'not particularly' when you asked if I wanted to talk about it didn't you get?" Sully turned and looked at his friend.

"The part where you really didn't mean it, boyo." Declan folded his arms over his chest and rocked back on his heels. "This could be the best thing that ever happened to you, if you let it."

"The best thing . . ." Sully stared at Declan. The man had to be kidding. If Sully didn't lose his job over the attack on that suspect, he sure as hell wasn't going to get his next promotion when he should. This situation was the farthest thing from being the *best* thing that any *thing* could be.

A red-gold haze settled over his eyes. He blinked and shook his head, trying to make it go away. A growl left his throat.

"And you goin' all wolfie on me isn't gonna change anythin', either." Declan's voice, the brogue a bit thicker, sounded tinny, yet loud.

Sully's breath came fast and hard, his lungs laboring to provide oxygen to a beast that wanted to be let loose. Looking at Declan, who stood alert, his shoulders slightly hunched and hands held loosely at his sides, weight balanced on the balls of his feet, Sully decided to let the fur fly.

With a growled epithet he launched himself at Declan. The other man met him halfway, his eyes wolf-amber and a snarl coming from his mouth. Their bodies came together, bones and muscles thudding, fingers gripping for purchase. Sully had one thought—get Declan on his back, make him show his vulnerable belly and throat.

And get him to admit that he'd ruined Sully's life.

Sully drew back his fist and slammed it into Declan's jaw. The other man's head snapped back, but he charged right back, his own fist flying toward Sully's face.

Sully ducked the blow and rammed his shoulder into Declan's belly, taking both of them to the floor. He ignored the pain in his knees as they smashed onto the hard tile.

Dimly he heard Pelicia's voice, vaguely saw her skirt around them to the patio doors, which she shoved open. Over the sounds of night creatures he heard the dryness in her voice as she muttered, "I meant for you to take it outside." A slight pause, then a disgruntled, "Werewolves."

Sully had no interest in stopping the fight long enough to be civilized and move it outdoors. If he ended up trashing Declan's house, so much the better, since Declan had trashed Sully's *life*.

He grunted as Declan slammed his fist into Sully's side. Another fist to his face, snapping his teeth together. Sully growled and mashed his fist into Declan's face. He winced at the pain of bone meeting bone, but when blood welled from Declan's split lower lip, raw, savage satisfaction rippled through Sully. He rolled off his friend, getting to his feet in one fluid move.

"You sure you wanna go here, boyo?" Declan stood.

Reaching up, he wiped blood from his split lip. When he looked at Sully, his eyes still held flecks of amber, though the wildness of before was muted. "It isn't going to change a damn thing."

"Might make me feel better," Sully muttered. He flexed his right hand, feeling the sting of battered knuckles already fading. That still surprised him. He and Declan could go ten rounds this way, and still be able to go ten more. Twenty, even.

"Gettin' that sour puss of yours pounded would make you feel better?" Declan's tone suggested he was surprised by the notion. Even as Sully watched, the wound on Declan's lip knit closed. Declan held up his hands in a boxer's stance. "Well, I'm more than willin' to oblige. Let's go."

Sully let out a sigh. "You're a son of a bitch, you know that?"

"Aye, I've heard it said before." He bounced around a bit, shuffling his feet and punching his fists toward Sully. "Come on, then."

"You're also an arse." Sully sighed again and plopped down on the sofa.

"I've heard that said before, too." Declan punched the air a few more times, eyebrows raised with a "Sure you don't wanna go again?" look, then shrugged and sat down in an armchair. "Well, that was highly . . . unsatisfying. I hope you did better with the woman out in the desert."

"Fuck you." Sully slouched down and leaned his head against the back on the sofa.

"Get in line."

There was silence between them for a few moments. Then Pelicia walked into the room. "Are you done? Or should I leave the doors open so even more bugs can get into the house?"

Declan got up with a grin. He closed the patio doors and went over to his fiancée. Enfolding her in a hug, he pressed a kiss to the top of her head. "She has a thing about bugs," he said to Sully.

"And wrongheaded men, too." She shot Sully a look. There was much less sympathy there than had been before. It appeared her patience with his whinging was nearing an end.

He couldn't blame her. There wasn't anything he hated more than a man who sat around pissing and moaning over the hand fate had dealt him. If you couldn't change what happened then you just handled it as best you could.

He hadn't done a very good job of handling it so far.

He'd have to do better.

The next morning, Olivia took her place in line at a small coffee shop near O'Connell's and tuned in on the conversation taking place a few tables away.

"I'm telling you, she tried to kill me. She had her teeth in my throat."

Even though their voices were muted, Olivia had no trouble hearing Sully and O'Connell as they talked at a corner table in the local coffee shop. She paid for her chai and took a seat nearby, out of Sully's direct line of vision but close enough he'd be able to spot her when she wanted him to. She made sure to slouch so that the big guy at the table in front of her further hid her from view.

She'd doused herself liberally with her citrus perfume, so she smelled very lemony. The big guy at the next table looked up at her and frowned.

Maybe too lemony, but she wanted Sully to see her when *she* wanted it to happen. She lifted an eyebrow at the guy blocking her view, and he shifted his gaze to look away.

"And so you had sex with her." O'Connell's voice was dry.

"Shut it." Sully huffed an aggrieved sigh. "There's something familiar about her." His voice dropped a notch. "I know I've seen her before. I just can't place from where."

Olivia scrunched down. The only place he could have seen her was outside his town house in London, when she'd gotten out of the cab. But he hadn't seen her face, she was sure of it.

"Does it really matter?" O'Connell made a gruff sound. "What we need to know is *why* she tried to kill you, boyo." O'Connell's Irish brogue thickened. "And knowin' who she is would get us started."

That was her cue.

She picked up her container of tea and started toward the door.

"That's her," she heard Sully mutter, then the scrape of chairs. Hard fingers wrapped around her arm, just above her elbow. "I think we need to talk, *Marie*. Don't you?"

Sully hustled the woman out of the coffee shop, Declan on his heels. Surprised that she didn't struggle, he nonetheless kept a firm grip on her arm as they walked to Declan's SUV. He was glad that Declan had decided to leave the Mustang at home and drive the big SUV instead. The larger vehicle would be much more conducive to holding a conversation with this tricky little wolf.

After Declan unlocked the vehicle, Sully opened the back door and helped her in, then climbed in behind her. Declan got in on the other side, effectively blocking her inside the SUV.

"Now, *Marie*. Let's start from the top, shall we?" Sully turned in the seat to face her, which crowded her back against Declan, who didn't budge.

Discomfort flitted across her face before she schooled her features to impassivity. "The top of what?"

Sully took the cup out of her hand and reached up to put it in the holder between the two front seats. He turned back to her with a low growl of frustration. "Don't play games with me, *Marie*. I'm not in the mood."

She stared at him without responding. When he let out another growl, she held up one hand and said, "All right. All right." She glanced over her shoulder at Declan and then looked back at Sully. "I thought"—she shrugged and glanced down at her fingers, twisting together in her lap—"I thought you would hurt me. It's all I've ever known."

Declan leaned forward. "You're the Omega of your pack." He caught the look Sully sent him and shrugged, a grimace tugging at the edges of his mouth. "I did a lot of readin' while I was at Ryder's."

Marie's dark head bobbed. She looked at Sully, her blue eyes wide and dark. "I figured, for once in my life, I'd make the first move."

"Hurt me before I could hurt you?" He could understand that, and it made him wonder just what her life had been like since she'd been turned.

She nodded and looked back down at her hands. "I am sorry. It was . . . instinctual."

"And the sex?" Sully stared at her, trying to figure her out.

She gave a little shrug, her cheeks tinged with red. She cast an uncomfortable glance at Declan but answered easily enough. "You know how it is after you shift."

"So I was handy?"

"Oh, I'd say you were a little more than just handy." A slight grin curved her pouty lips, and Sully found himself smiling in response. When she glanced at him, arousal flared in her eyes, flecking the blue with wolf-amber and driving away her slight embarrassment. "Cocky is the word that comes to mind."

He drew in a breath, his gut—and other parts—tightening in lust. Remembering what her silky cunt had felt like clasped around him, he wanted to plunge into her and lose himself in her again and again.

And again.

"All right, all right," Declan muttered.

By the look on his face Sully could tell that his friend had sensed the heightened sexual tension between the two of them.

"Maybe we should go back to the house where we can talk in private but a little more comfortably," Sully suggested.

"What, get to know each other a bit better?" Declan rolled his eyes. Opening his door, he got out of the vehicle. "Good idea. Before you two start up anythin'," he muttered. He slammed the door shut and opened the driver's door, glancing at Sully with one brow lifted as he climbed behind the wheel. "Of course, I don't want to be accused of kidnappin' here. You all right to come home with us, Marie? My fiancée will be there."

Sully reckoned that his friend tacked that on so she wouldn't feel threatened by going home with two men. The thought of sharing her with another man brought immediate and irrational jealousy.

It wasn't as if he had any claim to her. She didn't belong to him any more than he belonged to her.

And the absurd feeling of regret that followed that thought he ruthlessly pushed aside.

"Well, I . . ." Marie looked at Sully and then at Declan. She spread her hands. "Your fiancée won't mind?"

Declan shook his head and twisted around to face front again. "She won't mind. Probably will be glad to have another woman around." He pulled his door shut and fastened his seatbelt, then inserted the key into the ignition. When the engine kicked to life, he shifted the gear and pulled out of the parking space.

"Even if that other woman is a werewolf?" There was hesitation in Marie's voice.

Sully was quick to reassure her. "Pel's great. She'll be delighted."

Declan glanced to the side, lips pressed together, and Sully knew his friend fought a grin.

Damn. He was acting like a teenager with a crush on a pretty girl.

Well, she was more than pretty. She was beautiful.

Intoxicating.

And very likely habit-forming.

While in the past a thought like that about a woman would have had him running in the opposite direction, he felt at ease with it. Anticipated it, even.

Was that because he'd matured? Or because the wolf was wiser than the man?

"So, we're good to go, then?" Declan stopped the SUV at the end of the shopping center driveway, waiting to turn onto the main road, and watched them through the rearview mirror.

Marie nodded. "We're good to go."

They drove along in silence a few seconds. Sully glanced out the side window and watched the passing scenery, again noting the complete alien nature of this landscape compared to what he was used to. Turning back to Marie, he asked, "So, what's your real name?"

She went still, like a small prey animal sensing a nearby

hunter—or someone who expected retribution to be exacted. God. What the hell had happened to her to make her react like that?

The creamy skin of her throat moved with her swallow. Her expression flickered, and he knew she was weighing her options and deciding whether to tell the truth or continue lying to him. Finally, she whispered, "Olivia. My name's Olivia."

"Olivia . . . ?" He trailed off, prompting her for a last name.

Her dark blue gaze cut to him. Amid the submissiveness was clear irritation, perhaps even the beginnings of anger. "Let's just leave it at Olivia for now, okay?"

Damn, but she was beautiful when she was peeved. He was happy her spirit hadn't been completely broken by whatever life had done to her. Sully bit back a grin and gave a nod of agreement. "Fine. I'm Rory Sullivan—but everyone calls me Sully—and the bloke up front is Declan O'Connell."

Declan made the turn onto the rough road that led to his house. "Just another minute or so." His gaze met Sully's in the rearview mirror. He lifted an eyebrow as if to ask *You sure you know what you're doing*?

Sully gave a short nod. As soon as the vehicle glided to a stop, he got out and went around the SUV to Olivia's side, standing there as she hopped down. Unable to shake the feeling she'd take off the first chance she got—even though she hadn't fought them at all up to now—he wrapped his fingers around her elbow and guided her into the house.

"Pelicia, this is Olivia, a new . . . friend of Sully's." Declan bent and gave his fiancée a kiss on one cheek. "Let's pour some iced tea for everyone." He looked at Olivia. "Or would you prefer somethin' a bit stronger?"

"Tea's fine." Her voice was soft, her gaze sharp as she took in her surroundings.

"I'd like something a bit stronger," Sully muttered. "How about a beer?"

"It's in the fridge," Pelicia said.

As a fellow Brit, he knew she realized he'd be used to drinking beer at room temperature. "Lager or dark ale?"

She tipped her head toward Declan. "Guinness, what else?"

"Iced tea's fine." Sully ignored Declan's snort and looked at Olivia.

Declan and Pelicia headed toward the kitchen, and Sully gestured toward the sofa.

Olivia gave a little sigh and sat down on the end. Sully sat next to her, close enough to grab her if she decided to move.

Close enough that he could feel her thigh against his before she shifted and crossed her legs.

"So, Olivia"—he turned toward her, one arm along the back of the couch—"tell me more about yourself. I can't place the accent exactly, but I'd say you're from one of the Northeastern states, right? New York, or New Jersey maybe?"

Her brows dipped a little, but she replied easily enough, "New York. I'm originally from Virginia, but my husband worked in the city, so when we got engaged I moved there, too."

"So you're married?" He glanced at her ringless left hand.

She touched her ring finger with her right thumb. "He's dead. Almost six years now."

"I'm sorry." Sully lightly touched her shoulder and then put his hand back on the sofa. "Truly."

Her gaze met his. "Thank you. He was a good man." Sorrow darkened the vibrant blue of her irises before she shook it off. "But we had a beautiful little girl together, so I still have part of him with me."

"So, you're livin' here in Tucson now?" Declan asked as he walked back into the room.

"Ah, no. I'm here . . . on a job assignment." She looked uncomfortable with the line of questioning.

Sully decided to back off. Sometimes you got more information from a suspect by playing it cool instead of going after him—or in this case her—with both barrels blazing.

"You said you have a little girl?" Pelicia handed Olivia a glass of iced tea. "What's her name? How old is she?"

Olivia accepted the tea with a smile. "Zoe. And she just turned six."

"Just turned . . ." Sully did the math. "She was just a baby when her father died, then?"

She nodded and looked down. "He was a cop with the NYPD. He died in a shoot-out between gangbangers." She was silent a moment. "He was a good man," she repeated.

"I'm sure he was." Pelicia sat in one of the big armchairs opposite the sofa. "What was his name?"

"David." Olivia looked up. A sad smile flitted over her face. "He'd just welcomed his little girl into the world and passed his detective exam. He was so proud." She glanced down at her tea. Then she took a sip and seemed to shake herself of her sorrowful mood. She looked up with a genuine smile. "Anyway, that's ancient news, right?"

Pelicia returned the smile. "So, Declan was telling me that you and Sully met out in the desert when you were both in wolf form. Was that strange?"

"It was for me." Sully shook his head. "I hadn't expected to be able to shift so soon, regardless of what you said," he added with a look at Declan. "There I was, minding my own business, when I smelled something . . . different. Another werewolf." He raised his eyebrows. "I don't know why it seems so weird to be able to smell that someone's a werewolf, but it is."

"A dog's sense of smell is about a thousand times more acute than a human's." Olivia took another sip of iced tea. "And a werewolf's is even more acute than a dog's, so it stands to reason we'd be able to pick up on the most subtle of scents."

"Unless citrus comes into play." Declan scowled. "That trick was used on us back on St. Mary's. In the Isles of Scilly off the Cornish coast," he added for Olivia's benefit. "Couldn't smell anything except that."

"And yet you have lemon trees here." Sully tipped his head to one side.

"Which are going to go as soon as I can get someone out here to cut them down. But, enough about that." He set his glass on the small table at his side. He looked at Olivia with such intensity that Sully knew the idle chitchat was over. "You were going to tell us about trying to kill Sully."

She frowned and fidgeted a bit, uncrossing her legs only to cross them again. "I already told you." She glanced at Sully. "I was scared, coming across an Alpha so unexpectedly."

"Yes, but—"

"Declan, give the girl some room to breathe." Pelicia threw a glare at him. "The last thing we need right now is you going into your Black Ops Commando routine."

He scowled right back at her. "I'm not goin' into my Black Ops Commando routine. And even if I was—"

"They're like a little old married couple, aren't they?" Sully said from the corner of his mouth. He grinned at Olivia's muffled snort of laughter.

Declan and Pelicia both looked at him, and he could see laughter lurking in their eyes.

He shook his head. "They just do this so they can have makeup sex," he said. Pelicia blushed. "Come on, Pel. Americans are much more frank in their discussions, aren't you?" he asked Olivia.

She pursed her lips. "Some of us are, I suppose."

"Some?" Sully's lips twitched with a grin. "I seem to recall someone calling me cocky. And not in the arrogant sense of the word, either."

Olivia's gaze darted to his groin, and the body part in question stirred to life. He could smell the arousal building in her, could see it in the little amber flecks that appeared in her irises.

She abruptly leaned forward and set her glass of iced tea on the coffee table in front of her, then stood. "I, ah, thank you for the tea, Pelicia, and for allowing me into your beautiful home." Her hands clenched briefly. "But I really need to be going."

"Oh, so soon?" Pelicia seemed genuinely disappointed. "Well, as long as you promise to come back again."

"That's a guarantee," Sully said before Olivia could respond.

She gave him a sidelong glance but nodded. "Absolutely." She looked at Declan. "Can I get a ride back to my car at the shopping center?"

"Sure thing, lass." He stood and fished his car keys out of his front pocket. "You comin' along?" he asked Sully.

"Of course." He gave a nod of his head to Pelicia. "Thanks, love. We'll be back in a few minutes."

"It was nice to meet you," she said to Olivia as the other woman was already opening the front door.

"You, too," she responded. "I'll see you later."

Five minutes later, after a ride in which Olivia proved to be stubbornly silent, Sully stood beside Declan and watched her get into her modest four-door hired car. "Hey," he called out before she closed the door. He walked over to the car as she shut the door.

She started the car and rolled down the window, looking up at him with a questioning expression.

"Have dinner with me," he said. "Just you and me. We can get to know each other a little better."

Interest flickered in her gaze. "Sure."

He licked his lips and gave a nod. "I'll pick you up around six."

Her eyes narrowed slightly. "Why don't I just drive over to Declan's? We can leave from there."

"All right," he agreed slowly. If she wanted to stay mysterious, he was still willing to play along.

"See you at six." She waggled her fingers at him and put the car in gear.

He walked back over to the SUV and stood next to Declan, turning so he could watch Olivia leave.

"At least we know where she's stayin'." Declan folded his arms across his chest.

"If she was telling the truth." Sully couldn't be sure about anything she'd told them, though he didn't doubt that Olivia was her real name.

"You think she lied?"

"Most people lie, and I think this one's cagey. So I wouldn't put it past her." Sully glanced at Declan then put his gaze back on Olivia's car as she drove out of the parking lot and onto the main road.

"Whatever she is in her pack, she's definitely *not* an Omega." Declan's voice was thoughtful.

"What makes you say that?"

"She's spunky. If she's bein' made to bear the pack's aggression, it's unwillingly. It's not in her to be submissive like that." He looked at Sully and then opened the driver's door. "Couldn't you see that?"

Sully gave a nod. He climbed into the SUV, closing the door behind him. As he fastened his seat belt, he murmured, "She's not telling us the full truth, I know that much."

"Finally puttin' those acclaimed detective skills to use, are you?" Declan shook his head. "Nice to see you usin' your big head for a change."

"Shut it." Sully gazed out the side window, taking in the passing scenery with only vague interest. He kept turning the morning's conversation over and over in his head, trying to pinpoint exactly what it was that bothered him. But it was evasive.

Just like Olivia.

Chapter 5

Eddy stared down at the little girl quietly playing with her Barbies. He stretched one arm along the back of the sofa and contemplated the situation.

Olivia Felan had four days left in which to kill Sullivan. If she failed . . .

He sighed. He didn't want to hurt Zoe, much less kill her. He really did love her—who wouldn't? All those dark curls and impish face, along with a sweet, sunny personality. She was a joy to have around.

He would even go so far as to say he couldn't love her more if she were his own. But he hadn't gotten where he was today by being Mr. Nice Guy. He would do what was necessary and learn to live with it, just like he had everything else.

Another brick in the wall around his heart would be worth it to finally realize his dream. To make his life absolutely perfect there was no room for cousin Ryder. The bastard should have died in that cave-in when he was a child. Then Eddy would have had the loving family he deserved—been a son instead of the poor little orphan his aunt and uncle had taken in out of pity.

He should be the one with the fame and fortune.

Removing Ryder Merrick from the world would be like cauterizing an open, bloody wound. It would leave behind healthy tissue with all memories of pain fading away into oblivion.

Twenty years was enough time to wait. Olivia had better get a move on or there'd be hell to pay.

Starting with the little girl playing at his feet.

Leaning over, he ran his palm gently over the top of Zoe's head.

She looked up with a winsome grin. "Wanna play dolls with me, Uncle Eddy?"

"Sure thing, poppet." Eddy slid down to the floor, stretching his legs under the coffee table. He accepted the blond-haired doll she gave him and stared at it in his big hand. Fragile and vulnerable, just like Zoe, who he could also crush with very little effort.

And he would if he didn't get what he wanted. What he wanted was that miserable bastard Merrick to suffer before he died. By first losing the few friends he had—O'Connell and Sullivan, and from what he'd heard a new wife—well, that would be sweet vengeance, indeed.

Eddy wondered if he should head to Arizona so he could keep a closer eye on things—be more up close and personal so that if Olivia did screw things up, he could step in and take care of it himself.

Probably should have done that from the beginning. O'Connell and Sullivan would already be dead, and Eddy could focus all of his attention on Merrick and his new bride.

But what was done—or not done—was in the past. All he had was the present, and he would make the most of it.

Besides, that was why he had underlings—to take care

of the nitty-gritty things so he could focus on the bigger picture. And the bigger picture was Ryder Merrick.

He glanced over at Zoe. He had other things to attend to first. With a ruthlessness he was quite proud to possess, he pushed aside thoughts of vengeance and death and smiled down at the doll in his hand. He pushed up one plastic arm, then pressed it back down to the doll's side. "You sure you want me to be Barbie? Shouldn't I be Ken? I *am* a boy, you know."

Zoe giggled and shook her head. "I like it when you're Barbie. Your voice goes funny when you talk high."

He grinned. It *was* fun making his voice go falsetto so he could sound more like a woman. And listening to Zoe's sweet giggles made his day, every day. "So shall we be retail workers today, sweetie? Or office?"

Chapter 6

Olivia closed the door of her hotel room—not the hotel where she'd told Sully and O'Connell she was staying—and leaned against it a moment. Closing her eyes, she replayed the events of the day, lingering over the sense of camaraderie she'd felt with Sully and his friends.

Camaraderie she'd never gotten from her own pack. Probably would never get. Why couldn't she have met these people first, before Eddy had ruined her life?

Pelicia had been more than just a gracious hostess. She'd genuinely been interested in Olivia, wanting to befriend her with no agenda of her own that Olivia could discern.

O'Connell had been a likeable devil, full of mischief and endearingly affectionate with his fiancée.

Olivia could easily see herself becoming fast friends with those two. If things were different. They were hardly likely to become friends once she killed Sully.

She gritted her teeth and fought back despair. *Sully.* He'd been charming and attentive. Alternately teasing and intense, leaving no doubt as to his interest in her.

An interest that, in all honesty, she shared.

But an interest that could lead nowhere.

She straightened and walked into the room, sitting down on the queen-size bed. With a sigh, she toed off her shoes and plopped back onto the bed, arms splayed, and stared at the ceiling.

What to do? What to do . . .

Olivia brought one hand up and rubbed her forehead. She saw no way out of this. If she didn't kill Sully, she knew Eddy *would* kill Zoe.

And it wasn't as if she could go to the police. The first "law" of lycanthropy was to keep it a secret, at all costs. It was something as instinctive as the urge to run free.

Plus Eddy had enough clout with the authorities in New York that they'd never believe her about him. About any of it. Even if she could have him arrested for kidnapping, that wouldn't guarantee Zoe's safety. Olivia could take her daughter and run as far and as fast as possible, but someone, somewhere, would catch up with them.

Of course, there was no guarantee that successful completion of her "mission" would necessarily guarantee safety, either. As long as Eddy was alive, she and Zoe would never be assured of anything, including their next breaths.

He never really had explained—not to her satisfaction, anyway—why he was so desperate to have Sully and O'Connell killed. At least he hadn't asked her to do both of them.

Yet.

Olivia drew in a shaky breath. God, it would never end. She closed her eyes against burning tears. Killing Sully was just the first step down that slippery slope. If she did this, if she took the life of another person, it would only be the first in a long line of what would become nameless, faceless victims. Eddy would see to it that she became as indifferent to taking life as he was.

There are a lot of people on this planet, he was fond of saying. *In the overall scheme of things, a few here and there won't be missed.*

Becoming a killer would destroy her soul. Not becoming a killer would destroy her daughter. But what would it do to Zoe when she found out exactly how much of a monster her mother had become?

Turning into a werewolf was a thing over which Olivia had had no choice. Turning into a killer . . . well, that was something she *could* control.

With a sigh, she swung her legs up and turned to her side. She grabbed a pillow from beneath the covers and scrunched it under her head. She could just ask Sully for help. He was a cop, and O'Connell was former Special Ops or some such thing. They'd have the kind of combat training Eddy and his cronies didn't. But they hadn't been werewolves nearly as long as most in her pack. Eddy had been one for at least twenty years, and many of those in the upper echelons nearly that long.

But even if Sully and O'Connell could help, why would they? They didn't know her.

She'd just have to let them get to know her. In less than a week. And convince them that they had to go to New York for a fight in which they had no personal stake and in which they might die.

Good God. She sighed. It'd be easier to kill Sully, for crying out loud.

But then whoever said the easiest road was the right road?

Olivia flopped over onto her back and stared at the ceiling. It all came down to what she could do to save Zoe in the limited amount of time she had.

Her date with Sully—to go up to the small town of

Summerhaven on Mount Lemmon for dinner—could be the opening she needed. She'd play things by ear. Either she'd get a chance to ask him for help, or she'd have a window of opportunity to take him out.

Whichever happened first, she had to act.

Sully sat on the edge of the bed in the guesthouse and stared through the window at the desert beyond. It all seemed so surreal—do one little favor for a friend and have everything go completely sideways. In less than a fortnight he'd gone from being a highly valued member of the CID to one very close to official sanction. Not to mention he'd left the ranks of ordinary humans and had taken his place among movie monsters.

Only this wasn't a movie. This was his life.

He heaved a sigh. Goddamn. If someone had told him a month ago that he'd literally howl at the moon one day, he'd have thought them deranged. And while he couldn't deny the pluses that seemed to go along with turning furry once a month—the positives of which Declan continually reminded him—the negatives far outweighed them as far as Sully was concerned.

Every man had a dark part to his soul—the part that enabled him to take another life, whether justified or not; the part that could destroy as easily as create—and in his limited experience the wolf brought out that dark side much too readily.

His emotions seemed to roil just below the surface, especially the more aggressive ones—anger, hatred, fear. Always before he'd been able to channel those emotions into positive actions, notably when it came to bringing down the bad guys. This time when he'd brought the bad guy down, though, he'd done it literally, and those aggressive emotions had almost certainly cost him something when it came to his career.

And very possibly when it came to his soul.

The only good thing he could see coming out of this was Olivia. He would bet good money their paths would never have crossed if he hadn't been turned into a werewolf. There would have been no reason for him to travel to Arizona. When he left the Isles of Scilly he'd have gone back to his life and found it just the way he'd left it—neat, orderly, and sane.

He certainly wouldn't have entertained the notion of biting a suspect.

Or his sexual partner. Christ. He'd had strong reactions upon meeting a woman before, but never anything on the scale of what he felt with Olivia. Perhaps it was because everything seemed magnified because of the wolf. His senses and his emotions were enhanced.

Though he'd certainly never been careless enough to have unprotected sex before. But, God! What sex it had been. He was looking forward to getting her onto this nice, soft bed.

Not like that was going to happen any time soon, the way Declan kept poking his nose into things. First he'd almost interrupted them out in the desert and now, when Sully had invited her on a date, Declan had invited himself and Pelicia along as well.

Just what Sully needed. A double date with O'Connell.

He sighed and stretched his legs out in front of him, and leaned back with his palms braced against the mattress. He had a feeling there was more happening with Olivia than she was letting on. It was something he'd seen in her eyes—a hint of desperation, of . . . panic.

But except for that fleeting glimpse, she'd played it cool.

Her laughter had come easily and had seemed genuine. He thought she'd enjoyed herself. Certainly she seemed to have relaxed her guard, though every once in a while he sensed her tensing up and a shadow moved over her face as if her thoughts had turned dark. It was so fleeting he would have missed it if he hadn't been so focused on her.

He was determined to get to know her. To uncover her secrets.

And her body. He'd hoped they could make use of this big bed tonight, but with the way Declan was horning in on things . . .

Well, at least according to Pelicia, he'd get some decent pie up on the mountain.

"Mack, you've outdone yourself," O'Connell said as he sat back in his chair and looked up at the owner of the restaurant.

From behind him Olivia could see the outdoor patio where a few people sat at tables in the sun.

O'Connell went on. "That chili has to be the best yet." He lightly patted his flat stomach.

"Well, I hope you saved room for dessert." Mack propped his hands on his hips. "We make a killer chocolate cake here—the best Mt. Lemmon has to offer."

Olivia thought about telling him she was too full, but she had a definite weakness for chocolate and found herself ordering the cake. After the server placed a piece of three-layer cake in front of her, she was glad she had. The aroma of chocolate and raspberry—with the light scent of vanilla from the melting ice cream—was too tantalizing to pass up.

Licking her lips, she cut into the cake and pushed it through the raspberry sauce drizzled onto the plate. When the decadent flavor hit her tongue, she moaned and leaned back in her chair, her eyes fluttering closed.

A slight shiver of delight went through her, and she couldn't hold back another low moan. It was just so good.

She became aware that the others at the table had gone silent. Opening her eyes, she saw her companions staring at her, amusement on their faces. She also realized Mack was still standing there. With delicate care she placed her fork on her plate and lifted her napkin to her lips.

A grin creased the owner's face. Shaking his head, he murmured, "It's a pleasure to see someone enjoying my food the way you do."

Heat flooded her face. She must look like a piglet, eating like there was no tomorrow. While there was no denying that she'd always enjoyed food—the tastes and the textures—there was more to it than that. It was yet another aspect of the increased metabolism thanks to her inner wolf—which had apparently eaten the little pig.

Or all three of them.

Mack's hand fluttered near her as if he meant to pat her on the back but was unsure if he should touch her. "Oh, please, I meant it as a compliment." His cheeks colored as well.

Olivia couldn't help but feel bad. Her embarrassment had embarrassed *him*. "I was hungry," she said, trying to ignore the amused glances she was getting from her dinner companions, especially Sully. Amusement was so not the reaction she wanted from him—not if they were going to have wild monkey sex later on.

Which was certainly on her agenda.

"It's really good," she went on to assure the restaurant owner.

He smiled. "Well, I'm happy you like it." He looked

around the table. "Dessert's on the house, folks." He dipped his head and headed into the kitchen.

She saw Pelicia glance from her to Sully and back again. "Um, Declan, let's take our cake and coffee out onto the terrace, all right? It's too nice outside not to take advantage of the sun." Without waiting for his response, she stood and picked up her plate and coffee cup.

O'Connell shrugged and followed suit. "Guess we're goin' out onto the patio where the sun's shinin'. But it's bloody cold," he muttered and followed his fiancée.

Olivia's eyes partly closed as the smorgasbord of aromas hit her nose again. She looked down at the cake. *Just one more bite*, she promised herself. She forked up a piece and popped it into her mouth.

Okay, maybe two.

As before, she couldn't contain a low moan of almost orgasmic delight at the decadent taste.

"It's almost as good as sex, isn't it?" Sully's voice came as a low rasp.

Olivia looked at him. Gone was the humor. His eyes were heavy-lidded and glittering with sensual awareness. It gave him a dangerous, feral look that, combined with the testosterone oozing from him, brought her to instant, heady awareness. He was a big man, tall and broad, and she knew firsthand how he could use his size to his advantage over smaller, weaker prey.

That wasn't what worried her.

It was those hooded emerald eyes burning with restrained carnal hunger. If he didn't stop looking at her like that, she was going to jump his bones—well, one of them, anyway—regardless of how many onlookers there might be.

It was getting harder and harder to think about killing him.

She swallowed the bite of cake and licked her suddenly dry lips. His gaze tracked the movement. He leaned forward in his chair with a casual grace that made her heart beat a little faster. God, this man was sex on a stick. She'd never felt so aroused so fast by a man before, and it made her feel a little out of her element.

But, never one to run from a challenge, she took a deep breath and lifted her chin. She could give as good as she got. "Yeah, it's almost as good as sex," she agreed, if untruthfully. She couldn't imagine anything even coming close to how good sex was with this man.

Sully reached out and swept his thumb over the corner of her mouth. "You missed some," he said, his voice low and husky.

Before he could move his hand away, she turned her head and sucked his thumb into her mouth. Keeping her gaze on his smoldering one, she brought her teeth lightly down on his thumb, trapping it between her lips, and licked the chocolate off, swirling her tongue over the pad of his thumb.

His eyes darkened, the pupils dilating and amber specking his irises as arousal built. Lips parting, he stroked his index finger along her cheek and pressed his thumb a little farther into her mouth.

Oh, Lord. Her body responded, her core tightening, her clit setting up an insistent throb.

He slowly pulled his hand away and picked up her fork. He speared another piece of cake and held it to her lips.

"I shouldn't," she demurred, not wanting to ruin the erotic moment. She wanted him to think of her as a sexy beast, not a little pig.

But, dayum. That cake was too good to leave on the plate.

"I admire a woman who doesn't pick at her food. Besides, there's always room for . . . chocolate." Sully's voice dipped at the end, running over her nerve endings like rough silk. "Or so I've heard said."

Olivia let him feed her the bite. As her lips closed over the fork, his eyes glittered with heat. His face darkened with desire, and his other hand clenched on the table. He dropped his gaze long enough to scoop up another piece of cake.

She waited until he looked at her again to run her tongue over her lips. His nostrils flared, but he said nothing as he put the fork to her mouth. She clasped his hand, gently taking the fork from his fingers, and cut into the cake. She lifted the piece to his mouth, gaze focused on those kissable lips as they parted.

What was it about this man that made the simple act of eating cake such a turn-on? The muscles in his jaw bunched as he chewed. As he swallowed, the strong muscles of his throat making his Adam's apple bob, she drew in a breath.

A murmur of conversation from a couple at the next table brought her back to the realization that they were in a public place. And she wasn't *that* adventurous.

Olivia set the fork onto the plate and looked around the room, casting about for something to start up a conversation that didn't include sexual innuendoes. She leaned back, picked up her cup, and took a sip of coffee. The slightly bitter flavor blended with the chocolate, and she took another sip before saying, "It's really very pretty up here. So different from the valley."

Giving a mental roll of her eyes, she fought back renewed embarrassment. How lame, but it was the best she could do given the way he was looking at her and how her body was responding.

Holding her gaze, Sully speared another piece of cake and brought it to his lips. She watched, mesmerized, as his mouth closed around the tines of the fork. As he drew it away, his tongue swept out, licking away a smear of chocolate and leaving his bottom lip deliciously wet.

"So, Olivia," he said, leaning back in his chair and apparently willing—for the moment at least—to cease and desist in the sensual teasing department, "tell me why you're here."

"You invited me," she quipped. Even though she'd told herself to take an opening when it came up, she didn't want the conversation to head that way. She wasn't ready to end the day.

And end it most likely would, if she told him the truth.

"That's not what I meant, and you know it."

She sighed. This *was* an opening, and she should take it. "It's . . . complicated." At his narrow-eyed look she faltered. This wasn't going to be easy.

Not that she'd thought it would be.

With the ease and grace of an animal—a large, predatory animal that was looking at her as if she were good enough to eat—he leaned forward again and captured one of her hands where it rested on the table. Idly playing with her fingers, he murmured, "Uncomplicate it for me." He looked up at her then, his steady gaze snagging hers.

She stared down at his big hand, the blunt-edged fingers gentle around hers.

The wrong thing done for the right reason is still the wrong thing.

Olivia couldn't bargain for her daughter's life by killing

Sully when there might be another way. She had to at least give it a try. She licked her lips. "I told you that I have a daughter. I . . . could use your help."

He turned her hand over and began rubbing across the veins in her inner wrist.

Her pulse jumped, then pounded erratically. She hadn't realized before how much of an erogenous zone that was for her.

"Help with what?"

Olivia was so focused on that damn thumb of his she almost didn't hear the question. With a start, she looked into his eyes. There was no easy way to say it, so she didn't bother trying to dress it up. She kept her voice low so she wouldn't be overheard by the diners at nearby tables. "My alpha is holding my daughter hostage and will kill her if I don't kill *you*."

Chapter 7

"I beg your pardon?" Sully's thumb stilled. He surely hadn't just heard what he *thought* he heard.

He watched an inner struggle play across her face and, once again, felt a connection to this stranger. He hated to ask for help, too.

She glanced around the small restaurant. "Do you mind if we go outside? We can find a more . . . private spot to talk."

Without a word he snagged the server's attention and pointed to the patio. "Give them the bill," he said with a little smirk. The server nodded and headed out toward the table where Declan and Pelicia sat.

Sully grinned at the scowl Declan shot him, then got up and helped Olivia out of her chair. They walked outside, and he pointed to the far side of the parking lot. "How about by the fence there? Over by the trees."

Olivia gave a nod. They walked in silence to the spot he'd indicated. He rested his hands on top of the vertical log fence, then frowned and pulled his hands away.

"What?"

"It's sticky." Sully grimaced and pulled his handkerchief

out of his back pocket. He wiped his fingers off as best he could.

"I didn't think men carried those any more."

He glanced over at her.

She nodded toward the handkerchief.

"It's the mark of a true gentleman," he said, his lips quirking at the thought of his proper mother. "At least it is according to my mum."

Her eyes crinkled with a smile. "She's a slave to etiquette, I take it?"

"You could say that." He shrugged. "She's Lady Montescue-Sullivan. In her circles, etiquette rules."

She turned to face him, eyes wide. "Lady?" Her dark eyebrows rose. "So that makes you . . . what? Lord Montescue-Sullivan?"

"That would be my brother Ben, since my father's death ten years ago."

Those eyebrows rose even higher.

"I'm the younger son. I don't carry a title, so I'm not referred to as Lord anything." And he was heartily glad of it.

"Well, no wonder you . . ." She bit her lip and looked away.

When she didn't go on, he prompted, "No wonder I . . ."

She drew in a breath and let it out in a sharp huff. "No wonder you can afford that swanky town house in London."

"How do you know about . . ." Sully stared at her, his gaze taking in her profile, her long dark hair. He drew in a breath and beneath the light scent of citrus and the smell of the wolf was something familiar. "That was you I saw, by my terrace house in Lyall Mews."

Olivia nodded. "I followed you there from Scotland Yard. That's how I knew you were coming to Tucson. I heard you on the phone."

"I see." Sully stared at her, saw the lines of defeat in the slope of her bent neck. But her back was ramrod straight, and he realized she was tougher than she looked . . .

And that she'd brought more trouble into his life. Only time would tell if she was worth it. He had a feeling he would have to deal with it, regardless of whether he had the inclination to or not.

Life used to be so simple—go to work, try to catch bad guys, go out for drinks or dinner, and go home. Repeat. His job gave him plenty of excitement. Or, rather, it used to. Now it seemed rather mundane.

However, it was time to get down to business and stop letting her distract him. She'd dropped a bombshell back in the restaurant, and she needed to explain herself. "You said you were sent to kill me. Why?"

She didn't answer right away. Instead, she stared down over the slope of the mountain. Finally she sighed and said, "My alpha wants you dead." Her slender shoulders lifted in a shrug. "All I know is that he wants to use your death to get to someone else—he didn't say who," she added before Sully could ask. Her troubled gaze met his. "He tried to have your friend O'Connell killed, too."

Interesting. "And you don't know why?"

For a brief moment tears sparkled in her eyes. Then they disappeared, and he wondered—not for the first time— what kind of life she'd had to give her such strength and determination. "All I know is that Eddy Stone is holding my daughter hostage and will kill her if I don't do as he says." She shook her head and gazed out over the railing.

Sully doubted she even saw the beauty of the valley, with more mountains beyond, spread before her.

"I thought I could do it," Olivia murmured. "I thought, for my daughter, I could do anything. But what kind of message would I send her if I took an innocent person's life in exchange for hers?" She bent her head and rubbed the bridge of her nose. Her chest lifted with her deep inhalation. She lifted her head and met his gaze again. "I thought I could handle this on my own." Her eyes closed, and her shoulders slumped. Along with it went the image of strength. She looked tired.

Defeated.

It hurt him to see it.

"But I can't do this alone." She looked at him. "And I know you have no reason to trust me, or to help me. But I'm asking . . . begging you. Please." Her throat moved with her swallow. "Please help me get my daughter back. He'll kill her . . ." A shudder worked its way through her, stealing some of the color from her face. Her gaze searched his. "Please, Sully . . ."

His name on her lips sizzled like lightning through him. He wanted nothing more than to take her in his arms and protect her from the big bad wolf she was so afraid of.

God, how had he gotten in so deep, so fast? This strong yet softly rounded woman with earnest eyes and troubled soul was so beautiful that Sully had trouble breathing. In spite of her fear and worry, his desire surged just below the surface, like a hungry wolf circling its prey.

Unable to keep from touching her, Sully moved closer and brought his hands to her shoulders, stroking back and forth with his thumbs. "Where is he, this Eddy of yours?"

She lifted her gaze to his. This close to her, he could see flecks of dark yellow in the blue of her gaze—amber from the wolf because of her heightened emotions. "New York." She relaxed under his hands, as if by sharing this secret her burden had been lightened. "You'll help us?"

Doubt and fear colored her tones.

He slid his hands down her arms until he grasped her hands. "Yes. I'll help you. *We'll* help you," he added, committing Declan to her cause as well.

A six-year-old little girl was in danger, and he knew his friend wouldn't hesitate to jump in and help.

She reached up and traced her fingers along his jaw, then touched his lips, his nose, and skimmed along his eyebrow. "Thank you," she whispered.

Sully clasped her hand and placed a soft kiss in her palm, then drew Olivia's hands behind his back, enclosing himself in her embrace. He wasn't going to ignore his need any longer. He drew her closer, her softness affecting him in predictable ways. He had to get another taste of her. "Thank *you* for trusting me."

He tilted his head and took her mouth, drinking down her sigh. She tasted of chocolate and coffee, and something else entirely unique—a dark, rich flavor that only made him want more. He closed his eyes to better focus his other senses. Lifting his mouth for a moment, he dragged in a ragged breath, allowing the scent of her growing arousal to permeate his lungs.

Olivia's fingers twisted in the belt loops of his jeans, so he let go of her hands and brought his up to cup her face. Angling her head to the position he wanted, he brought his mouth back to hers and deepened the kiss, thrusting his tongue between her lips in blatant possession.

He turned her and urged her back until she rested against the thick log railing. He sucked and nibbled and bit at her lips, her gasping moans acting like a wick to his already enflamed cock.

Her nipples pressed like diamonds against his chest,

branding him through their layers of clothing. His entire body was taut, something dark and primal inside him urging him to strip her naked and mount her then and there.

Make her his again.

Savage possession surged through his blood. His hands tightened, holding her head still, and he crushed his mouth to hers, needing—*demanding*—a response.

Her hands left his waist and slid up his back, her fingers curling, digging into muscles hard with tension. Sully groaned and canted his hips, deliberately letting her feel his arousal against her belly.

He kissed a path over the line of Olivia's jaw and lingered beneath her ear. Then he mouthed his way down her throat. She sighed and tilted her head farther to the side. Bringing her hands up, she tangled her fingers in his hair. She shimmied her hips, rubbing against him.

Fire streaked through him. Sully groaned and moved his hands to her hips to hold her in place. God, she felt so good. So right.

Forcing himself to once again slow down, he moved his lips to her jaw, then down her neck to the curve where neck met shoulder. He rested his lips against the pulse pounding there.

Life thrummed beneath his tongue. Lust roared through him, drawing his wolf closer to the surface. With a low growl, he jerked, rocking his erection against her, and set his teeth into her flesh—not hard enough to break the skin, but enough to send the message.

She belonged to him.

"Sully . . ." Olivia's voice rasped in his ear, her hands sliding down to his biceps in a fierce grip.

He went back to her mouth. He slid his tongue over her bottom lip, then bit down lightly, eliciting another moan from her. He slanted his mouth over hers once more, nipping and licking and sucking until she cried out and clasped his head, holding his face to hers. Her tongue twisted around his, surging into his mouth when he retreated. He sucked on it, drawing her deeper, making them both groan.

"Jaysus." Declan's voice came from behind him. "Get a room." He gave a low grunt. "Unless you plan to charge admission to this show you're puttin' on for everyone." There was a slight pause, then he said in a musing tone, "Hmm. Might not be a bad idea, that. Could help pay for your board."

Drawing slowly back, Sully ignored his friend and rested his forehead against hers. "Olivia, what you do to me . . ."

"Yeah. I know what you mean." Olivia rolled her forehead back and forth on his, then put her hands on his chest and gave him a gentle push. "But Declan's right, this isn't the place." Her eyes darkened, and her lips bowed into a sad frown. "Or the time."

His erection, which had deflated at Declan's ill-timed interruption, drooped even more at her change in attitude. "Hey, none of that now." Sully curled his fingers around her nape and gave her a little shake. "You won't help your daughter by trying to cut off your feelings." He turned and looked at Declan. "We've work to do. Let's go."

The ride back down the mountain was accomplished amid explanations and apologies—the latter from Olivia. Once they'd reached Declan's house, they gathered in the cozy living room, where Olivia told them more of her story.

"Eddy moved in next door to me just over three years ago, and ingratiated himself with Zoe right away. And me," she admitted, staring down at her fingers twisting in her lap. "I didn't see the danger until it was too late."

"But *why* did he bite you?" Pelicia sat beside her and held out a cup of coffee.

Olivia took it from her with a sigh. "Apparently he saw me in a kickboxing class I teach twice a week, in the evenings after work." She glanced around the room, gaze skittering past the sympathy she saw in the others' eyes. "He followed me, found out where I lived, and took an apartment next door. And once he found out what my last name was"—she shrugged and brought the coffee to her lips, taking a careful sip of the steaming brew—"he saw, he wanted, he took."

"And that last name would be . . ." Sully's voice ended on an up-note.

She fought back a blush. She'd had sex with him, had exchanged heated kisses with him up on Mount Lemmon, and he didn't even know her full name. "Felan."

She saw the way the others looked at each other, as if that name meant something to them.

Olivia looked back at Sully. "It means 'little wolf' in Gaelic."

"Aye." Declan sat forward in his chair, propping his elbows on his knees. "It's an unusual name, too, I'm thinkin'. Interestin' that you share the same name as an ancestor of our friend Ryder."

Olivia looked at him with a frown. "Ryder?"

"He's the reason I'm now a werewolf—well, in a roundabout way." Declan stood and paced to the wide patio doors. With his back to the room he said, "A friend of mine, now his wife—Taite—was being stalked by a werewolf, but only because he'd been sent to kill me. Because of my friendship with Ryder." He turned back to face the room, his expression grim.

Pelicia stood and walked over to his side, sliding one arm around his waist. He looped an arm over her shoulders and gave her a hug. The affection between the two of them, while nice to see, reminded Olivia of what she no longer had.

She glanced away from them. "That must be who . . ." Olivia trailed off and thought back over the conversation she'd had with Eddy when she'd stopped off in New York.

"Just so you know, love, you didn't finish that sentence out loud." Sully stood and walked over to her. He sat on the edge of the coffee table in front of her, his legs bracketing hers, and rested his hands on her knees. "What's going on?"

"I already told you. Edward Stone, the man who turned me, sent me to kill you because of your relationship to someone else. He didn't say who," she said before anyone could ask. "But it's too much of a coincidence, don't you think?"

"Well, did he say why?" Pelicia asked.

"Only that this other man had what Eddy deserved. I got the impression that he had—or has, rather—wealth, and that he's a werewolf." When Sully frowned, confusion evident in the downward turn of his mouth, she added, "He said this other guy didn't like not being normal." At his raised eyebrows, she shrugged and said in a dry tone, "You can't get much more abnormal than being a werewolf."

"Isn't that the truth." Sully cleared his throat and stood. Back rigid, he thrust his hands into the front pockets of his jeans.

Olivia saw Pelicia bite down on her bottom lip. Declan murmured, "It's not your fault," and shot a glare at Sully.

Sully scrubbed one hand across the back of his neck. A slight blush tinged his ears and skated along his cheekbones. "Sorry."

Olivia swallowed. God, Pelicia felt guilty for Sully being in the situation he was—for having had his life twisted inside out—when it was all Olivia's fault. She opened her mouth, ready to confess, then shut it. If she told them she was the wolf who'd bitten Sully, they'd never be willing to help her.

Why would they? She'd brought nothing but chaos into their lives, and for them to try to save her daughter put them at even more risk. Yet she couldn't *not* ask them.

They were her only hope. Because she couldn't kill Sully.

She kept her mouth shut and said nothing.

Chapter 8

"The first thing we need to do is call the police in New York." Pelicia came around the coffee table and sat back down on the sofa. "Or the FBI, since it's a kidnapping. Isn't that the way it works over here?" she asked, looking at Declan. "That's how it's done on the shows on the telly, anyway."

"Aye," he said. "But—"

"We can't!" Feeling the need for space, Olivia stood and stalked to the other side of the room. She turned and faced the other three, trying to quell the rising anxiety that twisted her gut. "Let's say we did call the police. What're they gonna do? Knock on his door and ask him if he's holding Zoe? Assuming that they're not already part of his pack."

"Yes." Sully walked closer but stopped when she waved him off. "Sweetheart, we should let the proper authorities handle this."

Even as she thrilled at the soft-spoken endearment, the rest of his words made her give a soft growl, a mixture of aggravation, fear, and long-bottled rage. "When it comes to this, *we're* the proper authorities. You send a couple of

New York's finest to Eddy's front door, and I guarantee you they'll either end up dead or turned. Either way, he'll know I was behind it."

"How?" This from Pelicia, who had also stood, an expression of concern on her lovely face.

"He already has a couple of his minions on the force. An innocently asked question here and there, and they'd know that a call came in from Tucson. As far as I'm aware, I'm the only person here that Eddy knows. It wouldn't take long for him to figure out cops showing up on his doorstep and me being in Tucson wasn't a coincidence."

"So if a couple cops can't make it past the front door, what makes you think any of us will?" Sully shoved his hands in his pockets and stared at her with eyes dark with frustration.

"Because we're werewolves, too," she said. "Eddy's only as good as the guards he surrounds himself with." Of course, a couple of those guards were big and as vicious as Eddy. But she had a feeling Sully and O'Connell weren't above fighting dirty.

"Still . . ." Sully didn't seem convinced. "He'd be on his home turf, which would give him the advantage."

"I've a thought about that." Declan leaned back against the wall, one ankle crossed over the other, the pose one of negligent grace but power in every long line of his body. "For this to work, we have to put him off his feet. Knock him off balance," he clarified when everyone looked at him uncomprehending. "We need to get Ryder here."

"Ryder?" Pelicia looked from Declan to Sully and back again. "But this Eddy person wants to kill Ryder."

"He wants to kill all of us, darlin'," Declan reminded her dryly. "But it's Ryder he wants the most, which makes me think that this . . . Eddy person, as you call him, is none other than Miles Edward Hampston the Third."

Olivia saw Sully's eyebrows raise and a flash of recognition cross his face. Pelicia also seemed to know whom her fiancé was talking about, so Olivia was the odd one out. "Um, just who the hell is Miles Edward Hampston the Third?"

Sully approached her. She didn't bat him away, so he put one arm around her and tugged her close. His body heat warmed her, comforted her, and she slid her arm around his waist. She rested her head against his shoulder. *Just for a moment,* she told herself. *I'll lean on him for a minute or two. Then I'll go back to being strong.*

"He's Ryder's cousin. He wanted to be a werewolf from the time he was a boy and first found out about Ryder's . . . condition. Or, rather, the condition he'd inherit upon turning twenty-five." Sully's breath stirred her hair just before he placed a tender kiss on the top of her bent head.

She pulled far enough away to look up at him with a frown. "What are you talking about?"

"Ryder's werewolfism—is that a word?" he asked, glancing at Declan.

The other man grinned. "The proper term is lycanthropy." He shrugged. "I practically read his entire bloody library, learnin' what I could about this . . . thing we have. Some of it's utter rubbish, of course."

"What about the non-rubbish parts?" Olivia asked, beginning to lose patience. Damn, but this Irish devil could spin a tale out until it was threadbare.

"Werewolves are either born or made. Werewolves who are born usually come about because of a curse of some sort." Declan shifted his stance, straightening away from the wall. "Ryder's great grandfather was cursed by a *cail-*

leach—an Irish witch—because he turned down her daughter's hand in marriage." He grinned. "From the description of that old biddy, I'd have turned the daughter down, too."

"O'Connell!" Patience never being one of her virtues, Olivia straightened, dislodging Sully's arm from her shoulders, and took a couple of steps forward. She clenched her fists to try to retain her control. The wolf struggled to be let loose, to do something it rarely got to do—beat up on someone. And she didn't care who that someone might be—either of the other two wolves in the room would do.

Focus on your breathing, girl. In, out. In. Out. "Would you please stick to the point? It's my daughter's life we're talking about here." She looked at Pelicia. "God, how do you put up with him?"

"It's bloody hard sometimes," the blond woman murmured, unsuccessfully hiding her grin as she sent a sidelong glance to her fiancé. "But I manage."

"Well, I guess he has other, less obvious virtues that redeem him," Olivia muttered. "Because this smartass routine is fucking irritating."

"How can you not know this stuff?" Declan asked. Dark brows drew down in a frown. "You've been a werewolf longer than we have."

"I haven't had much"—she shook her head—"I haven't had *any* freedom to do anything other than go to work and come home again for the last few years. Eddy keeps me and my daughter under his thumb."

"No Internet connection?"

"No nothing." She sighed. "I tried to use the school computer a couple of times, but when the administrator asked me why I was researching werewolves and was it job related"—she shrugged—"I didn't want to put anyone else in danger, and telling her what was going on wouldn't have accomplished anything other than to get myself fired for being a crazy person. How would I have explained that to Eddy?" She bit her lip. "I didn't push it too much because of Zoe. Not that that helped." Olivia swallowed, trying to ignore the gnawing fear for her daughter. She knew Eddy wouldn't harm Zoe while he thought Olivia was doing his bidding, but the second he believed Olivia had stepped out of line he would act. Brutally and without hesitation or remorse.

She'd seen him do it before to other pack members' families. She wasn't about to let him do it to her child. Not while she still had a breath in her body.

She looked at Sully. God, had she made the wrong decision? Should she still try to kill him?

That would satisfy Eddy, for the moment at least. And it might give her time to figure something else out—a way of escape, a way to get her daughter out of from his sphere of influence.

And what then? Even on the remote possibility that she could kill Sully, a man—werewolf—stronger than her, what were the chances of escaping from O'Connell with her life? And if she wasn't around to protect Zoe . . .

In twelve or fourteen years' time Eddy would turn Zoe into the same soulless creature he was. He'd have a dozen or so years to mold her into the kind of woman he wanted her to be. Without her mother's influence, Zoe wouldn't stand a chance.

But if Olivia killed Sully, what message would that send to her daughter? Because eventually Zoe would find out. One way or another, secrets always had a way of coming back to bite you in the ass.

"I don't think I like the way you're looking at me, love." Sully cocked his head to one side. "Having second thoughts?"

She drew in a sharp breath. "Of course not," she denied, trying her best not to look guilty. Time to steer the conversation back to Declan. "You were saying about werewolves being born that way?"

Declan gave a short nod, as if recognizing the very thin wire her emotions teetered upon. "Every male of the Merrick family becomes a werewolf upon his twenty-fifth birthday—the age Ryder's great grandfather was when he was cursed. Ryder had no choice but to become a werewolf, as will any male children he has."

"You and I didn't get a choice, either, remember?" Sully scowled and crossed his arms.

Olivia tamped down her guilt. The last thing she needed was for him—any of them—to see that on her face. Too many questions that she didn't want to answer. Not yet.

"Oh, bloody hell. Let it go, boyo." Declan shook his head. "There's no use cryin' over spilled milk, now is there?"

Olivia saw Pelicia's lashes flicker, then the other woman excused herself with a murmured, "I'll just go put on more coffee."

As soon as she was out of the room, Declan threw up his hands. "Now look what you've done." After sending a frown Sully's way, he followed after Pelicia.

Sully heaved a sigh and looked down at the floor. "Sorry. It's just"—he muttered a curse—"I hate this. This constant feeling that I'm about to spiral out of control." He looked up, his green eyes glistening. "And the knowledge that I'd fucking enjoy it."

"I'm sorry." The words were out before Olivia could stop them.

"For what?" Sully turned toward her.

For making your life a nightmare was what she wanted to say, but didn't. Couldn't. "For what you're going through," she finally offered.

He must have thought it was lame, too, because he rolled his eyes. "Oh, thanks for that. I appreciate it."

The wolf surged inside her, howling with pent-up rage. "Hey! I'm not the one who made you take a vacation in the Isles of Scilly in the middle of a bunch of werewolves."

"No, you're not. Declan is." He shook his head. "No, that's not true, either. I did it as a favor and, even knowing what I know now, I'd do it again to keep Pelicia safe." He frowned and stared at her. "How did you know I was on holiday when it happened?"

Oops. Think, think, *think.*

"Pelicia mentioned it earlier, when the two of us were in the kitchen," she lied. "When we were making coffee and having a chat between us girls."

He seemed to accept that. She just hoped to God he didn't ask Pelicia later, because it had never happened. She couldn't tell him she knew about his vacation because she'd been there.

"So," Olivia went on, desperate to turn the conversation, "your friend Ryder was born a werewolf?"

Sully nodded. "I didn't know anything about it until after I went to the Isles of Scilly to help Dec protect Pelicia." He pursed his lips. "Then I found out at the same time that Dec had just been turned." He huffed out a sigh. "Well, looks like I've joined the club, too."

"What club would that be?"

"The Hair Club for Overachievers."

She pressed her lips together against a grin, but couldn't maintain her sober expression for long.

"Go ahead," he said on a sigh. "I'd be punching holes in the walls if I didn't find something to laugh about in this mess."

Just that quickly her humor fled. How could she be so jovial when her little girl's life was in danger?

"Anyway, I think Declan has the right idea. We should have Ryder come to Tucson. That'll flush your boy out of New York and get him here on our turf." Sully walked over to a leather recliner and plopped down. He yanked on the lever and raised the footrest, stretching out with a sigh. "Well, out of his own territory, at any rate. It's not like he'd bring the entire pack with him, right?"

One could never tell with Eddy, but she doubted it. "He'll have a few of his 'lieutenants', as he likes to call them," she said. God, but she was tired of living like that—the constant fear, agitation, uncertainty. She rubbed the back of her neck and headed toward the sofa.

"Come over here with me," Sully murmured, holding out one long arm.

"All right, but behave yourself. I don't want to be embarrassed in front of Declan and Pelicia." She changed course and settled onto Sully's lap, her legs dangling over the side of the recliner.

"Well, between the four of us, we can take out a few of Eddy's lieutenants." He leaned his head against the headrest and closed his eyes. "This is nice."

Olivia had to agree. It was the kind of thing she and her late husband used to do after he'd had a hard day. They'd snuggle after dinner and just be together. No need for words; just each other.

She was amazed that she not only wanted this with Sully after knowing him for such a short time, but that she needed it, too. The feel of his breath tickling the hair at her temple, his arms holding her securely with gentle strength, the reassuring thud of his heart against her palm.

The growing hardness beneath her buttocks.

She grinned and wiggled a bit. Just to get more comfortable.

"Enjoying yourself?"

She glanced up to see one of his eyes was open. The corners of his mouth twitched, and she laughed. "I am, as a matter of fact." Even though she felt divided—worrying about Zoe one minute and doing her best to give Sully a hard-on the next.

He closed his eye. "It's worth the torture to hear you laugh."

Olivia looked at him, seeing lines of strain feathering from his eyes and his mouth, and wanted to ease the burden she'd placed upon him. Leaning up, she kissed one side of his mouth, then the other. She planted soft kisses along the sculpted edge of his jaw to his ear and followed the firm tendon that ran down the side of his neck.

"You know, it occurs to me," he whispered without opening his eyes, "this would be a prime opportunity for you to rip out my throat."

Her breath hitched, and she stilled. It would. And she should take it, for Zoe. But she couldn't. Also for Zoe.

And for herself.

"We have another plan now, right? Or will, anyway." She moved her mouth to the hollow of his throat and touched her tongue to the dip there.

She felt him shudder, his erection pressing against her buttocks. She'd love to take it farther, to feel his thick length inside her again, but not with Declan and Pelicia in the other room.

Olivia frowned and lifted her head. Come to think of it, she hadn't heard anything from the kitchen since Declan went in there. She focused her attention, and her frown deepened when she realized that they weren't in there.

"They went to their room."

She looked at Sully, who had lifted his head and looked at her through heavy-lidded eyes.

"About two minutes after Dec went into the kitchen," he added. His hands slid up her back. "So it's just you and me." He drew her closer.

An inch away from his mouth she murmured, "I am not making love to you on their recliner."

His breath wafted over her face, warm and smelling faintly of coffee. "But you will make love with me?"

"Yes." She could resist him no more than she could resist taking her next breath. With his hands at her hips she jumped out of the recliner.

He kicked down the footrest and stood, taking her hand in his. The trip from the living room of Declan's house to the small *casita* out back took only a few seconds. Ripping off their clothes took even less time.

Growling his pleasure, Sully nipped at Olivia's lips. When she reached around and grabbed his buttocks to hold him against her, he moaned. Pulling away from her, he picked her up and tossed her onto the bed.

She landed with a bounce, her soft laughter echoing in the room. She held out her arms in sensual invitation.

He paused, getting his first real look at her nudity. Her pink-tipped breasts billowed above a narrow waist and generous hips. Dark hair flowered between creamy thighs.

Sully came down on top of her and kissed her, his tongue sweeping into her mouth to mate with hers. Her hands came around him, and he felt her fingers flex into his back. She moved her legs restlessly, and he slid between them, his cock stiff against her belly.

Drawing back, he braced himself on one elbow and brushed the hair away from her face. He skimmed his fingers along the curve of her eyebrow, over long, silky lashes, across satiny lips. Then he curled his hand around the back of her neck and smoothed his thumb along her jawline just below her ear.

There was strength there, too, yet fragility. He knew he could snap her neck with ease, and the fact that she trusted him enough to be vulnerable to him made his gut clench.

The fact that he was just as vulnerable to her didn't escape him.

Olivia's eyes heated to a slumberous amber, and her lips parted. "Sully." She brought one hand to the arm braced at her side and the other to his face. She touched his cheek, his nose, the center of his chin, lightly, wonderingly, as if she couldn't believe he was really there.

Her teeth came down onto her lower lip as she brought her hand, and her gaze, to his shoulders. She traced the lines of his collarbones, pausing at the dip at the base of his throat. Then she trailed over his Adam's apple to his chin, putting the tip of her finger beneath his lower lip.

"What is it?" he whispered, stroking his thumb along her jaw.

"I just . . ." She shook her head. Her gaze met his, that look of wonder still in her eyes. "If someone had told me a week ago that you and I would be like this"—she sighed—"I'd have told them they were crazy."

He smiled and pressed a kiss to the corner of her mouth.

"Sometimes being crazy can be a good thing." When her hands came up and clasped behind his head, fingers sifting through the short strands of his hair, he slanted his mouth over hers. Her lips clung to his, her fingers tightening in his hair as she held him as if she never meant to let him go.

One kiss blended into another. Tongues twined and danced. Breaths mingled. His heart thudded against his ribs; an answering pulse pounded in his cock.

He mouthed his way down her throat, scattering kisses across her chest. He tongued each stiff nipple before making his way down her flat stomach.

He parted her legs wider, stroking his fingers in the moist folds between her thighs. She jerked when he touched her, a sharp cry of pleasure escaping her.

Sully pushed a finger slowly inside her tight, hot sheath. At once her muscles clenched around him, velvet soft yet firm. And God! So wet.

His cock swelled in response.

Her hips pressed forward wantonly. He thrust another finger into her, stretching her, preparing her. More than anything, her pleasure mattered to him, after their first primal, rough mating.

Her cunt pulsed for him, wanting, demanding, and he fed that hunger, pushing deep, retreating, thrusting again so that her hips followed his lead.

"That's it, love," he breathed against her stomach. "Just like that. I want you ready for me."

"I am ready for you." She panted, her slender hands grasping his hair, trying to pull him up to her. Or push his face farther down. She couldn't seem to make up her mind.

"No, you're not. Not yet." He dipped his head to her folds, tasting her, holding her flavor, her essence, on his tongue. Tart. Spicy. Hot and slick.

Her breath hissed out, his name a whispered plea.

He lifted his head and looked at her. "Open your legs wider, Olivia. I want to feast."

Her thighs moved farther apart. He pressed his finger into her again. She was tight and hot and wet, and he groaned her name before lowering his head to her once more.

He licked his way up her folds, teasing and sucking at her until she was sobbing, writhing beneath him, thrusting helplessly against his mouth. He built her passion and gentled her, taking her higher each time so that her body shuddered with pleasure over and over.

Sully knelt between her legs and guided his cock to the entrance of her body. She was unbelievably wet, her cream trickling down her thighs. He pushed his hips forward, saw the moist tip of his cock slide past the slick folds of her sex, and felt her, tight and hot, close around him. The sensation shook his control. "Olivia!" Her name burst from between his clenched teeth. He grabbed her firm ass and lifted her as he slid in another inch. "You okay?"

"Fine. I'm fine." Her eyes were bright, amber flecks sparkling in the blue depths of her irises. "I'd be better if you'd just hurry the hell up." She reached down and grabbed hold of his ass, squeezing hard. "I don't need soft and gentle, Sully. I'm not some delicate flower. I can take it. Give it to me hard."

He laughed, a short, sharp burst of sound from a throat tight with need. With a hard flex of his hips, he buried his cock deeper. It had been a long time since he'd felt such ecstasy, perhaps never. Lowering his head, his tongue flicked the taut peaks of her breasts. The action tightened her body around him even more.

"I feel full," she whispered. "But I want more. I want all of you." She tightened her grip on his buttocks.

"Me, too." Sully surged forward. Her sheath was slick, hot, velvet soft, and so tight it was just about to kill him. He buried himself deep, withdrew, thrust hard again. He watched her face for signs of discomfort, but her expression held only a look of passion, her eyes glazed and glowing amber, her breath coming in fast pants.

Satisfied she felt the same pleasure as he, Sully began to move, gliding in and out of her, deeper with each stroke. He tilted her hips so he could thrust even deeper, wanting her to accept every last inch of him.

Accept his soul.

He buried himself to the hilt, shoving so deep he felt her womb, felt the spasms of her climax beginning. His rhythm became faster, harder, his hips surging forward, beyond any pretense of control. Olivia cried out and stiffened, and Sully felt the strength of her inner muscles gripping him in the intensity of her orgasm. He pumped into her frantically, the explosion ripping through him from his balls to the top of his head. Helpless against the raging beast his hunger had awakened, he bent and sank his teeth into the meat of her shoulder.

He shuddered against her when another orgasm rippled through her. Her hips slammed against his, her mewling cries echoing in the small room.

Sully let loose of her shoulder and threw his head back, her name a muffled shout as his cock pulsed, flooding her with hot seed. The small explosions jetted from him again and again until, finally spent, he exhaled and slumped against her, resting his head against her heaving breasts.

Olivia wrapped her arms around him, holding him close. Her hands stroked over the moist skin of his back.

He flicked his tongue against her nipple, a languid back-and-forth motion that sent renewed shock waves through her body. Her pussy rippled and tightened around his still-hard shaft.

And the primal dance began anew.

Chapter 9

Olivia rested her cheek against Sully's shoulder and sifted her fingers idly through the dark hair on his chest. It felt good to be in his arms, feeling the warmth of his skin, the bulk of his solid body against hers.

She'd missed this. Being with a man in the aftermath of sex, listening to his heartbeat, the sound of his breathing. Any sex she'd had since becoming part of Eddy's pack had always been fast and furious, animalistic in the truest sense of the word, with very little tenderness in the coupling. But with Sully, it was like . . . before. Before she'd become a werewolf. Before her life had turned into a nightmare.

Too bad it couldn't last. Once he found out she was the one who'd attacked him, had been the one to turn him into a werewolf, well, he'd hate her. They all would.

She pushed that thought aside. There would be time enough later for regrets. She'd enjoy what she had at this moment. She'd hold on to this, hard, so she'd have something to remember in all the lonely nights ahead.

The time had come for planning. She rubbed her palm over his ribs. "So, you think if your friend Ryder comes to Tucson that will bring Eddy running?"

He squirmed and clamped a hand over hers. "Yes, I do."

She rose up on one elbow and looked down at him. Pursing her lips, she wiggled her fingers and managed to skitter over his ribs again.

He grimaced and jerked.

She laughed. "You're ticklish." How delightful.

"Just a bit." He quirked his eyebrow. "Don't be getting any ideas, you hear? Because I'm bigger than you are."

Olivia grinned. "Yes, you are." Her smile faded as her thoughts turned once again to her sweet little Zoe. "It will take Ryder a day or two to make arrangements and get here, Sully. I don't have much time left."

"How long do you have?"

She shook her head and sighed. "Eddy gave me a week. I've already lost three days. I'm afraid that"—she bit her lip—"when I check in with him later, if I tell him I'm still working on it, he's not gonna be happy." She blinked back tears. "He wanted Declan dead and that didn't happen; he wanted you dead, and it didn't happen. He's running out of patience."

"You said he loves your little girl. How can you be so sure he'd hurt her?" Sully reached out and stroked his hand down the side of her face, leaving a sparking trail of warmth in his wake.

God, she wanted to stay in his arms forever, be comforted and encouraged by this man for the rest of her life. However long that might be—and it wouldn't be long if Eddy had his way, she knew. A six-year-old orphan would be much easier to mold without her pesky mother getting in the way.

"He's done it before to other children." At Sully's shocked expression Olivia went on. "Just after I joined the pack, one of his lieutenants failed at turning a councilman that Eddy wanted in his back pocket. The councilman ended up dying." She pressed her lips together.

Remembering her horror at witnessing what followed that failure, she could hardly believe she'd been so naïve, so ill-prepared for the terrible new world she'd found herself in. "He brought the werewolf and his family—he had four children—in before a 'tribunal' as Eddy called it. A tribunal where Eddy was the judge, jury, and executioner."

Olivia paused, swallowing back the bile that rose even now, two years removed from that horrendous scene. "He made Calvin—his lieutenant—choose which of his children would pay for his failure." She shook her head and stared down into Sully's compassionate gaze. "How can a parent choose which life to end?" She swiped at her eyes. "Eddy's a monster. When Calvin said he couldn't choose— that he *wouldn't* choose—Eddy killed them all." She drew in a deep breath and held it a moment, then exhaled in a loud puff. "He killed them all without breaking a sweat, even though he used to treat the youngest just like he does my daughter—like a doting uncle. That's just how much of a monster he is. And that's how I know he would kill Zoe in a heartbeat."

"Goddamn." Sully put his arms around her and drew her down to his chest, pressing her face against his shoulder. "Sweetheart, the life you've had to lead . . ." His sigh ruffled her hair. "I wish . . ."

When he didn't finish, she prompted, "You wish?" She tilted her head to look up into his face.

He bent his head and placed a soft kiss on the end of her nose. "I wish I'd been there for you. That you didn't have to go it alone."

Oh, God. It was too much. *He* was too much. And he

wouldn't want to be anywhere near her once he found out she was the one who'd turned him.

Olivia pasted a smile on her face. "We should get with Declan and make plans, don't you think?" She pulled away from him and got off the bed. "I'll just take a quick shower." She grabbed her clothing and headed toward the bathroom.

Without waiting for a reply, she closed the bathroom door behind her and leaned against it for a moment. Hot tears burned beneath her eyelids, finally escaping to roll down her cheeks.

This thing had gone sideways from day one. She'd dilly-dallied when she'd first started trailing Sully back in the Isles of Scilly. She'd had more than one opportunity to attack him, to do what needed to be done in order to save her precious baby.

But he'd been so caring of Pelicia—a woman he didn't even know—out of loyalty to his friend. Add to that the face and body of a god, and it had made it even harder.

Maybe if she'd been a stone-cold killer it wouldn't have mattered. But she wasn't, and it had.

She'd been able to attack him, all right. She just hadn't been able to kill him.

Now . . . now she'd gotten to know him even more, and she was very much afraid she was falling in love with him. Even knowing that another plan was in the making, or soon would be, she couldn't shake the thought that the option of killing him was also still on the table.

To try to cover up the sounds of the sobs she could no longer contain, Olivia twisted the faucet to the shower and didn't wait for the water to warm up. She stepped into the stall and stood underneath the stream, the water making her skin as chilled as her soul.

As the water quickly heated, she wished it could warm her on the inside as well.

Sully stayed on the bed a moment, his keen hearing picking up the sounds of Olivia's distress. He'd seen the tears that brightened her eyes and could now hear the soft sobs over the sound of the water running in the shower.

He rubbed his forehead. He hated feeling helpless. He wanted to do something—take away her pain and fear.

He guessed that killing the fucker who'd taken her daughter would work.

He rolled off the bed and pulled on his clothes. She was right—they needed to nail down a plan, and the first thing that had to happen was a phone call to Ryder.

But she was also right that it would take Ryder at least a day to make travel arrangements and get there from the Isles of Scilly. So, what to do in the meantime?

He paced in the confines of the small bedroom, his thoughts racing. He and Declan could go to New York, at the very least get a scope of the situation—see just how many bodyguards this Eddy fellow had and suss out a way to get the girl.

And if they were seen? If Eddy—who most likely *was* Ryder's cousin Miles—was the one behind this, he knew what both Declan and Sully looked like. Sully had met the man once—at the memorial service for Ryder's parents.

Even though he and Miles had both been eighteen at the time, Miles had seemed much younger. He'd been silent and sullen, even pouting. Not grieving, at least not that Sully had seen. He'd wondered about that reaction then, but in the intervening years—and especially in light of the most recent events—he had to wonder if Miles had instigated the elder Merricks' murder/suicide.

Given the fact that Ryder's cousin was so desperate to

make Ryder pay for whatever imagined slight he'd given him, it made more and more sense. At any rate, the fact that they'd met—that each knew what the other looked like—made a trip to New York less and less feasible. Because if they were seen, Eddy would know that Olivia had confessed the plan to kill them.

So . . . scrap that idea.

They could call the New York police, even though Olivia had said no. While he didn't have any contacts there, he wouldn't be surprised if Declan did. If he didn't, well, the cops in New York could make a call upon Eddy out of courtesy to a fellow officer, even if he was from across the pond.

When they got there and asked questions . . .

Sully sighed. As violent as Eddy seemed to be, what Olivia had predicted might happen would very likely be the outcome. A couple of New York City's finest would find themselves becoming furry once a month.

That wasn't a secret you told. Because who in the ordinary world would believe it?

So, scratch that idea, too.

He paced over to the doorway and stared into the living room. While his eyes looked ahead, he trained his ears toward the bathroom, waiting for any sign that Olivia was done with her shower. He hated that she was in there crying. Alone. Hated that she felt the need to hide her tears, her grief, and fear from him when all he wanted to do was comfort her, care for her.

Did she believe he'd think less of her if she wasn't strong one hundred percent of the time?

He snorted. That sounded like him. He'd always believed any sign of weakness was unacceptable. That to show a momentary chink in the armor he presented to the world would somehow decrease him in the eyes of his friends, his subordinates. His boss.

The irony of the situation didn't elude him. Now that he was as much animal as man he realized he couldn't always be strong. That sometimes he had to lean on somebody else.

Needing someone—and being needed in return—was one aspect of what made him part of the human family. With the wolf always lurking just below the surface, Sully was finding he needed that connection more than ever.

Which was yet another reason he wanted to save Olivia and her daughter from Eddy. Not just because the little girl was an innocent—although that was enough. But because he cared for Olivia more than he would have thought possible after such a short time. He was old enough to know it was more than mere physical attraction, even if they had that in spades.

The attraction went much deeper. On some level he felt he recognized her. He wasn't enough of a romantic to say they shared the same soul or any such nonsense as that. But there was something. . . .

Something that compelled him to help her.

He focused his thoughts back on the problem at hand. After casting off another couple of idiotic ideas, he finally lit upon one that he couldn't shake.

Eddy wanted him dead? Then he'd have to die.

Or, at least, make it look that way.

He and his squad had faked a witness's death once in order to keep her safe until she could testify. It would be a simple matter of placing an obituary in the local paper, maybe even create a bit of sensation around his "death" by having Declan or Pelicia talk to a reporter about the "dog" attack that killed him.

They'd have to go with a dog, because Eddy would no doubt expect Olivia to kill him while in her wolf form and, as far as he knew, there were no wolves in southern Arizona. Just the smaller, scrawnier coyotes. He couldn't see a small animal like that being able to take down a man as big as him.

When they got Ryder on the phone, he'd talk to Taite about the idea. As a former investigator with the local County Attorney's Office, she had to have contacts they could use if needed.

He gave a wince and rubbed the back of his neck. He didn't imagine she'd be too happy with the idea of them asking her husband to fly thousands of miles just to put himself in harm's way. For a woman he didn't even know.

But though Sully didn't know Taite well, she struck him as a compassionate sort, one who wouldn't keep her husband from doing what needed to be done in order to save an innocent child.

Not to mention his friends and family.

Sully glanced toward the bathroom door. Olivia had stopped crying, for which he was glad. He usually didn't have a problem with weeping women. He dealt with them all the time as crime victims. It was part of the job. But there was always a sense of detachment in those cases.

A detachment he sure as hell didn't have with Olivia.

He scowled. How had this woman gotten under his skin so quickly? He sat on the edge of the bed and waited for her to come out of the bathroom. Was it just because he felt a bit vulnerable, trying to deal with being a werewolf and all? Or was it—could it be—something deeper?

The bathroom door opened, allowing steam to come billowing out of the room.

Sully turned to see Olivia walk out, her dark hair, still

wet from her shower, tucked behind her ears. Her face was scrubbed clean, her skin clear and soft-looking. She looked . . . young. Even more defenseless than before.

As if she, too, had shed her armor.

"Are you feeling better, love?" Sully took a few steps toward her.

Before she could reply, the phone in the living room rang.

Sully turned and walked into the other room, and picked up the receiver. "Hullo?"

He was aware of Olivia padding quietly into the room. She stood just behind him, and he glanced over his shoulder to give her a reassuring smile.

She didn't return it.

"Come up to the main house," Declan said without any preliminary niceties. To the point, that was Dec. "We've work to do."

Without breaking eye contact with Olivia, Sully said, "Aye, aye, Captain." As he put the receiver down, he clearly heard Declan's muttered, "That's Major to you, smartass."

Sully couldn't deny that having werewolf hearing was a good thing. He certainly would not have been able to hear that muttered comment before. Imagine the kinds of intel he could pick up from suspects without the aid of electronic listening devices.

His lips tightened. If he kept on like this he'd be as excited about being a werewolf as Declan was. He reminded himself that he had been ready to rip out a suspect's throat and that was why he was here in the States.

You don't like being an animal, remember?

Though he had to admit he did enjoy having more . . . stamina.

He turned and pulled Olivia into his arms. She stood as rigid as a board for a few seconds and then relaxed against him with a small sigh.

"Declan wants us up at the main house," he murmured, "to put a plan together." Rubbing his hands up and down her back, he tried to bestow comfort as best he could. "Are you up for this right now?"

"Do I have a choice?" She pulled back enough to look up into his face. "I'm sorry."

"For what?"

"For . . . everything. For complicating your life. I sense you're the kind of man who likes to keep things simple."

"You're not the one who complicated it, love." He leaned down and placed a soft kiss on her forehead. "The bastard who attacked me and turned me into a werewolf did. And if I ever find out who he is . . ." He bit off the rest, clamping down on his anger. Now wasn't the time. He needed to focus on the problem at hand. The bastard who'd turned him could wait.

After all, revenge was a dish best served cold.

Olivia's throat moved with her swallow, and she dropped her gaze to his chest. Bringing her hands up between them, she fiddled with one of the buttons on his shirt. "Yes, well. I haven't exactly helped to make things any simpler, have I?"

Sully cupped her chin. "Look at me." When she kept her eyes downcast, he repeated, "Look at me." As soon as her gaze lifted, he said, "You were doing what you felt you had to do in order to protect your little girl. I can't fault you for that." He didn't like the shadow that moved through her eyes. There was something more going on than she was telling him. But that was all right. He'd ferret the entire truth from her sooner or later. "Let's focus right now on getting your daughter back, all right?"

She gave a small nod.

"All right." He put his arm around her waist and turned toward the door. "Let's go figure out how to save Zoe, shall we?"

Chapter 10

"**Y**ou want to do what?" Declan propped his hands on his hips, the gaze he centered on Sully full of incredulity.

Sully leaned back on the sofa and stretched his arms along the back. He didn't take his eyes off his friend, but he was acutely aware of Olivia sitting beside him. She'd been quiet since they'd joined the others, and he knew her thoughts were on her daughter.

Only a first-rate bastard used children. But then Miles had always been a bastard.

"You heard me," he said to Declan. "We should fake my death."

"Do you have any idea how complicated that is? Not to mention illegal?" Declan's broad shoulders lifted in a shrug.

Sully grimaced. "Since when does complicated or illegal bother *you*?" Not waiting for a response, he asked, "Anyway, just how is it illegal? We wouldn't be doing it to commit any sort of fraud. We're doing it to save a little girl's life."

"If he wants Olivia to provide proof? What then?" Declan raised one dark eyebrow.

"Then we take a picture." Sully frowned and leaned forward again, resting his elbows on his knees.

"The proof I'm thinkin' of is more along the lines of a finger. Or your head."

Pelicia scrunched up her face in a grimace. "He wouldn't really ask for something like that, would he?" She glanced from one person to the other. "Couldn't you post an obituary as proof?"

Olivia shook her head and finally spoke up. "It's too easy to run an obit in the paper. Eddy would never accept that as proof." She sighed.

"What about talking to a reporter?" Pelicia looked at Declan. "Surely there's something else we can do."

"Don't call me Shirley," he muttered with a flash of a grin, and just as quickly grew sober again. "A reporter will try to verify the truth of what we're saying. No body, no police report." He shook his head. "Thinkin' on it further, I don't know how it would work without getting the police involved."

"You see why I took the course of action I did?" Olivia sent an apologetic look to Sully.

He straightened from his slouch and put his arm around her, hugging her to his side. "Don't you dare apologize again, love. What's done is done. We need to move forward." When she gave a small nod, he looked at Declan. "What about that idea you had of getting Ryder here?"

"I really think that's the way to go, don't you?" Declan scratched his chin. "I mean, if Miles—we're all in agreement it probably is Miles, right?"

Everyone nodded.

But just to be sure. Sully glanced down at Olivia. "Tell us what this Eddy of yours looks like."

She jabbed him in the side with her elbow. Her gaze ferocious, she said, "He's not *my* Eddy."

"Sorry. Eddy, then. Tell us what Eddy looks like."

She briefly closed her eyes and muttered a cross "Sorry." She looked a little shamefaced, as if she knew she'd overreacted and was embarrassed by it. "He's average height, I guess—five-nine or ten. Medium brown hair, somewhat husky build, though he's not fat. Slight cleft in his chin."

"Sounds like Miles. Damn bugger." Declan rubbed his chin against his shoulder. "If he knew Ryder was comin' here, I think he'd have to come, too. His obsession wouldn't allow for anythin' else." He walked over to the plush armchair where Pelicia sat. He parked one buttock on the padded arm. "That will get the bastard to Tucson." He looked at Olivia. "Would he bring your daughter with him?"

"I don't know." Olivia chewed on her bottom lip a moment.

In spite of the gravity of the situation, Sully's body reacted to seeing those white teeth digging into soft, plump flesh. He wanted to be the one doing the biting, damn it. Then he'd kiss it better.

Need flared. His cock stiffened, growing thick along his thigh. He shifted against the sofa and, with a grimace, pulled a pillow onto his lap. Damn wolf, always randy, always ready for a hard fuck. *Now isn't the time.*

"I think he would bring Zoe with him," Olivia finally said. "He wouldn't trust anyone enough to leave her behind in New York. He'd be too afraid that someone would have sympathy for me and let me have her. But how would we find him?" She glanced at Sully, frowning a little when she saw the pillow.

An unmistakable sweet musky smell hit his nostrils. God, she was getting aroused again, too. "Olivia . . ."

"You started it," she muttered with a light smack to his shoulder. She stood and moved away from him, going over to the patio doors and opening them. She leaned against the door frame, arms folded as she faced the room.

A fresh breeze swept into the room, carrying with it the odor of lemons from the trees in the side garden. The citrus scent did what it did best—blocking other more tantalizing aromas.

Though it didn't help alleviate his ill-timed erection.

He noticed Pelicia looking from him to Olivia and back again, curiosity plain on her face.

"Don't ask," he muttered before she could say anything.

Her fine eyebrows went up, but all she said was, "Okay."

"So, if we can get Miles here . . . aye, the question is, how do we find him?" Declan glanced at the pillow and lifted one brow but otherwise didn't comment, though Sully suspected it was more for Pelicia's sake than his or Olivia's. Declan rubbed one hand over his face. "He was a slippery one, even as a youngster. He won't be easy to fool."

"He will be if I can be convincing enough." Olivia shrugged. "He should believe me if I tell him I overheard a conversation between the two of you. And that I thought it best to pass along that information and see what he wanted me to do." She spread her hands and grimaced. "Seeing as how I screwed up my assignment, I don't think he'd trust me with killing Ryder. Plus, he told me that was something he wanted to do himself. After . . ."

When she didn't complete the sentence, Sully prompted, "After?"

Her lips thinned. "After he rapes and kills Ryder's wife in front of him." At their shocked looks, she pursed her lips, then added, "I did warn you—he's a monster."

The thought of Taite and Ryder being put through something like that caused Sully's hopeful arousal to die a quick death. He stared at Olivia, disbelief warring with outrage. "Son of a bitch."

"Aye." Declan stood and walked to the phone. His face was hard. "Well, we can handle the bastard."

"He won't come alone." Olivia's eyes darkened.

"How many do you think he'll bring with him?" Sully went over to her and put his arm around her. He was gratified when she slid her arm around his waist and gave him a small squeeze.

"I dunno." She blew out a breath. "Probably at least four—his most trusted lieutenants."

"Well, then. Between the three of us we can handle five werewolves." Declan picked up the phone and dialed.

"Three?" Olivia crossed her arms.

Declan didn't look up from the phone. "Aye. Me, Sully and Ryder."

Uh-oh. Sully pressed his lips together to hold back a grin. Declan was about to get his ass chewed off by an irritated female—one who was a hot-blooded werewolf to boot.

"And just what is it li'l ol' me is supposed to be doing while all you heroic menfolk are off saving my daughter?" Olivia began tapping her right foot.

The sarcasm in her tone caught Declan's attention. He looked up, seemingly unfazed by her attitude, a slight smile curling his lips. "Waitin' in the getaway car for us to bring her out to you."

Pelicia cleared her throat. "And just what am I supposed to do?"

Declan's grin faded. "You can't be thinkin' to go along with us, darlin'." At her raised eyebrows, he slashed his free hand through the air. "No! I am not takin' you literally into a den of wolves."

Her lovely face darkened with a scowl. "Just how stupid do you think I am, O'Connell? I don't want to go fight a bunch of werewolves, you dolt."

Sully kept his lips firmly pressed together. Declan should stop while he was ahead, though his friend did seem to have a knack for just digging himself in deeper.

"Don't you now?" In his agitation, Declan's rich Irish brogue thickened. "That seems to me just what you were suggestin'."

"*I* could drive the getaway car."

He frowned, opened his mouth to respond, then turned his attention to the phone. "Get Ryder." He paused, his scowl deepening. "Yeah. Hello, Cobb. Get Ryder." He huffed a sigh. "She's fine, an' I'll be happy to let you talk to her. *After* you've put Ryder on the line."

Pelicia stood and walked over to the phone, one hand outstretched. "Let me talk to him."

"We haven't the time—"

"Oh, for God's sake, O'Connell. Two minutes for me to say hullo to my father isn't going to make a bit of difference." She thrust out her hand. "Give me the bloody phone."

Declan handed over the receiver.

Pelicia brought it to her ear. "Hi, Dad." Her face blossomed with a smile.

"She doesn't look at me like that," Declan muttered.

"You don't deserve it." Olivia shifted against Sully, tucking her shoulder tighter under his arm.

Sully grinned. Every facet of this woman's personality he uncovered just made him like her more. That she wasn't going to take any of the crap Declan was so good at shoveling was a good sign.

"And just so we're clear—I am *not* gonna sit around in the damned car. She's my daughter." Olivia's voice was tight but low enough to not disturb Pelicia on the phone. "If I have a chance to remove that monster from my daughter's life once and for all, I'm taking it."

"Even if it means you could die?" Declan studied her for a moment, then looked at Sully. "You all right with this?"

Sully stared down at Olivia. Did he want her in harm's way? No. Did he think he could stop her if that was really what she wanted to do?

Hell, no.

But he understood and admired the fierce determination she had to protect her daughter. "She has to follow her heart, Dec. As much as I don't want her to get hurt, she does know Miles better than any of us. She's been around him for the last three years, so she'll be an asset when it comes to fighting him."

Olivia tightened her arm around his waist. "Thanks."

"You're welcome." Sully pressed a kiss to her temple. "Just don't get yourself killed. You'll make me regret supporting you in this."

She smiled and rubbed her cheek against his shoulder.

Declan made a gagging noise, but when Sully looked over at him, his face was all innocence.

Pelicia got off the phone and handed it back to Declan. "Dad's gone to fetch Ryder." She met his frown with one of her own.

Sully bit back a grin. Dec had landed himself just as feisty a female as he had. The next several years for those two promised to be full of fire.

"I'll say it again. I don't know how you put up with him." Olivia shook her head and sighed.

Pelicia quirked an eyebrow at her fiancé. "Oh, he certainly tries my patience." She sat back down in the plump armchair. "But I've loads of practice and know how to handle him."

Declan rolled his eyes. Before he could respond, Ryder must have reached the phone, because Declan turned his attention away from Pelicia and her teasing. "We have a problem," he said, his voice low and terse.

As Declan explained to his friend what was going on, Olivia leaned into Sully and fought to breathe. What if Ryder said no? The entire plan hinged on him coming to Tucson to lure Miles out of hiding.

She sighed. She really needed to keep thinking of him as Eddy. That way she wouldn't mess up and inadvertently call him by his real name. Though she'd be happy to call him Miles when she killed him. To protect her daughter, Olivia was more than willing to kill the monster who'd put both of them—and so many others—in danger. An innocent Eddy was not.

But first they had to get him there. She was sure Ryder Merrick in Tucson would be an effective lure. *If* he agreed.

As Declan talked to his friend on the phone, his eyebrows rose. "Really?" He grinned and shot a glance at Pelicia. "Congratulations, boyo!" He listened to Ryder, his smile fading. "Well, you'll cross that bridge when you get to it. In twenty-five years, give or take. So, for now, give Taite a kiss for me, and tell her I said congratulations." He paused. "Aye. E-mail me your itinerary, and we'll pick you up at the airport." He said his good-byes and disconnected the call.

Olivia breathed a sigh of relief. Obviously Ryder had agreed to come. Now all they had to do was iron out some of the details.

"What was that all about?" Sully asked.

"You're goin' to be an uncle." Declan wore the biggest shit-eating grin Olivia had ever seen. He walked over and took up his perch on the arm of Pelicia's chair again.

Sully shook his head and stared at Declan. Then the meaning sunk in, and his eyebrows shot up. "They're pregnant?"

"Aye. Ryder said Taite's just about four months along." Declan's grin widened.

Olivia clenched her jaws to keep from spoiling the moment. A few seconds to let them talk about their friends' good news wouldn't kill her. But they'd better get back to planning Zoe's rescue soon.

"Four months? And they're just now telling us?" Pelicia crossed her arms.

"Apparently Taite didn't want to tell anyone until she made it through the first trimester. Just in case." Declan's smile faded. "Plus Ryder's having a hard time dealing with the fact that he's perpetuatin' the family curse by continuin' the bloodline. It doesn't matter if it's a girl or boy—

the boy will become a werewolf upon reaching twenty-five, and a girl will pass along the curse to any boy children she might have."

Pelicia sighed. "Poor Ryder. I wish . . . Well, I thought he'd finally come to accept what he is."

"Aye, I think he has. He just isn't keen on passin' this on to a child." Declan shrugged. "Me, I like bein' faster and stronger." He looked at Pelicia. "I can protect what's mine better."

"We'll talk about your caveman attitude later, sweetheart." She gave him a saccharine smile and a pat on the knee. "I can sympathize with what Ryder's going through, though. Perhaps especially because *you* won't pass this along to a child." She looked at Olivia. "Right?"

Olivia nodded. "Everyone in the pack who's had children after they became werewolves had normal human children. From what I've been told, if it weren't for Eddy, they'd live normal human lives." She bit her lip, not liking the memories of just how many turnings she'd been forced to witness over the last three years. "But he makes sure that the children are turned on their eighteenth birthdays. He considers it a coming-of-age. If they don't . . ." She met Sully's gaze. "People don't leave his pack. Ever. Unless they're carried out in pieces."

Sully cupped her face. "I am so sorry for what you've had to go through, love." He placed a light kiss on her lips. "We'll stop him, Olivia. I promise you that."

"We have to." She turned away from him and looked at Declan. Just to make sure, she asked, "So your friend is coming, right?" At his nod, she went on. "When should I call Eddy and let him know? After Ryder's arrived? Or just before?"

"You tell us." Declan stretched his arm along the back

of the chair. "How would Miles react if he thought you knew of Ryder's pendin' arrival at least a day before you told him?"

"He wouldn't be happy." Boy, was that the understatement of the year.

"Well, we don't want to give him too much of a head start," Sully protested in his crisp British accent. He crossed his arms and leaned one hip against the narrow table behind the sofa. "Giving him time to dig in somewhere won't help our cause a bit."

Olivia couldn't help but stare at him. He was such a handsome man. Dark brown hair fell over his forehead, giving him a young appearance. Two days' worth of stubble lined his strong jaw. The rolled-up sleeves of his shirt exposed strong, hair-covered forearms. Narrow hips made keeping his pants in place a fight against gravity. And green eyes that went tawny when his emotions were aroused never failed to arouse *her*.

She caught his eye and grinned at his satisfied smile.

Yeah, he liked her ogling him.

She hoped she'd have time to concentrate on him later.

She took a deep breath and tore her gaze away from temptation, looking at Declan. "Did Ryder say when he thought he'd be arriving?"

"He was goin' to see about gettin' the first flight out of Heathrow that he could, so sometime tomorrow, I reckon."

"Then I should call Eddy."

"You mean Miles," Pelicia corrected softly.

Olivia shook her head. "I have to keep thinking of him as Eddy. If I slip up and call him Miles, he'll know something's wrong." She swallowed. "I can't give him any hint at all that we're planning something. Zoe's life depends upon it."

"Call him after we find out Ryder's itinerary, once we know he's well on his way," Sully murmured. "That way, even if Miles is able to get a flight out that day, he'll still arrive after Ryder has." When she nodded, his lips curved in a slow smile. "In the meantime, you can stay here with us. With me."

Chapter 11

"I want you two to go to Tucson and keep an eye on Olivia. I don't trust her to complete her assignment." Eddy stared at one of the men in front of him with a steely gaze, directing him without words. In addition to finding a place in Tucson, he wanted Peter to keep an eye on Calvin to be sure the man either passed this final test of loyalty or, if he failed, to make sure that his failure was fatal.

Peter gave a short nod. "We won't let you down," he said. He glanced at Calvin. "Either one of us."

"See that you don't." Eddy directed his gaze to Calvin. He knew the other man hated him for what he'd done to his family, but it didn't matter. Eddy was pack leader. His word was law.

He was law.

"Hell, they're in the middle of a desert. You two hole up somewhere isolated. It shouldn't be too difficult to find a place sitting out in the middle of a few dozen acres or so." As he looked at Calvin, displeasure tightened his lips. "Even for you."

Calvin kept his gaze lowered, showing the proper subservience, but Eddy knew behind those hidden eyes seethed hatred. He should just kill him and get it over with, but Calvin had garnered a lot of sympathy from many in the pack. To kill him without provocation might be Eddy's right as pack leader, but it would cause more problems than it would solve.

Of course, if something happened while Calvin and Peter were out in the Sonoran Desert . . .

"Go get ready," he told Calvin. "Peter, stay," he said to the other man. When the door closed behind Calvin, Eddy lowered his voice, even though the soundproofing he'd had installed in the room should block anyone from eavesdropping. "If you find a place that's occupied but otherwise is suitable, kill whoever's there. You should only need the place for a day or two at the most. Livvie's deadline is fast approaching. But be careful. Keep it under the radar of the police."

Peter nodded again, his pale blue eyes sparkling with anticipation of meting out violence. Of all of Eddy's lieutenants, Peter was the biggest sociopath, which made him ideal as Eddy's prime enforcer.

He was also the most ambitious, which made him a likely candidate for mutiny. Eddy knew he had to keep his eye on him because it wouldn't be long before Peter believed he could win a pack challenge. But, until then, he'd do Eddy's bidding because it was in his best interests to do so.

Eddy could live with that. For now.

He leaned back in his chair and steepled his fingers, tapping his fingertips together. It was one of the things he liked to do, using body language to drive home the point that he was the one in charge. "Once you're out there and have done what needs to be done, take care of Calvin." He jabbed a finger toward Peter. "I want him taken care of, you hear me?"

Peter nodded. "Gotcha."

"If anyone in the pack asks what happened, you can just say that Calvin tried to kill you, and you acted in self-defense." As a thought occurred, he narrowed his eyes. This would be an opportunity for Peter to throw an unfavorable light on Eddy. He had to nip that in the bud right now. "And don't think about pointing the finger back at me. I'll disavow all knowledge. As far as anyone else is concerned, I was trying to salvage Calvin as a valuable pack member."

"Whatever you say. You're the boss." Peter clasped his hands behind his back. "Is that all?"

Eddy planted his palms on the top of his desk. He pushed to his feet and, bracing himself on the desk, said, "Just remember one thing. I made you; I can unmake you." He gave a jerk of his head toward the door. "Go."

Peter inclined his head, the light glinting off the blond strands of his perfectly layered hair. "I'll call you as soon as it's done."

Eddy stared at the doorway long after Peter was gone, his thoughts churning. He hadn't yet gotten a call from Olivia letting him know she'd completed her task. He was very much afraid he'd have to carry through with his threat against Zoe.

If he did, he'd take her to Tucson and take care of her there where Olivia could see up close and personal what failing him meant. As much as it would hurt him, he'd leave Zoe's little body out in the desert for the coyotes and other scavengers to feed on. By the time the police found her remains, there would be nothing left of her to identify.

Just as there'd be nothing left of Olivia.

He shook his head and sat back down. It was a shame, really. At one time he'd given serious consideration to taking Olivia as a mate. One of many, of course, but she would have held precedence in his favor.

Until she'd proven to be so stubborn, so . . . intractable. It had seemed poetic indeed to turn a woman whose married name meant "little wolf" and whose maiden name, also Gaelic in origin, meant "warrior." While she was certainly that, especially where her daughter was concerned, she had failed completely in proving she could be a warrior for *him*.

He blew out a sigh and rubbed his forehead. Live and learn. It was easier dealing with people who weren't parents before they were turned. From now on, he'd only turn single people who were unattached—no children, no significant others.

People who were desperate to belong, who would eagerly accept a place in his pack. And who would be proud to add children to the pack as well. Children who, upon reaching adulthood, would also join the pack as full-fledged werewolves.

Just a few more loose ends to take care of and life would be . . .

Perfect.

Chapter 12

Sometime after midnight, Sully propped up on one elbow and stared down at the woman beside him in bed. Kindred spirits, that's what they were, he and Olivia. Two of a kind—proud, independent, unwilling to let others see the chinks in their armor.

As much as he'd tried to deny it, he knew it to be true. They did share the same soul.

Wonder gripped him anew at how important she'd become to him in such a short time. It had to be more than his admitted savior complex—his deep-seated need to safeguard those in need of protection. It had to be more than his profound respect for the fervent love she held for her child. That was to be expected of any parent, though many fell short.

He couldn't shake the sense of familiarity, and it was more than the fact that he'd seen her outside his terrace house in London. He felt close to her in a way that defied definition. For the moment, at least. Sooner or later he'd put his finger on it.

One thing he did know—it wasn't important. He felt; therefore he was.

He rolled his eyes at his fancifulness. What was it about love that made men sodding idiots?

He held his breath a moment. Love. Was what he felt really love? Olivia being important to him was different than him loving her.

Wasn't it?

For God's sake, he didn't know enough about her to love her. She was a single parent, but he didn't know anything about her deceased husband, and next to nothing about her child other than that she was a girl named Zoe, and she was six years old.

Sully didn't even know how old Olivia was. She appeared to be in her early thirties, but according to Declan werewolf metabolism slowed down the aging process, so she could be older than she looked.

He didn't know what she did for a living. She'd mentioned teaching kickboxing, but that was it.

Did you ask?

No, he hadn't. Apparently she was supposed to become this fount of information, spilling details about herself without being asked. He knew enough about her to know she was a private person, just like him. With the situation she found herself in, he knew she'd feel that the more information someone had about her, the more it could be used against her. So she'd keep as much as she could to herself.

It was all about trust. Not only him trusting her, but vice versa. What had he done to show her *she* could trust *him*, other than have the best sex of his life with her?

You couldn't base a solid relationship purely on sex, though as far as Sully was concerned good sex went a long way. Great sex went even further.

He stared down into Olivia's face, able to see her features clearly even though the room was dark. A sliver of light from the security spotlight outside came in from around the edges of the curtain, allowing him to make out the graceful slant of her jaw, the sultry curve of her lips, the sweep of dark lashes against her cheek.

Christ, she was beautiful. At that moment, with sleep cradling her in its peaceful arms, she looked content. Almost happy without the lines of care creasing her forehead and bracketing her mouth.

He shook his head. There he went again, being poetic. What had happened to the hardnosed, tough DCI Sullivan?

"Sucked into the quagmire," he murmured.

Olivia must have heard him, for her brows dipped, and she sighed. Her eyes fluttered open, but he could see she wasn't really awake. "Wha . . ."

"Nothing, love." He stroked her hair, tucking a few strands behind her left ear. He pressed a kiss to her temple. "Go back to sleep."

She sighed again and closed her eyes. "'Kay."

And just that quickly her breathing evened out.

Poor little thing. She'd probably been running on adrenaline for the last three years. This could very well be the first solid night of sleep she'd gotten in quite a while.

He was glad he could calm her fears enough so she could get a much-needed rest.

Now, if someone could just settle him down and help him accept his new life . . .

Late the next morning, Olivia glanced around the breakfast table at her companions. She held her cell phone in one hand. "You're sure about this?" She hoped they wouldn't back out, but to be fair she had to give them the chance to change their minds. They were getting ready to walk into a very dangerous—maybe even deadly—situation. She had no right to ask it of them, yet she knew they were her only hope.

If they decided not to help . . . She didn't even want to think about what that would mean for her.

"Make the call." Sully leaned forward and took her left hand in his.

"Aye." Declan reached out and pulled Pelicia closer to him, the legs of her chair screeching against the tile floor. He twined his fingers through hers, grinning at the shake of her head. "Ryder's e-mail last night said he managed to book a flight out of Heathrow this morning. It's roughly a fifteen-hour flight. With just the one layover, he should be in tonight around five-thirty." He tipped his chin toward the cell phone in her hand. "Call Miles and tell him the news."

Olivia nodded and took a deep breath, holding it in for a moment. After she exhaled, she punched in Eddy's number and brought the phone to her ear. It was answered on the second ring by a deep, melodious voice with an Hispanic inflection.

Olivia tightened her fingers on the phone. "Hello, Rico. It's Liv. Let me talk to Eddy."

"*Por qué, chica?*"

She'd long ago ceased to find anything even remotely sexy about his deep, accented tones. Rico was almost as slimy as Eddy. As far as she was concerned, that took away any positive appeal his dark Latin good looks might have otherwise held. A pretty face didn't make up for a black soul.

"I have news for him, and I don't have a lot of time."

She made sure to keep her voice hushed and put as much urgency into it as she could. "Come on, Rico. Put him on the line."

"All right, all right. Hold on."

She heard a rustling noise as he transferred the phone to Eddy, then Eddy's voice came on the line, hard with displeasure and impatience. "Livvie? You'd better have good news."

"I do." Olivia bit her lower lip. Please, God, let this work. Now that she had him on the line, all she could think about was her daughter. "Let me talk to Zoe. Please," she tacked on, not wanting him to interpret it as a demand, though it was.

"Give me your news first then I'll determine if it warrants a reward."

She swallowed and crossed the fingers of the hand Sully still held. "I've been trying to get close to Sullivan to find the opportune moment to strike." She met Sully's gaze and inwardly winced at the sympathy she saw in his eyes. God, when he found out she was the one who'd turned him . . . She blinked and pushed that thought away. She'd deal with that later, once she had Zoe safe and sound.

If her daughter was protected from Eddy, then what was the sacrifice of Olivia's happiness? It was nothing. She'd give her life if that's what it took.

She realized that Eddy hadn't yet said anything. "Eddy? Are you still there?"

His words came out in measured cadence, evidence that he was furious. "You mean to tell me that Rory Sullivan is still alive?" His voice ended on a rasp.

Oh, boy, he was really, really mad.

"Go get Zoe," she heard him say.

Her heart leaped into her throat, then dropped and began thudding hard behind her ribs. "Eddy, wait! There's more."

"More than the fact that you've been in Tucson for three days already and have yet to complete your task? Tick-tock, Livvie. Ticktock." He cleared his throat. She could see his expression in her mind's eye and, knowing he was about to say something sarcastic and hurtful, she braced herself. "It's not that hard, even for a stupid bitch like you. Isn't that right, Livvie?"

God, but she hated it when he called her that. He'd get his, and soon. For now, she had to agree with him that she was stupid. "Yes."

"Yes." He sighed. "What else?"

She paused for effect then said softly, "Ryder Merrick is coming here."

"What?" His voice was incredulous. "What did you just say?"

"I said that Ryder Merrick is coming to Tucson. I overheard Sullivan and O'Connell talking about it when they were out at a local coffee shop this morning." She paused, then fumbled her words a bit to make him think she was nervous. Well, she was nervous, but not for the reason he would think. She hoped.

She met Declan's encouraging gaze. "Go on," he mouthed with a slight smile.

Olivia nodded. "I . . . I figured that's, ah, who you've been trying to get, you know, revenge on. You almost said his name when you told me a little bit about the reason you wanted me to"—she softened her voice even more—"to kill Sullivan."

"I did?" His voice had softened as well.

She cleared her throat. "Yeah. You, well, you said 'Merr' and then trailed off." She drew in a breath and quietly exhaled, knowing his werewolf hearing would pick up the sound. She made sure there was a slight tremble in her voice as she asked, "Was I wrong? Should I not have bothered you with this?"

The other three around the table were tense, sitting straight, their gazes fixed on her as they listened to the one-sided conversation.

Well, as Pelicia listened to the one-sided conversation. Olivia suspected that Sully and Declan could both hear Eddy.

"No, no. You did absolutely right in calling me with this news." As it usually did when he was feeling particularly pleased about something, a slight British accent had crept into his voice. "When is he due to arrive?"

"This evening, sometime around six p.m." She fudged the arrival a little, just to give them some more time.

"That soon?"

"I called you as soon as I knew," Olivia hastened to say, making her voice sound defensive.

"Of course you did, pet. Give me a minute to think."

Silence was broken only by the intermittent static on the line.

She looked at the others and gave a slight shrug, and tried not to panic. If he didn't take the bait, she was SOL.

And so was Zoe.

Finally he said, "I'm coming out there."

She removed her hand from Sully's and gave a thumbs-up signal. "When?"

The others relaxed, Sully slumping back in his chair and Declan pulling Pelicia closer in a silent hug.

"Don't you worry about when," Eddy said. "You worry about Sullivan."

She frowned. "You still want me to—"

"Yes, I still want you to kill him. Why would you think that had changed?" His voice was hard again, full of irritation.

Olivia tightened her lips at his aggrieved tone. Please, God, soon this would all be over and she'd be done with him. For now, she kept her voice soft and timid. "Well, I just thought that—"

"Don't think, pet. You'll overheat." He laughed at his own joke.

She grimaced, not appreciating his humor. Not that she ever had, even when she'd first met him. BC. Before the Change. He had a mocking sense of humor that frequently belittled others. She told herself it was because he felt inferior and had the need to make others feel bad in order for him to feel good. But that didn't always help when she was on the receiving end of his insults.

"I don't need Merrick to witness it." Eddy went on in a musing tone. "As a matter of fact, I'd like that to be the first news he hears when he gets off the plane this evening. It'll distract him. So, make it happen."

Olivia swallowed. "Today? In the next"—she glanced at her watch—"eight hours?" She looked at Sully with a frown.

"It's okay," he mouthed.

"Stop fucking around, Livvie, and get it done." Eddy's indrawn breath was sharp. "I'll call you when I get into Tucson, and you'd better tell me then that Sullivan is dead. You hear me?"

She sighed. "Yeah, I hear you." He sounded like he was about to hang up, and she yelled, "Eddy! Wait! Please let me talk to Zoe." When he didn't respond, she repeated, "Please."

She heard him snap his fingers and hardly dared to breathe while she waited. But soon she heard Zoe's dulcet tones. "Mommy?"

Olivia closed her eyes against the urge to weep. Zoe sounded all right. Not scared, not unhappy. Just her sweet, lovely little self.

"Hello, baby. How are you?"

"I'm okay. Me and Calvin's been hanging out, but he had to go away." She sighed. "I miss you."

"I miss you, too." Olivia propped her elbow on the table and bent her head, resting her forehead against her fist. God, it felt so good to hear her daughter's voice. She'd been so scared for her. "But I'll be home soon."

"Uncle Eddy said you had something you had to take care of." Her daughter's voice became muffled as she added, "Isn't that right, Uncle Eddy?"

"That's right, poppet." Eddy's voice was indulgent. Full of affection. But Olivia knew that affection could turn deadly in a heartbeat. She could almost see his hand stroking over Zoe's shiny dark hair as he murmured, "Very important business your mommy has, and she mustn't fail."

"Oh, my mommy won't fail. She's smart."

Olivia laughed at that. From the mouths of babes . . . She only hoped she was as smart as her daughter believed her to be. "Sweetheart, I promise I'll be home just as soon as I can, all right?"

"Okay, Mommy." Her voice was still muffled.

Olivia shook her head. Her daughter was notorious for covering up the receiver area when she used a cell phone. "Zoe, honey, take your hand off the bottom of the phone."

She heard Eddy say, "Tell your mother good-bye, poppet, and give me back the phone."

Ever obedient, Zoe said, her voice no longer muffled, "I have to go now, Mommy. I love you."

"I love you, too, baby. Zoe—"

"Go on back to your room and play with your dolls, Zoe," Eddy told the little girl. Olivia realized he'd taken the phone from her daughter and was waiting for Zoe to leave the room before they went on with their conversation. "Today, Livvie," he said as he came back on the line. "I want confirmation *today* that Sullivan is dead. And more than just your word that the deed is done."

She frowned. She had to ask, but dreaded his answer. "What kind of confirmation?"

"Hmm. Well, there aren't all that many things that would be certain proof, are there?" He laughed. "Once I'm in town I'll call you with my location. You can bring me his head. In a sack." He hung up without waiting for her response.

Olivia held the phone to her ear for a few seconds after he disconnected the call. She wasn't sure why, but somehow she'd had the feeling that he'd tell her to hold off on fulfilling her assignment until he got to town.

Figured she wouldn't be so lucky.

But at least she knew that, for now, Zoe was all right.

She drew the phone away from her ear and slowly closed it. She looked at Sully. "He still wants me to kill you."

"I heard."

"And bring him your head in a sack."

"I heard that, too." Sully grimaced, then leaned forward and took her hands in his. "So instead of bringing him my head, you'll take me, Declan, and Ryder to him. And we'll put *his* head in a sack."

She was werewolf enough to appreciate that visual. And mother enough to be willing to do what it took to make sure Eddy never bothered her daughter again. If that meant separating his head from his body, she was up for the job.

A far cry from the small town Southern girl who taught physical education. *You've come a long way, baby.*

"Well, now that that's settled . . ." Declan pushed away from the table. He stood and stretched, his dark green T-shirt riding up at the waist to show tanned, hair-roughened skin. "Pelicia and I are goin' to run out and pick up some steaks for dinner. You two want to tag along?"

"No, thanks." Olivia stood and pushed her phone into the front pocket of her jeans. "I think I'm going to take a long walk. It helps me relax."

"As a human or as a wolf?" Pelicia stood and walked over to the kitchen counter. She opened her purse and pulled out a pair of sunglasses, which she perched on top of her head, then clicked her purse closed.

"As a human." Olivia made a face at the other woman, who just laughed and gave her a wink.

"Well, you never know around you lot." She winked at Olivia again. "Would you like to borrow a pair of shorts? It will be more comfortable." She eyed Olivia up and down. "We seem to be about the same size."

Olivia's eyes widened in surprise. Pelicia really was a sweet, kindhearted person. "If you don't mind."

"Of course not, or I wouldn't have offered. I'll be right back." She headed toward the bedroom.

Declan grinned. "I think I'll help her." He went after her.

Sully asked, "Do you mind some company on your walk?"

For the next few hours there wasn't anything she could

do for Zoe, and worrying would only sap energy she didn't have to spare. Plus, she was determined to enjoy her remaining time with Sully. But she couldn't resist teasing him. "Not as long as you can keep up."

"Keep up?" His dark brows drew down in a frown. "I thought you were going for a walk."

"I am." She grinned. "But it's not going to be a measly little stroll along the Thames."

He raised his eyebrows. "I believe I'm up for the challenge. What does the winner get?"

"It's not a race, you goof." She leaned toward him. "But if you do manage to keep up with me, I'll make you very glad you did." She shivered at the carnal thoughts racing through her mind, some of which involved the use of whipped cream and chocolate. It would be messy but oh, so worth it.

"Lead the way." Sully held out one arm with a flourish. "I'm curious, though. What happens if I don't manage to keep up?"

"Well, I suppose if you can't keep up I may just have to punish you."

Which might also involve the use of whipped cream and chocolate.

She looked him up and down. He was dressed in blue jeans and a button-down shirt. Even though the sleeves were rolled up, it wasn't an outfit made for a brisk walk. "You might want to change, too."

"All right." He turned and started toward the front door. "Be right back."

She watched him go, admiring his lean physique.

Pelicia walked back into the room, her face flushed and lips swollen, eyes sparkling. "Where's Sully?"

"He went to change." Olivia pressed her lips together

briefly to keep from commenting on Pelicia's somewhat disheveled appearance. She longed to tease the other woman, but not knowing her well enough, she didn't want to take the chance that it would embarrass her. "He's going with me."

"Good. Dec has his mobile phone, so if you need us, just call." Pelicia paused, her pretty face sobering. "We'll get your daughter, Liv. Try not to worry."

Olivia nodded. "I am trying, believe me. It's hard," she admitted softly.

"I can't begin to imagine what you feel." Pelicia pulled her into a hug. "But you're with friends now, you know that, right?"

As she drew away, Olivia forced a smile. "I do. Thanks."

They were friends now, but for how long?

Chapter 13

For about the first mile, once they'd moved onto the main road with its wide bike/pedestrian lane, Sully deliberately stayed behind Olivia as she gradually increased her speed. Soon she was walking as close to a run as she could get without actually running. Her arms were bent and pumped furiously at her sides.

But it was her derrière that had his gaze riveted—the firm cheeks swaying from side to side with her gait. He wished the shorts she had on were more formfitting.

Something made of a clinging knit would have been so much better—at least from his unbiased point of view.

"Stop staring at my ass," she threw over her shoulder.

He jerked his gaze to her face and shrugged. "Can't blame a man for admiring the view, love." Lengthening his strides, he easily caught up to her, and then went on past. "Come on, slowpoke."

"Barmy smastard," she said without heat.

He grinned. Flip those letters around, and she'd just called him a smarmy bastard. He felt the heat of her gaze on him and for good measure said, "Stop staring at my ass."

She laughed, a light tickle against his eardrums.

He'd bet she'd been a carefree woman prior to Miles Edward Hampston the Third coming into her life.

"Just admiring the view, my lovely man." She laughed again. The sound made him feel lighter, as if it lifted the burden his own descent into lycanthropy had caused.

They walked in silence then, their quickened breathing the only sounds they made. A few cars went by periodically, but gave them plenty of room. He supposed drivers around the area were used to people taking advantage of the sunshine.

He looked around, taking in the awe-inspiring majesty of the mountains and surrounding desert terrain. In just a few short days Tucson had gone from being completely alien to looking like something he could call home. Before he realized it, Olivia had caught up to him and pulled slightly ahead.

Still walking.

He broke into a jog to overtake her.

"Hey!" She smacked him on the shoulder blade as he passed her. "That's cheating. This is a power walk, bub. W-a-l-k. Not r-u-n." She made a razzing sound with her lips. "Don't they teach you the basics over in Britain?"

"They teach us just fine."

"Huh. Coulda fooled me."

He glanced over his shoulder and saw her pause.

"Hey! Here's another path. Wonder where it goes?" She started off down the rabbit trail, ducking under the branches of a couple trees, almost disappearing from sight.

He was about to head after her when a car passed a little too close for comfort, coming far over the solid white line that separated the driving lane from the pedestrian lane. "What the fuck?"

Olivia called out, "What is it?"

"That bloody car nearly hit me." He glanced over his shoulder. The vehicle was nowhere in sight. "He must have pulled onto another street."

"Well, I'm sure sometimes people get distracted looking at the mountains." He could only see her head as she turned and started back toward him. She paused and looked over her shoulder, motioning with one hand. "I mean, look at them. Who wouldn't?"

"I agree." Sully glanced at the mountains and gave a quick grin. "I just don't happen to appreciate nearly being the recipient of their distraction."

She laughed. "No, I guess not." She stopped with a curse.

"What is it?"

"I just ran into a damn cactus." She bent, going out of sight. "Let me just get these stickers out of my leg."

A vehicle gunned its engine. Sully looked around to see that same late-model sedan on the wrong side of the road barreling straight toward him.

He started to jump out of the way but moved too late. The car slammed into him, catching him in the thighs and knees and catapulting him through the air. He barely had time to register the pain in his legs before he slammed onto hard, unforgiving ground and skidded several yards. The air forced from his lungs, he lay there gasping for breath.

Vaguely he heard Olivia scream his name and realized his body was already going into shock. Regardless that his broken bones would heal, being hit by a car, he discovered, hurt like hell.

"I'm all right," he said, or at least tried to. But he couldn't get the words through his pain-tightened throat. He heard the screech of tires and Olivia's yell.

"Get up! He's coming back." She knelt beside him, putting her hands in his armpits and trying to drag him away from the road. "Rory, come on!"

He couldn't even process that she'd used his first name, or acknowledge the fact that he liked hearing it in that husky voice. He could only groan. "God, stop. Olivia, stop." The pain was excruciating. "Just . . . stop." He craned his neck around and saw the car was almost upon them. With a groan, he shoved Olivia away seconds before the car ran over him. It ran over grass and scrub bushes at the edge of the road before maneuvering back onto the tarmac and speeding away.

"Oh, God. Sully!"

He felt Olivia's fingers stroke down his cheek. A rich copper scent filled the air, and he knew it was from him. From his blood.

He could taste it in his mouth—rich, dark, and hot. He coughed and more blood came up his throat and filled his mouth. He realized at least one of his lungs was punctured by broken ribs.

"Stay with me, Sully. Don't you dare quit on me."

"Werewolf metabolism," he managed to croak.

She scowled, though he saw worry shadowing her eyes. "It doesn't mean you can't die from blood loss, you idiot." She bit her bottom lip. "You need to shift. Now."

He gave her a matching frown. "It hurts enough . . . to change to . . . a wolf under normal circumstances." Breath hitching, air wheezing through the puncture in his lungs, he moved against the hard ground and winced. "No way . . . I'm doing it . . . now."

"The process of shifting will help you heal." She took a breath. "But you can't do it here on the roadside where everyone can see you." She glanced around. "There are a couple of trees down that little path I was just on. I think that should be enough cover." She looked back down at him. "It's only about a hundred yards or so."

He swallowed. She was right, of course. If he was going to shift, he couldn't do it there. He was amazed that no other cars had come along and stopped to help. Even as he thought that, his keen ears picked up the sound of a vehicle. "Do it, quickly."

She nodded and grasped him under the arms again. With a minimum of fuss and a multitude of whispered apologies, she dragged him over to where she'd pointed, then hunkered down beside him.

In spite of the pain, Sully noticed she was barely out of breath. She was strong for a woman. He corrected himself. She wasn't just a woman, she was a werewolf. So of course she was stronger than a normal human woman.

He clamped his jaws together, ragged moans muffled behind his teeth. He'd never felt that kind of pain in his life. Not even the first time he'd shifted, and that had been painful to the extreme.

Olivia looked toward the road. "Okay, they didn't see us. At least if they did, they're not stopping." She stared down at him. "I can haul your carcass back to Declan's, but in the condition you're in right now that will only aggravate your injuries." She held his gaze. "You need to shift."

He recognized the truth in her words, but couldn't ignore his misgivings. "It's not exactly as if I enjoy—"

"And you think I do?" She slashed one hand through the air. "I hate Eddy for what he did to me. He turned me into something less than human. More than human." She shook her head. "Sometimes I don't even recognize myself,

I've changed so much in the last three years." Leaning over him, she placed her hands lightly on his shoulders.

It was about the only part of him that didn't hurt.

"I'm sorry. This isn't about me." She held his gaze, hers searching and serious. "You can do this, Sully. You have to."

"You called me Rory before." He closed his eyes.

"Shut up." She started pulling at his clothing.

He opened his eyes. "I'm not in the mood right now, love."

Her scowl deepened. Beneath the irritation lay fright and worry. "You'll need to put these on again. I'd rather they not be all ripped up from your shift. Hold on. This is gonna hurt."

She pushed his shirt carefully up his torso and drew in a quick breath. "Oh, God."

"It's bad. I know. It hurts to breathe."

"From the looks of things, you have several broken ribs." She exhaled. "Okay, here we go."

She worked his shirt up over his shoulders and head, and drew it down his arms. It was agony. Then she unfastened his shorts and pulled them over his hips along with his underwear. When she pushed them down his legs, he couldn't help the moan as she jarred him.

"I'm sorry." Olivia untied his shoes and pulled them off, then his socks. She sat back on her heels. "All right. That's it. You can shift now."

Sully took a few deep breaths, trying to contain the fresh pain the removal of his clothing had caused. He focused his attention inward, finding his inner wolf with very little effort. It always simmered just below the surface anyway, as if it knew how much he didn't want it. It was like a dog—or pesky little kid—that sensed the one person in the room that didn't like it and so gravitated toward that individual.

"Come on," he heard Olivia mutter. "You can do this. You *have* to do this."

As bones and muscles began to shift, broken bones scraping against each other as they went into their new form, he couldn't hold back a yell of agony.

Deep breaths were impossible as the pain seemed to constrict his lungs. The few seconds it took to transform into his wolf were the longest moments he'd ever had to endure.

When it was over, he lay on his side, panting softly through the lingering pain. Olivia stroked her hands lightly over his fur, not touching his legs or rib cage. When she brought one hand up and touched his muzzle, he gave her fingers a soft lick.

"Okay, sweetheart, I know you're hurting," she crooned, still rubbing her fingers along his muzzle. "But you need to shift back again. And then," she muttered, "we need to figure out how to get you back to Declan's without anyone seeing you." Then she flipped a finger against her forehead. "Duh. I have my phone." With an embarrassed chuckle, she pulled her cell phone out of her front pocket. Then she looked back down at him. "Change back, Sully."

He whined. He couldn't help it. He was in pain and didn't look forward to the agony another shift would cause.

"Don't be such a baby." Olivia tapped one finger between his eyes. "You have to do it, so just . . . do it and get it over with."

He lifted one lip in a snarl to let her know he didn't appreciate her sniping at him, and her total lack of sympathy was unappreciated as well.

Never mind that he knew her hard words were all an act. He could see the emotional pain in her eyes.

Turning his attention inward, he forced the wolf back. Three shuddering heartbeats later he lay once more in his human form.

One thing he'd learned from the experience—being in so much pain made having the usual hard-on after a shift impossible.

"What's Declan's number?" Olivia's voice was as soft as the fingers she sifted through his hair, brushing strands away from his sweaty face.

"Don't . . . know." Sully struggled to sit up but collapsed back onto the sand. "Phone's . . . on . . . my belt. Number's . . . programmed."

She reached over him and grabbed his bloodstained shorts. After she slipped his phone from its holder, she quickly figured out how to get into the directory and called Declan. She explained in abrupt, worried tones what had happened, then disconnected the call. "He said they'll be here in just a few minutes."

"Good. That's good." He wasn't looking forward to trying to walk the distance to the road, let alone all the way back to Declan's house.

She glanced at his shorts. "These actually aren't in too bad of shape." She grimaced. "Well, other than being covered in blood." She sighed and shook her head. "But it's better than having you running around naked. Let's get them back on you."

He groaned and closed his eyes. Pain racked his body, especially his legs, and he just wanted to lie there and not move.

"Come on, Sully. Declan and Pelicia will be here soon, and it won't look nearly as strange to passersby if we're helping a man in bloodstained shorts rather than a naked one. I think we'll get some really hard stares—and most likely a few calls to the police—if you're seen naked." She stroked her fingers across his forehead. "Come on. You can do this, Rory."

It was his name on her lips that made him open his eyes. It was the worry in her eyes that made him nod and do what he could to help as she pulled his shorts onto his legs. It was the sight of her teeth worrying her bottom lip that made him grind his jaw against the pain and lift his hips to allow her to pull the shorts to his waist.

He squeezed his eyes closed and collapsed onto the ground, holding the moans in, breathing through his nose with quick, shallow pants. God, he hurt. And he'd be hurting even worse if . . .

If he wasn't a werewolf.

Hell, he'd probably be feeling no pain by now if he were still human, because he'd be dead.

Being a werewolf had just given him a second lease on life.

The thought of whether werewolves had nine lives like cats flitted through his mind. It was probably a grave insult to compare them to felines, but who cared right at that moment? Certainly not him.

The sound of car doors slamming made him open his eyes again.

"They're here." Relief was rife in Olivia's voice. "Hang on, honey." She stood and waved.

Getting hit by a car might just be worth it if he could get a few more endearments out of her.

In a matter of seconds, Declan and Pelicia stood over him.

"Bloody hell." Declan muttered a few more curses. "Who did this?"

Olivia shook her head. "I have no idea. It was a dark four-door—black or maybe dark blue." She sighed and folded her arms over her breasts. "It all happened so fast. But I have to believe it was deliberate. It hit him and then came back and ran over him."

Pelicia put her arm around Olivia's waist and looked down at Sully. "Is it as bad as it looks?"

"Not now. It *was* pretty bad, but he's already shifted to wolf and back once." Olivia started chewing her bottom lip again. "Both his legs were broken and are probably still very fragile."

"Bloody hell." Declan shook his head and scowled.

Olivia looked at him. "You should carry him to the car. Once we get back to your house—"

"Back to the house?" Pelicia looked from Olivia to Declan and back again. "Shouldn't we take him to the hospital?"

Olivia shook her head. "They'll only ask questions we don't have answers for. If he goes through at least one more shift, he'll be fine. If he can stand the pain."

"He *is* right here, you know," Sully muttered, peeved they were discussing him as if he were unable to contribute to the conversation. "There's nothing wrong with his hearing."

"Or his mouth, it appears." Declan hunkered down beside him. His light tone and teasing words did little to hide the concern in his eyes. "You've gone an' done it up right, haven't you?"

"It was on my list of things to do—ride up to Mt. Lemmon, stand next to a saguaro, get run over by a car." Sully struggled to a sitting position, grateful for Declan's strong hand behind his back helping him up, chagrined that he needed the assistance. He huffed a few pain-filled breaths between his lips. "Been the . . . highlight of . . . my trip so far."

"You must not be feelin' too bad, boyo." Declan shook his head. "Come on, then. Up you come." He grabbed Sully's left wrist and hauled him up and into his arms. "Jaysus. You've put on a few pounds, haven't you?"

Sully gasped with pain, and in a gruff voice repeated the only Irish Gaelic phrase he knew, one he'd heard Declan say often enough during their university days. "*Póg mo thóin.*"

"No, thank you. If I'm goin' to be kissin' anyone's ass, it sure as hell won't be yours."

"Oh, for crying out loud." Olivia smacked Declan on the shoulder as she walked past him. "Can you be serious for even one goddamn minute?" She reached the SUV and opened the back door.

As Declan came nearer to the vehicle, Sully closed his eyes and clenched his jaws, preparing himself for the transfer to the backseat.

The pain wasn't as bad as before, but still bad enough to make him break out in a fresh sweat. One ragged moan rasped from him before he could contain it. Thinking to give Olivia room to sit next to him, he opened his eyes and tried to maneuver to a normal sitting position.

"What're you doing?" she asked, her lovely face scrunched in a frown.

"Making room for you." He grunted as pain shot through his legs. But at least it was getting more bearable.

Maybe.

"I'll ride back there." She pointed to the cargo area of

the SUV. Without giving him a chance to reply, she closed the door and went around back.

Declan helped her up and shut the door behind her. He and Pelicia got in front, and he started up the vehicle. "How're you doin' back there?"

"Fine." Sully's entire body was beginning to throb, and not in a pleasant way.

"We need to get him home so he can go through the change at least one more time. Maybe twice." Olivia scooted forward. Lifting her arm over the seat, she stroked the back of his head.

Her touch was soothing, but even so, Sully didn't think he could go through that again. As a matter of fact, he was sure he didn't want to do it again. Changing from human to wolf and back again was extraordinarily painful under the best of circumstances. He'd discovered that doing so while grievously injured made the agony a hundredfold worse.

"God, no." He shook his head then looked at her. "It's too much."

"Declan and I will get you through this, Sully." Olivia rested her hand along the back of his neck. Her fingers felt cool against his heated skin, and he waggled his head against her touch, not caring that he rather resembled a dog begging for its master's caress.

She stroked his neck, sifting her fingers through the hair at his nape, and he felt himself calming. Even knowing how much pain he had yet to endure, he knew he could do it with this woman at his side.

"Here we are." Declan pulled the vehicle to a stop in front of the guesthouse. "We'll get you into the bedroom, and after you've shifted a few times, you can have a wee lie down."

"Are you sure we shouldn't take him to the hospital?" Pelicia asked as she got out of the SUV.

"I'm sure Olivia knows best, darlin'. She's had more experience with this sort of thing." Declan opened the back door and glanced at Pelicia. "Go help Olivia out, would you, darlin'?"

Pelicia came around to the back of the vehicle and opened the hatch, then pulled down the tailgate. Olivia climbed down and walked to the side, standing behind Declan as he helped Sully out of the SUV.

"Lean on me," Declan murmured, putting one arm around Sully's waist. He glanced at him from the corner of his eye. "Want me to carry you in?"

"No. I can walk." Sally took one step and bit back a groan at the pain splintering through his legs. Not to mention that the slight jar of motion set cannonball fire off in his head, making it pound and roar in protest.

Pelicia fished keys out of her pocket and opened the front door of the *casita*.

"Maybe I'd best carry you." Declan stooped and picked Sully up again, and carried him into the guesthouse. Once he made it into the bedroom, he set Sully onto the edge of the bed.

Sully looked up at three very concerned faces. "I'll be all right," he murmured. He really didn't want Pelicia to have to witness him shifting into an animal—and viewing the pain that went along with it. He looked at Declan. "You and Pelicia go on up to the main house. Olivia can help me."

Declan lifted his chin. "You sure?"

Sully gave a nod. "We'll be up later. We still need to finalize some plans, right?"

"Aye." Declan flipped his wrist and looked at his watch.

"Ryder will be here in about six and a half hours." He looked at Olivia. "Before we go, though, you answer me this: what are the chances that the driver of that vehicle was sent by Miles?"

She swallowed, hard. "Like I said, it seems too much of a coincidence for it not to be." She shook her head. "Though I don't know how he could have gotten someone here that fast. As far as I know, he doesn't have any contacts in Tucson. But . . . it was clearly not an accident. Especially since the driver came back to make sure the job was done. So to speak."

"Yeah, running over me after he hit me going at least fifty miles an hour was the mark of a true professional, someone who takes great pride in his work." Sully made sure there was a wealth of sarcasm in his pain-laden voice.

"Yet if he'd been aware you were a werewolf, I'd hardly think a car would've been his weapon of choice." Declan gazed down at him. "So let's be thankful of that, at least."

"Oh, yes, indeed. Thank God for small favors." More sarcasm.

Olivia sighed. "Oh, brother. Don't you start, too. One smartass around here at a time is about all I can take." She drew in a deep breath. "I can help him. I've had to do this before. Don't ask," she said as Declan opened his mouth. "It's not a pretty story, and it's one I really don't care to discuss at the moment."

He raised his eyebrows but otherwise didn't comment.

"Well, if you're sure you don't need us . . ." Pelicia seemed torn between wanting to stay and help—because she was a compassionate woman—and wanting to get out of there as fast as possible.

Sully forced a slight grin. "I'm sure, darling. You and Dec go on."

She leaned over and gave him a quick kiss on the cheek. "We'll see you later."

He waited until the front door closed behind them before he closed his eyes and heaved a long sigh. "I don't want to do this, Liv. I really don't."

"I know, honey. But it has to be done, or you'll have a hell of a lot longer recuperation. And we don't have time for that."

He looked at her. She was right, damn it. If they meant to take on Miles in the next day or so, he had to be in top shape. He'd be of no help to anyone—and, actually, much more of a hindrance—if he were anything less than in his best fighting form.

With a sigh, he eased down onto the floor and turned his focus inward once more.

Chapter 14

"What do you mean, you've taken care of things? And where the hell is Peter?" Eddy tapped his fingers on the top of his home office desk.

Calvin cleared his throat. Even across the phone line Eddy could hear the underlying satisfaction in Calvin's voice as he said, "Peter tried to rip my throat out. It was self-defense."

"Was it?" Eddy leaned back in his chair. Had he miscalculated? He'd thought that Calvin had learned his lesson after losing his family, but perhaps not. Perhaps he still ached for revenge. "I'd hate to think you took it upon yourself to scratch an itch."

"He tried to rip out my throat," Calvin asserted, his voice hard and ringing with sincerity. "I have a new wife and a baby on the way. I wouldn't jeopardize them by acting without provocation."

Eddy wasn't so sure about that. *He* wouldn't let anything stand in the way of what he wanted, even a wife and unborn babe. Wives were easy enough to come by, and it was equally as easy to get children.

But he'd let it go for now. He'd have a better sense of

what had happened once he got to Tucson himself. "And the other matter?"

"We saw Sullivan out walking along the road, and Peter ran him over. He's dead."

Eddy sat forward. His eyes narrowed, and he pushed down the sense of elation threatening to overtake him. He wouldn't celebrate until he had it confirmed. "How can you be sure? Perhaps he was only injured, not dead."

"It's not the first time I've seen Peter use a car as a murder weapon. He made sure to run over Sullivan's chest— broken ribs ripping into his lungs. I saw blood coming out of his mouth before we took off. He's dead, believe me."

Eddy pursed his lips. So, Merrick would receive the news of his friend's death when he got off the plane. Most excellent. He frowned. "I wonder why Livvie hasn't called with the news."

"It's possible she doesn't know yet. It only happened about half an hour ago."

There was something in Calvin's tone that Eddy couldn't put his finger on, but it made him a little uneasy. He pondered it a few moments, but finally shrugged it off. No matter. He'd figure it out.

He always did.

"I've booked a flight for three p.m. today out of La-Guardia." Eddy switched the phone to his left ear and reached for a copy of his itinerary. "My plane should land at Tucson International Airport at ten twenty-four. Pick me up."

"Of course."

"And not in the vehicle you used on Sullivan."

"Of course not." Calvin's voice was even, but Eddy caught the underlying thread of annoyance the other man couldn't hide.

"Don't you take that tone with me. Did I give you the order to take out Sullivan?"

"Ah . . . no."

"That's right. I did not. That was something I wanted Livvie to do. Now she'll be stuck at the bottom of the pack for who knows how long. This was her chance to shine, to prove she's more than an Omega. But you've taken that away from her."

"It wasn't me, it was Peter. We thought—"

"Don't think, Calvin. Just do what I tell you, when I tell you to. That's all you need to do." Eddy heaved a sigh. "God. I should have . . ."

"You should've what?" More hardness crept into Calvin's voice.

I should have killed you along with your family. "Never mind. Just pick me up tonight." Eddy hung up before the other man could respond. "When did I surround myself with idiots?" he asked himself.

"Sir?" Rico paused at the doorway, his dark eyes holding a false subservience that made Eddy want to puke. His second-in-command might think he had Eddy fooled, but he didn't. Eddy knew it was just a matter of time before Rico got tired of being the second and struck out for his chance to be first.

Eddy had surrounded himself with wolves just as ambitious as he was, but he knew how to handle them. He was older and wiser, and he knew a lot more dirty tricks than Rico ever would. "What is it?" Eddy stood and thrust his hands into his pockets. He morphed his fingers just enough so that his fingernails sharpened into werewolf claws. He never let his guard down.

Never.

"Will you be requiring any of us to go with you to Arizona?"

"Why? Wanna work on your tan?" Eddy pursed his lips.

"That would be a nice side effect." Rico shook his head. "But you know I'm more than willing to go with you if you need me."

Eddy clenched his fists, welcoming the pain of his claws slicing into his palms. "I'd rather you stay behind and keep things under control here. I'll take Walter and Aaron with me."

"Of course." Rico turned to leave.

"A moment." Eddy called him back. "If Livvie calls, make sure to put her through to me right away. No vetting her calls anymore, you understand?"

Rico inclined his head and walked toward the living room.

Eddy closed his eyes, rotating his head to work the kinks out of his neck, and let his hands turn back to normal. Taking them out of his pockets, he sauntered into the kitchen, where Zoe was finishing up the cereal she'd insisted on having for lunch. He ruffled her dark hair and then bent and placed a kiss on top of her head. "How's my poppet doing?"

"Good." Her little feet swung in the air beneath her chair. She lifted the cereal bowl to her mouth and slurped down the milk in big long gulps. When she set the bowl on the table, he saw a rivulet of milk dribbling down her chin.

He shook his head. "That's not very ladylike, Zoe."

She grinned. Grabbing a napkin from the holder in the middle of the small table, she wiped her mouth and chin. "Mommy says it'd be a waste of milk to just pour it down the sink. Besides, it's sweet."

He smiled and gave his head a slight shake. She was precocious. Sometimes she acted so mature he forgot she was only six. But at that moment . . . definitely childlike. Give her something sweet, and she'd gobble it right up. That was the way of children.

His penchant for sweets lay along another path.

He pulled out a chair and leaned his elbows on the table. When in Rome and all that. "How would you like to go to Arizona with me?"

"Arizona?" She frowned. "I don't know where that is. What about Mommy? When is she coming home?"

He was getting tired of her asking him that. It seemed like every hour on the hour she would sniffle about her mommy. But it wasn't the time to lose his patience with her. "Mommy's actually in Arizona, sweetie. So you'll get to see her there."

Zoe's face brightened. "I will?" She jumped down off her chair and came over to him, going up on tiptoe to throw her arms around his neck. "Uncle Eddy!"

"Yes, you will, poppet. So, you'd better go pack your smallest suitcase, okay?" He glanced toward the living room. "Rico!"

When Rico walked into the kitchen, Eddy said, "Take Zoe over to her apartment and help her pack for a couple of days in Arizona. Shorts and short-sleeved shirts, plus at least one pair of jeans and a light jacket in case the evenings get cold." He flicked a glance at Zoe, who was hopping impatiently from one foot to the other. "And the other . . . essentials." He looked at Rico, at a loss for what other things a little girl might need to pack for a trip. "You know, little girl stuff."

"*Sí.* I'm sure *la chica hermosa* will know what she needs, eh, little one?"

"Sure, Rico." She grabbed Rico's hand and tried to drag him out of the room. "Come on! We're gonna go see my mommy!"

Rico grinned and allowed her to lead him away.

Eddy sighed. Once he had Merrick and O'Connell out of the way, he'd really have to do something about Rico, too.

Chapter 15

Olivia sat on the floor and stroked the wolf's heaving side. Poor Sully. Even in those amber doggy eyes she saw the pain he was feeling. He'd already shifted twice, and she knew he wasn't going to like it when she told him he had to shift one more time. But she could tell that his healing still wasn't complete. He needed another shift.

He gulped down air and closed his eyes, and in a few seconds was back in his human form. "Oh, God," he muttered with his eyes still closed. Sweat coated his skin, made his dark hair stick to his forehead. "I think I'm going to throw up."

With so many shifts in a row, that reaction wasn't at all out of the ordinary. Olivia pushed to her feet and ran into the bathroom. She wet a washcloth with cold water and wrung it out, then grabbed the wastebasket, just in case.

Returning to Sully's side, she patted his face with the cold cloth, then held it across the back of his neck. "Is that better?"

"Mmm." He opened his eyes and turned his head slightly to look at her. "Thanks."

She nodded. Brushing his hair from his forehead, she murmured, "You need to shift one more time."

His brows drew down. "I don't think so. I feel fine."

"Do you?" Olivia sat back on her haunches. Voice firm, she said, "Get up then."

He stared at her, determination in his eyes. A muscle flexed in his jaw, then the stubborn son of a bitch tried to do just that. To give him credit, he actually made it to a hunched-over position before he fell back to the floor, clutching his legs and cursing.

She did her best not to flutter over him, or smack him for being so thickheaded. "Once more, Sully. Then you can rest."

He turned to his side, breathing heavily. He gave a short nod, muttered another curse, and closed his eyes.

As many times as she'd seen a shift, it never ceased to amaze her, how bones and muscle, tendons and cartilage could transform themselves from one form to another. And in such a short time. Yet the proof was before her, as Sully lay on the floor, panting. His tongue lolled from one side of his muzzle, and his eyes were half closed.

From what she could tell, he had just about enough energy to get back to his human form, and that was it. She sifted her fingers through the heavy ruff at his nape. "Okay, honey. Come on back."

He turned his head and swiped his tongue along the inside of her arm. Then he closed his eyes and a few shuddering breaths later rolled onto his back, once again human.

Olivia helped him onto the bed, then grabbed the washcloth and wet it again. Returning to the bedroom, she lightly ran the cloth over his arms, chest, and belly, then down his legs, wiping away the sweat and trying to cool him down. By the time she finished, he was asleep. She pulled the sheet over him and sat on the edge of the bed, staring down at his still form. The fear for him still ate at her like a living thing, telling her most clearly that she had, indeed, fallen in love with him.

Not that she could tell him that. Not yet. Not until after she confessed all of her secrets. Then she'd see where she stood.

He frowned in his sleep, his unhappiness with his current situation clear even in slumber. She knew his legs still ached, though he had pretty much healed. At any rate, by the time Ryder was to arrive at the airport, Sully would be in tip-top shape.

There were a few upsides to being a werewolf. Speed healing was one of them.

She let her gaze travel over him, covered with just a sheet, and saw the bump caused by his penis. Usually when a male shifted from wolf to human he had a hard-on; with Sully being in so much pain and exhausted by the last shift, no matter how strong he was, his body couldn't produce an erection.

Minutes passed, blending into an hour, then another as she watched over him. She'd just closed her eyes, trying to clear her mind of worry over him, over Zoe, over the mess her life had become, when he spoke.

"Hullo." Sully's voice came out a deep rasp, sending shivers skating over her skin and heat straight to her core.

Olivia smiled at him. Leaning over, she stroked her fingers across his jaw, letting her thumb rub gently over his lips. "How're you feeling?"

"Better." He lifted his arms above his head and stretched, a low moan coming from him. The sheet slipped to his waist, and she admired his long lean torso and ridged abdomen, and tried to push aside the compulsion to trace her tongue over the small muscles covering his ribs along his side. He levered himself up against the headboard, arms loose at his sides. "What time is it?"

She glanced at the clock on the side table in the living room. "Just past three."

"So just another couple hours until we need to head out to pick up Ryder."

Olivia nodded. "Yeah. I was thinking about that, actually." She met Sully's gaze and curled her hand around the back of his neck, rubbing her thumb beneath his ear. "I think you need to stay here. Out of the public eye. Just in case."

He drew in a breath and held it a moment, then puffed it out through his nose. "You mean in case whoever hit me might be watching." He brought his hand up and covered hers, pulling it to his mouth to plant a soft kiss in her palm.

"Yeah." A deep thrumming started inside her, one which she tried to ignore. He really wasn't in the best shape to be doing the horizontal mambo, for crying out loud. Her timing could have been a bit better. She cleared her throat. "If whoever hit you has reported back to Eddy that you're dead—which is what I'd have done—then you're the one advantage we might have in this whole mess."

She should probably call Eddy and tell him the news herself. But how would she explain that she'd been close enough to witness the accident but hadn't been the one to "kill" Sully?

"Hmm. I like that. Being an advantage." Sully moved her hand and pressed his lips to her inner wrist.

"Keep that up, buddy, and you might find yourself being taken advantage *of.*" Olivia pushed aside thoughts of Eddy and focused on the man at her side. She tried to pull her hand away, but he tightened his grip, his mouth lingering on her pulse.

Sully's gaze turned thoughtful. "I don't think I've ever been taken advantage of before." His lips tilted in a lopsided grin. "You never know. I might like it."

She wasn't going to turn down an invitation to take advantage of him, that was for sure. She'd just make sure she was gentle. "Want to find out?"

His eyes sparkled with amber heat. "Absobloody-lutely."

"Well, then, my good man," Olivia said with her best British accent, "lie back and prepare to be advantaged." She wiggled her hand, and this time he let her go.

She'd long ago divested herself of her shoes. "I think I'll get a bit more comfortable while I'm at it." She slid off the bed and yanked off her T-shirt, then took off her shorts, keeping her peach-colored panties and matching bra on for the moment. "Now, where to begin?"

She tapped her chin with one finger, letting her gaze rove him from the top of his head to his sheet-covered feet. On her way back up, she noticed the bulge at his groin had grown considerably and now tented the sheet. "You *are* feeling better, aren't you?"

"Good enough to be taken advantage of." His face lightened with his quick grin. "So . . . what are you waiting for? I'm ready."

She got back on the bed on her knees, kneeling at his hip, and leaned forward, bracing herself with one hand gripping the solid pine headboard. She placed a soft kiss against his mouth, gave his bottom lip a sharp nip, then laved away the sting with her tongue. Another kiss to the corner of his eye, his nose, beside his ear.

Her kisses wandered across his strong, stubbled jaw and down his neck, lingering in the hollow at the base of his throat. Sully tipped his head back, his low groan vibrating against her lips.

Olivia couldn't resist following the line of his nearest collarbone, her tongue lightly tracing a trail out to his brawny shoulder. She kissed her way over the bulge of his biceps, paused at his inner elbow, then picked up his hand and brought his fingers to her mouth. After kissing each fingertip, she pulled his index finger into the wet heat of her mouth, laving it with her tongue, then added his middle finger and gently sucked on them.

"Oh. My. God." Sully looked down at her. His tongue flicked out, leaving his lower lip wet and inviting. "I don't think this is being taken advantage of, love. I think you're still trying to kill me."

Her heart stuttered. He couldn't really think that. She looked up again and realized he hadn't meant it literally. She released his fingers and murmured, "You ain't seen nothin' yet, honey."

She let his hand drop back to his side and leaned over him again. She nuzzled under his jaw, enjoying the solid feel of bone, the softness of flesh, then moved down to his chest, darting her tongue out to flick at one hard nipple. His indrawn breath sounded like the sweetest music to her ears. Bringing up her free hand, she rubbed her fingers back and forth over one of his nipples while she licked and sucked the other one.

Deciding she needed both hands, she swung one leg over him and straddled his thighs. His erection bowed beneath the pressure she put on the sheet still covering him, and his breath hissed between his teeth.

"Poor baby," she murmured with a glance down between her legs. There was a small wet spot on the sheet and the clear outline of the head of his cock. "Your turn's coming soon," she promised.

"From your lips to God's ears," Sully muttered with a low chuckle.

Olivia met his gaze and ran her tongue over her bottom lip. "That's the idea, big boy. From my lips . . ."

His nostrils flared. "Well, get on with it, then."

"Aye, aye, sir." She gave him a mock salute and then bent over him. Her lips followed the smattering of hair that bisected his tummy, her hands pushing the sheet away as she went. She scooted down, pulling more of the sheet with her until his cock was bared to her gaze. And her hands.

And her mouth.

Her breath quickened, but she made herself keep a slow pace. She wasn't going for the gold just yet. Anticipation was the greatest aphrodisiac of all.

She ran her hands lightly down Sully's legs, taking care not to exert too much pressure, loving the feel of warm, hair-roughened skin covering hard, flexing muscles. Her pussy thumped with emptiness; her nipples hardened beneath her bra.

But it wasn't about her. It was all about him. She kissed a path over one hip to his leg, lingered on the sensitive flesh of his inner thigh, feeling his cock twitch against her cheek.

"Oliviaaaaaa . . ." His voice rasped against her eardrums, setting up another set of shivers.

She planted another slow kiss on his thigh, then wandered down his leg. Tilting her head, she placed her mouth on the sensitive skin behind his knee. His muscles tensed and relaxed, tensed again as she curled her hands around the back of his thighs and kissed her way down to his ankles.

Every inch of this man was special to her, from his long toes to the dark, spiky hair on top of his head. And before she was done, he'd know it.

She started her way back up his legs again, lightly massaging with her hands in the wake of her mouth.

"Olivia, sweetheart." His voice was a low husk of sound. "Put that gorgeous mouth of yours on my cock before it explodes."

She looked up at him and grinned. With gentle fingers she took his erection in one hand.

"God, yes." He groaned, his eyes fluttering closed.

He was so hot and heavy in her palm, his skin silky smooth. She rubbed the fingers of her other hand lightly over his hair-dusted balls. "What do you want, Sully? This?" She leaned down and pressed her open mouth against one testicle, letting her warm breath blow against him as she swirled the tip of her tongue in a slow circle. Lifting her head, she whispered, "Or this?" and nibbled her way up the underside of his cock to his tip.

She licked the pre-cum that wept from the slit, and with her tongue spread it around the ruddy head. His hips punched upward, driving more of his length into her mouth. Olivia pulled away and *tsk*ed him. "I'm the one doing the taking advantage of, remember? You're just supposed to lie there and let me do all the work."

"Then get to it." Sully's irises were wholly amber now. The wildness of the wolf swallowed up the green and blazed from his eyes. "Stop teasing."

"But the teasing will lead to so much more," Olivia promised and stuck out her tongue to lap at the head of his cock. She held his gaze, exulting in seeing a muscle flex in his taut jaw. He was on the fine edge of his control. She wanted to see if she could shove him over it. Making him shed his cool, calm Brit exterior was her new calling in life.

For however long that might be.

For however long he might be hers.

She looked down at his erection. He was thick and long, wide veins running the length of his shaft. More clear liquid hovered at the tip, and she leaned forward, swiping it with her tongue.

His hands came up and fisted in her hair. "More," he demanded, his voice guttural.

Olivia took the head of his cock into her mouth and sucked lightly. She stroked one hand down his shaft and cupped his balls, rocking them in her fingers.

Sully groaned and bucked against her. "God. Take more!"

She opened her mouth wide and took as much of him as she could. He was so thick she couldn't take all of him, so she stroked her hand from her mouth down to his base. When he grunted and thrust against her, she drew slowly away until he left her mouth with a soft, wet *pop*.

"Olivia . . ."

"Anticipation, remember?" She pressed his cock up against his belly and licked a path on the underside from the crown to the base. He tipped his hips toward her, and she smiled in feminine triumph. There was something very empowering about having a strong man like this silently— and sometimes not so silently—begging for more.

She was only too happy to oblige. In her own way.

In her own time.

Olivia swiped the flat of her tongue over his sac and pulled one of his balls into her mouth. Beginning a slow steady stroke of one hand along his shaft, she fingered his balls with the other hand, rolling them back and forth as she nibbled and sucked. She slipped her fingers from his sac to the sensitive skin behind, rubbing gently.

She licked her way back up the length of his cock, then pulled him into her mouth. Keeping one hand beneath him, she palmed his sac and rubbed the skin behind it. He pumped his hips, thrusting more of his cock into her mouth, and she hummed, knowing the vibration would shoot straight to his balls.

"Christ!" Sully's hips bucked and surged, driving more of his thick length into her mouth. The head of his cock hit the back of her throat, triggering her gag reflex. She pulled back slightly to catch her breath, then went back down.

He tried to push her away, but she swatted at his hands and stayed where she was. She put her hands on his thighs and kept sucking.

"I'm going to come, sweetheart," he muttered, his muscles tensing beneath her hands. His hands went to her hair and gripped, holding her steady.

She hummed again and brought his cock deeper, to the back of her throat, and swallowed.

Sully growled and took over the rhythm, fucking into her mouth with short, hard thrusts. Olivia opened her mouth as wide as she could and sucked him on each outward stroke. She reached one hand between his legs and grasped his balls, tugging on the hard globes.

His roar reverberated through the small room. Hands tightening in her hair, he held himself still while his release jetted into her mouth. He tasted salty and tart, and her throat kept moving until she'd swallowed every last drop.

Hard hands around her arms hoisted her up, and he clamped his mouth over hers in a possessive, demanding kiss. Drawing back, he cupped her face in his hands.

"Damn. I think you've about killed me." He kissed her again. "Let me return the favor."

With a quick twist of his lean torso, he flipped her over onto her back. He stared for a moment at her lying there, clad only in her bra and panties. His eyes narrowed, and he placed one palm on the slight rise of her tummy. Heat from his big hand permeated her skin, fired her blood. She couldn't stop the slight shimmy of her hips any more than she could keep from breathing.

He drew in a deep breath through his nose and groaned. "God, you smell so fucking good when you're aroused." He reached behind her and undid her bra, pulling the filmy material away and letting it drop to the floor. Then he pulled her panties off and let them drop, too. "That is one aspect I'm willing to admit is helpful about being a were-wolf." His gaze held hers a moment. "That I can smell even the smallest hint of your arousal."

His hands slid from her ankles up to her knees, parting her legs. He bent over her and pressed his lips to one calf, mouthing a path up her leg to the back of her knee. He draped her leg over his strong shoulder and lifted her other leg. After placing a soft kiss on her inner thigh, he let that leg rest over his shoulder as well.

He spread her slick folds apart with his thumbs. With another rough growl, he dipped his head and swiped the flat of his tongue along the length of her slit.

Olivia moaned and jerked, tilting her hips and letting her thighs fall apart even more. Sully's hands slid under her and lifted her closer to his mouth. His low groan vibrated against her clit just before he sucked it into the wet warmth of his mouth.

She helplessly thrust her hips against his face, seeking more of his touch. As he suckled her swollen bud, his fingers kneaded her buttocks. He brushed against the puckered rosebud of her ass, and she shuddered as her climax began to build.

He licked through her folds to her slick opening. His tongue swirled around and around, making her cry out. She gripped his hair, holding his head close to her, crying out again as he fucked his tongue into her sheath.

Sully moved back to her clit. One last suckle, and she fell over the edge with a scream. He brought one hand between her legs and slid two long fingers into her pussy, thrusting in and out while she moaned and quaked around him.

When she was finally still, he wiped his hand across his mouth. She let her legs fall to the bed, and he came up over her. He kissed her, giving her a taste of herself.

Olivia tried to calm her breathing. He settled at her side, moving one thick thigh over hers, cupping her breast with his hand. His thumb swept languidly over her tight nipple.

She sighed and rested her hand on his forearm, feeling the muscles flex with the movement of his thumb. She closed her eyes, feeling sated and content for the first time in a long time. "Well, Mr. Sullivan, I think you've about killed *me*."

His low chuckle stirred the hair at her temple. "Just returning the favor, love."

All she wanted to do was lie there in his arms and not face reality. But she couldn't. She stirred. "We should get up to the main house."

Sully's arms tightened around her. "In a minute. I want to hold you a while longer."

Olivia settled down against him again and rubbed her cheek against his hair-roughened chest. It felt good to be in a man's embrace again.

In *this* man's embrace.

He was good and honorable, and . . . fucked up because of her. She had to make sure he didn't find out about that until after Zoe was safe. She didn't think that would make him change his mind. He wasn't the sort to allow an innocent to suffer because he was in a bad temper. But she also didn't want him or the others distracted by the knowledge.

She would come clean once she had Zoe in her arms again, once she was sure Eddy was no longer a threat.

Then she and her daughter would go back to New York long enough for Olivia to quit her job, pack up what few belongings she didn't want to part with, and get the hell out of the City.

They'd start over again somewhere else. Somewhere new and, if they were lucky, devoid of other werewolves. Hopefully her daughter never had to find out what a monster her mother had become.

Olivia would pack away her heart and her love for Sully, and go on as before.

Just her and Zoe.

"Tell me I'm not the only one that feels a connection here." Sully's hand rubbed up her arm from elbow to shoulder and back again. "I don't even know if I can explain it, but you feel so familiar to me. Almost as if . . ." He made a gruff sound in his throat. "Never mind. Being run over apparently has made me a sentimental arse."

Way to go, twist the knife of guilt even deeper, why don'tcha. And he didn't even know it. As her heart thrilled that he felt more for her than mere lust, Olivia couldn't let him soul search any deeper. Rather than tell an outright lie, she gave a laugh and shook her head. She pressed a kiss to his pec and then pulled out of his arms. Sitting for a moment on the edge of the bed, she stared down at her knees and sighed. "We need to get up to the main house, Sully."

She got off the bed and began to dress. After a few seconds, Sully did the same. She could feel him staring at her and knew if she turned around she'd see confusion on his face, in his eyes.

Better to see confusion than revulsion and hatred. There was time enough for that later.

Chapter 16

A few hours later, Sully sat on the sofa next to Olivia and looked again at Taite Merrick. Her tummy had a noticeable bump, but still just a little one. The knowledge of new life sparkled in her eyes, glowed on her skin. Unable to hold it back any longer, he finally interrupted the current conversation by frowning at Ryder and asking, "What in the hell were you thinking?"

Voices stopped. Ryder glanced at him with a muttered, "I'm sorry?"

Sully gestured at Taite. "What were you thinking, bringing her here? In her condition?"

Taite's eyebrows shot up. "Excuse me? Just what are you saying there, Mr. Sullivan? That I should've stayed home barefoot and in the kitchen like a good little woman?" She crossed her legs and her foot started tapping the air.

He rolled his eyes at her sarcasm, though he made a mental note to stay clear of that foot. "Of course not." Unable to resist, he added, "Cobb wouldn't let you hang out in the kitchen barefoot."

"Oh, hardy-har-har." She leaned back in her chair and

folded her arms across her breasts. "Aren't you just the co-median?"

"No, seriously, I just mean"—he looked again at Ryder—"things are going to get dangerous. Perhaps even deadly." To emphasize his point, he added, "She won't be safe."

"Which is why she isn't going anywhere near Miles and his minions." Ryder's eyes darkened with annoyance. "Just how much of a noob do you think I am?" he asked with a sidelong glance at his wife. He looked once again at Sully, one side of his mouth lifted in a wry grin. Or maybe it was a grimace, it was hard to tell. "Besides which, *you* try stopping her when she has her mind set on something."

Sully snorted. He didn't know Taite all that well, but he'd been impressed with her no-nonsense attitude. "Has you running scared already, does she?"

"You'd better believe it." Ryder shot a grin toward his wife, trying to duck the hand she smacked down on his arm.

"Hey!" Taite scowled at Sully and then turned her frown on her husband and waggled her index finger at him. "Watch it, buster. You *can* sleep on the sofa, you know."

"Oh, he wouldn't have to sleep on the sofa," Declan chimed in. As usual, his eyes glimmered with merriment, though the look on his face remained sober. "We've another guest room."

Taite threw her hands into the air. "I give up." She snuggled under the arm Ryder draped over her shoulders. "It's a good thing the three of you can't get together very often. Look what happens." She shook her head and sighed, an exaggerated expression of sadness on her face. "Everything degenerates to a shit-fest." She glanced at the other women. "It breaks the heart, doesn't it?"

Sully noticed that Olivia was the only one not joining in the fun. Her lips were held tighter than normal, and he got the feeling she was holding back her impatience with the lot of them.

Before he could bring the conversation back to business, Declan leaned forward and said, "Aye. All sorts of mayhem ensues." Declan winked at Taite. "Which I happen to know you enjoy."

She stuck her tongue out at him and grinned. Declan laughed. Sully was struck again by how much their relationship was like that of siblings. They had that kind of closeness. It made him, for a brief moment, miss his brother. Wouldn't Ben be properly flabbergasted if he could see the mess his little brother had gotten into?

One day, maybe, he'd tell Ben what had happened. But maybe not. The less he knew, the more Ben's insular world would remain intact.

He glanced over at Pelicia to see how she was taking the byplay between her fiancé and Taite. Pelicia must have had the same view of her fiancé's relationship with the other woman, or she just wasn't the jealous sort, because she watched the interplay with an indulgent smile on her face.

Taite turned to Sully. "I came because I have contacts here," she said in all seriousness. She glanced at Olivia, her expression suggesting that she, too, realized Olivia endured the turn in conversation by a thin thread of tolerance. "If we want to make Miles think you're dead, I can probably pull some strings and have an official investigation announced to the media."

"How would we explain the aftermath?" Olivia leaned forward and clasped her hands between her knees. Her eyes darkened. "We're not just getting my daughter back, we're going to kill Eddy, too." At everyone's silent response, she spread her hands, a look of surprise on her face. "What? Am I the only one who wants him taken out? If he's allowed to live, he'll just keep coming after all of you, you must know that."

The others exchanged glances. Sully could see from the men's expressions that they knew killing Miles would be the only course of action open to them. The women—except for Olivia—seemed less convinced.

"As much as it goes against all of my training, I realize we're not in a situation to turn him over to the authorities." Sully reached up and stroked his hand across Olivia's back. If she was bloodthirsty, well, then, so was he.

He guessed it was in his blood. He pushed that thought aside to be dealt with at a later date. It was not the time to be sidetracked with feeling sorry for himself.

"Aye." Declan's eyes glittered. "Anyway, I'm itchin' for a little payback. He's the one who sent Sumner after me and Taite. If that little prick had had his way, I'd be dead and Taite would be whelping little bastards for him."

Taite grimaced, her hand coming up to grip Ryder's where it rested on her shoulder.

Pelicia murmured, "It just seems so—"

"It's so what?" Olivia stood and paced to the patio doors. With her back to the room, she folded her arms, her hands cupping her elbows. "So brutal? So cold?"

Sully was struck again at how strong yet fragile she could appear at the same time. A woman of contradictions, yet one he'd trust with his life.

Olivia spun around, her eyes glittering with tears and the amber heat of the wolf. "So justified?"

"Perhaps to you it is." Pelicia's voice was as calm as Olivia's was fraught with tension. "But there are other ways to handle him." She glanced around at the others in the room. "Aren't there?" She shook her head and murmured, "There has to be another way. I can't believe that killing him is the only answer."

"We're werewolves." Olivia looked around the room and shook her head. "The court system isn't set up to deal with people like us. We're stronger, faster, and a hell of a lot meaner when things go wrong." She took a deep breath and some of the dark yellow flecks faded from her irises. "Don't let yourself think for even one second that Eddy would allow himself to be arrested, let alone put on trial and sent to prison. He'd die first. And take as many people with him as he can."

"She's right." Ryder's shoulders moved with his deep breath. "Even as a kid he was frighteningly determined and callous."

"Yes, she *is* right." Sully went over to her and pulled her into a loose embrace. "Taking Miles out is the only way any of us—or our children," he said with a pointed glance at Taite's midsection, "will be safe."

"We're werewolves," Olivia said again. "We handle things differently." Olivia rested her forehead against Sully's chest, and he felt the shudder that went through her as she fought for control. God, once they had her little girl safe and Miles was completely out of the picture, he was going to take Olivia and Zoe someplace special so they could relax and have fun like they hadn't been able to do in the last few years.

As Pelicia went and sat beside Declan, Sully addressed the room at large. "Miles has to be put down like the dog he is. Olivia's right. None of us will be safe." He shook his head. "Not to mention how many more lives he'll ruin by turning people into werewolves and killing others who are in his way. Including children like Zoe."

Olivia swallowed. "I won't let him hurt my daughter!"

"No, of course not!" Pelicia stood and walked over to Olivia, and put one hand on her arm. "Darling, I wasn't suggesting . . . I didn't mean . . ." She lifted her shoulders in a shrug. "It just seems so bloodthirsty."

"You fight fire with fire, Pel." Sully looked down at Olivia. "We're not going to let anything happen to Zoe, all right?"

She turned in Sully's arms. Reaching up, she touched his cheek with a fleeting, loving gesture, and then stepped away from him. She glanced from person to person. "Regardless of what a coldhearted bitch you think it makes me, I don't plan for Eddy to survive more than another couple days."

"No one thinks you're coldhearted." Taite rested one hand low on her belly. "Sometimes being a bitch is the only way to get things done."

"Well, then," Ryder said. "We should make our plan."

"Right." Sully wrapped his arm around Olivia and urged her back to the sofa. He didn't know why she kept trying to distance herself from him, but he did know he didn't like it. He wasn't going to let her. He sat, tugging her down beside him. "We reckon Miles will arrive in Tucson tonight or tomorrow, right?"

Nods came from the group.

"And . . . what? Will he find out where Dec lives and come here with his gang?" He looked at Olivia.

"He probably would, unless . . ." She broke off, her expression turning thoughtful.

"Unless what?" Sully prompted.

"Give me a minute." She put her thumb to her mouth and chewed lightly on the nail. After several minutes she took a deep breath and dropped her hand to her lap. "If I know Eddy—and I do—he'll bring Zoe with him. He's not going to bring her here for a bloody fight. So, that means he'll need to have a hidey-hole somewhere. If the person who ran you over"—she glanced at Sully—"was a front man, then he already has somewhere to go."

"So how do we find out where that is?" Taite leaned forward in her chair.

Olivia raised her eyebrows and grinned. "I call him again. He said he was coming to Tucson. It's a simple matter of me demanding to see Zoe." She shook her head, her smile fading. "Of course, he'll probably want to see me anyway and ask why I wasn't the one who killed Sully."

"Well, let me make a couple of calls first." Taite got up and walked over to the phone. "At the very least, we can allay any suspicions he might have by planting a phony story in the local paper—with some help from friends," she added with a slight smile. She took the handset off the base and walked to the patio doors. As she dialed, she pulled open the slider and went outside, pushing the door closed behind her.

Ryder shook his head. "That woman. She's such a sun worshipper."

"The heat does feel good, especially after London this time of year." Sully leaned against the sofa and stretched his arms along the back. He looked at Olivia. "So, what now?"

She took a deep breath. "Now I call Eddy. Then we get to work."

He was amazed at how good it felt to hear her use the word "we." It was time she realized that she didn't have to go it alone anymore. She had friends who were willing and eager to help her.

She stood up and pulled her phone out of her front

pocket. "Here goes nothing," she murmured, and flipped open the phone and dialed a number. He saw her cross her fingers on her free hand and grinned at the display of superstition.

He crossed his for good measure, too. Just in case.

"Eddy? It's Olivia." She paused and bit her lower lip. "Yeah, well, things have been . . . hectic." She met Sully's gaze, her eyes worried. Then her brows dipped slightly. "What?" She listened to whatever Eddy was saying, then replied, "But that's why I was calling you."

Sully stood and went over to her. She gave him a small wave as if to say "I'm fine, don't worry" or "Don't bother me." He wasn't sure which. But she was looking more and more anxious by the moment.

And he hated the feeling of helplessness that that engendered in him.

Olivia swallowed. Hard. "Eddy, if you'll just let me—"

"Yes. You explain why Sullivan was hit and killed by a car several hours ago and you're just now calling me."

Think fast, Liv. "I was waiting for something I could offer as proof." *Wait. Did he know I was with Sully when it happened?*

His sigh came across the line. "Well, I must tell you, Livvie, I am disappointed. I wanted *you* to be the one to take him out. I'm not sure now what to do about you."

Oh, God. He was going to use this as leverage for Zoe. But it didn't appear that he knew she'd been witness to the hit-and-run. "Eddy, please. I tried, you know I did. It's not my fault that someone hit him with a car before I could take him out."

"Do you know who that someone was?" He paused. "And just where were you when all this was going down?"

"Um . . ." She racked her brain. The way he'd asked made it sound like she should know. But how could she? *Oh, God.* Unless he did know she'd been there. "I was there, tracking him. I was getting ready to attack him when—"

"Save the excuses. Anyway, you can thank Peter and Calvin for doing your job for you."

"They're here, too?" She looked around at the others with wide eyes. They might have just been handed another advantage, if neither man had disclosed she'd been with Sully.

Though why they hadn't caused her some worry. Were they waiting for a more opportune time? Or was this something they would use against her later on?

"Yes, they're here, too. I sent them down to check up on you. In retrospect, it was a good thing I did, I guess. Because they now have a cozy place for me to plan my final revenge on Merrick. It's that one," he muttered, his voice muffled.

"Sorry, what?"

"Wasn't talking to you. Wait a minute." She heard a shuffling noise, a couple of grunts. "And that one."

She frowned. What the hell was he doing? She closed her eyes and focused her sense of hearing onto the phone, and tried to block out the noises she could hear inside the room. She disregarded the sounds of breathing, the rustle of clothing as people shifted in their seats, heartbeats that picked up in speed the longer she was silent. From the phone she could hear other people's voices in the background, then what sounded like an announcement over a public address system. "Eddy, where are you?"

"I'm at the airport."

"In New York?"

"No, here in Tucson."

That made her eyes go wide. She sent a startled glance at Sully.

"What?" he mouthed.

She held up one finger in a gesture for him to wait.

"Just arrived," Eddy went on. "I'm getting ready to head out to the ranch."

"What ranch?" Olivia switched the phone to her other ear and grabbed a pen lying by a small notepad on the table near the landline phone. She wrote HE'S HERE in big block letters and showed it to Sully.

Sully picked it up and showed the others.

"I don't know. Some place that Calvin and Peter found." Eddy gave a few more directions to whoever was with him, once again ignoring her.

Just then, Taite pushed open the slider and came back into the house. Sully put his finger to his lips to forestall her saying anything. She nodded and quietly pulled the door closed, then went over to Ryder's side and sat on the arm of his padded chair.

Eddy's voice came back on the line. "Okay, Livvie. As soon as I get settled in, I'll phone you and you can come join us."

"And . . . Zoe?" Olivia held her breath. God, it would be just like him to do something to Zoe anyway, as a lesson for Olivia.

He sighed. "Now, you don't think I'd have left her in New York, do you?" His tone suggested he thought her lacking in intelligence. Something she was used to. "She's with me, of course. And she's fine—sleeping on Walter's shoulder right now."

Walter, one of Eddy's lieutenants—a big, beefy man with an absurd loyalty to their pack leader. Whatever his life had been like before, he seemed to look on Eddy as some sort of savior. There'd be no help there.

"Is it just you and Walter, then?" She pressed her lips together as she awaited his answer.

"No, Aaron's with me, too." He sounded preoccupied.

Aaron, Walter, Peter, and Calvin—four other werewolves with him. She glanced around at her soon-to-be-ex-friends. Four of them against five. It was doable. More than doable, if Calvin was on her side. But if he was on her side, why did he try to kill Sully?

"God, the weather here is perfect. It was fucking forty degrees and raining when we left the city." Eddy paused and took a deep breath.

He must have just walked outside the airport. "It's very nice," Olivia agreed, though her mind was still on the fact that he'd also brought Aaron along. Aaron was newer to the pack than even she was, but moving very fast through the ranks.

A werewolf that could go with either side, depending on which side looked to be winning.

"Anyway," Eddy continued, "I'm going to have a small chat with Calvin as soon as I . . . Ah, speak of the devil." He huffed a sigh. "Let me get settled, Livvie, then we'll catch up and you can tell me again and in more detail exactly why you failed me, not once but twice."

"But . . . can I talk to Zoe, please?" She chewed her bottom lip.

"She's sleeping, I told you." His voice went hard. "Have I ever lied to you?"

As far as she knew, he'd always been brutally honest. Though he'd at times withheld the truth, he'd never lied to her. "No."

"Then believe me when I tell you she's sleeping. You

know how traveling exhausts her. I don't want to wake her up. You can talk to her in another couple hours." He told Calvin to take his luggage and asked how long it would take to get to the ranch. After he received a reply, he said to Olivia, "It will take us about an hour to get where we're going. I'll call you once I'm settled in."

"Eddy. Eddy!" She snapped her phone shut with a scowl. "He hung up."

"What did he say?" Sully stood close, not touching, but his expression held such care and concern that she had to fight to keep from moving into his arms. It wasn't the time for comfort. She needed the grief, the anger to help her get through the coming hours.

To prepare herself to kill Eddy.

And to say good-bye to the man, she admitted to herself, she had fallen in love with and would love until the day she died.

Chapter 17

Sully couldn't stand the tortured look on Olivia's face. He reached out and hauled her into his arms.

She stayed there a moment, resting her forehead against his shoulder. "Why did you have to be so nice?" she whispered and then fought her way clear of him. "Don't!" She waved him off when he attempted to hug her again. "I can't . . . Don't be nice to me. I can't take it. Not now."

And there was yet another layer to her, peeled away. She could be strong but not if she was shown gentleness.

God, he would kill Miles for what he'd done to this beautiful, vibrant woman.

"Eddy's here. In Tucson. He was just leaving the airport when he hung up." She wrapped her arms around herself. "He said he'd call when he got settled." She drew in a deep breath and held it, then exhaled slowly. Eyes closed, she tipped her head to one side, then the other, working out the kinks in a neck he knew was tight with strain. "He has Zoe with him."

"Good. That's good," Sully said. "That was what we'd hoped he'd do. We'll make sure to get her to safety before anything else happens."

"Aye." Declan's voice was quiet. "Did Miles say *where* he was gettin' settled?"

With eyes still closed, she shook her head. "He didn't say. He mentioned a ranch." When she opened her eyes, tears shone in their depths. "Apparently he sent two of his goons here a day ago or so to"—she made quote marks in the air—"check up on me." She dropped her hands and looked at Sully. "One of them is the one who hit you. They've rented or . . . taken a ranch somewhere here in town. Or at least one nearby. Eddy said it would take an hour from the airport to get there."

"What do you mean, they've 'taken' a ranch?" Pelicia asked.

Olivia's lips tightened. "If they found a place that suited their needs and it was occupied, they would have made sure it became unoccupied."

"You mean"—Pelicia's eyes widened—"they just killed whoever lived there?"

"If that's what it took." Olivia lifted her shoulders. Her gaze hard, she gritted out, "How many times and in how many different ways do I have to say this? Eddy is an amoral, unconscionable monster." Before anyone could respond, she sighed. "I'm sorry, Pel. I didn't mean to snap at you."

"It's all right. I understand." Pelicia gave Olivia a sympathetic look.

"How many are with him?" Ryder stretched his legs out in front of him, looking unconcerned that his cousin was back in his life, wanting to kill him and his family and friends.

"From what I can tell, four. Peter and Walter are loyal and will fight to the death to protect him. Aaron is fairly new. He's only been with our pack about a year and a half.

But he's ambitious." Olivia spread out her hands. "If he sees the fight isn't in Eddy's favor, he might cut and run."

"Might." Sully shifted on his feet. "But you're not sure."

She shook her head. "He could go either way, but initially he'll be on Eddy's side, I guarantee it."

"And the fourth?" Declan slipped his arm around Pelicia and settled back against the sofa.

"Calvin. He's the one I told you about—the one whose family Eddy murdered. He has a new wife and a baby on the way. I don't know that he'd jeopardize that." She frowned. "But, again, if he sees the battle's not going Eddy's way, he might help us."

"There's another 'might.'" Declan shook his head. "I'm thinkin' we need to be prepared for no outside help. It's just us, as we'd planned. Five of them against the four of us." He grinned. "I like those odds."

Olivia nodded. She looked around at everyone in the room, and Sully noticed a slight tremor in her lower lip. "I haven't said this yet, and I should have. Thank you." Her eyes shone with tears she was too stubborn to let fall. "You don't even know me, yet you're risking your lives . . ."

Ryder straightened from his slouched position, though he didn't leave his wife's side. "This was my fight long before it was yours, Olivia." He glanced at Taite. "And now that I have more to protect than just myself, I'm willing to take it all the way, do what has to be done to keep my family safe."

"Aye." Declan tugged Pelicia a little closer. "We all have somethin' at stake here, lass. You're not alone."

Olivia's throat moved with her hard swallow. Sully knew she'd always considered herself as alone, and perhaps she had been. Zoe was too young to be much support, and the less the little girl knew about what really went on the better. He hated for any child to lose their innocence too early, but especially Olivia's child.

"Miles made it my fight when he sent one of his wolves after Declan and the bastard got me instead." Sully cracked his knuckles. "I've been looking for a bit of payback."

Something flickered in Olivia's eyes, there and gone so fast he couldn't tell exactly what it was. But it wasn't the first time she'd gone funny when he'd said something about his own turning experience. Perhaps it brought back bad memories of when Miles had first bitten her.

In a softer voice, he added, "Now it's even more personal."

Olivia shot a startled look his way. She cleared her throat. "Yes, well. Still, I appreciate it. For the first time in three years I actually feel some hope that I can get Zoe out of this *Twilight Zone* episode my life's turned into."

"We're glad to help." Taite shifted her weight from where she perched on the thickly padded arm of Ryder's chair. "Is he asking for proof of Sully's death?"

Olivia shook her head. "He apparently took Calvin's word for it."

"So we don't need to run an obit or get the authorities involved in any way?"

"No."

Which, in Sully's mind at least, was in its own way a relief. The more convoluted the plan was, the more likely something would go wrong. The fact that Miles thought Sully was dead—and that he didn't know Olivia had enlisted the help of Sully and his friends—meant he would be taken completely by surprise. Since Calvin hadn't disclosed that Olivia had been with Sully at the time of the hit-and-run, either he hadn't seen her or for his own reasons he'd kept it to himself.

Either way, it meant that Eddy was clueless. Which was fine by Sully. It was about time they got a break.

Olivia tried to bat down the jitters that set her stomach tumbling. Things seemed to be falling into place quite nicely—and that made her nervous. Calvin had left out one tiny detail in the hit-and-run story he told Eddy—that she had been with Sully at the time—and that made her even more anxious.

Why hadn't he told Eddy? He had to have seen her dragging Sully away from the road. Or he would have seen her with Sully before she'd started down that little rabbit trail.

"You know, they had to have seen me." She looked at the others and tried to stay calm when her insides were jumping. "Why didn't he tell Eddy I was with Sully?"

Sully and Declan exchanged a glance. "Well, I know if the bastard had killed my family," Sully said, his deep voice flinty, "I'd be doing everything I could to undermine him. If Calvin saw us together and didn't say anything, maybe he reckons you've switched sides."

"I don't know." She sighed.

What was Calvin's game? Would he be on her side, or Eddy's? Would he try to blackmail her later, when this was all over?

She'd like to think he still had enough integrity—that Eddy hadn't crushed it out of him completely—that he would stand and fight on the side of right. But he had a new family to think about, and after losing four children to Eddy's depravity, she couldn't imagine him risking yet another child.

"I guess we'll find out soon enough, won't we?" She gave a halfhearted smile at a murmur of sympathy from Pelicia.

Olivia wouldn't be surprised if she walked into her meeting with Eddy and he told her he knew Sully wasn't dead. At the moment Eddy seemed to be clueless, and that was rare. He was usually so tapped into everything that happened with his pack she'd often wondered if he had some psychic ability.

She'd come to accept that he didn't. He just had a lot of loyal minions out there.

And, if luck was on her side, some not-so-loyal ones.

She leaned against the wall and watched the other people in the room. It was so obvious that Ryder and Taite, and Declan and Pelicia loved each other.

Her gaze centered on Sully. What she'd give to have that same relationship with him. But she didn't dare hope that he'd forgive her for what she'd done to him, because when that forgiveness wasn't forthcoming she'd be heartbroken.

Better to have low expectations and not be crushed when they weren't fulfilled than to wish for the stars and always have them be out of reach. She'd learned that lesson first when she lost her husband after only being married two years, and then again with Eddy making promise after promise only to break them and, along with those broken promises, trying to break her.

"Regardless," Sully said, the roughness of his voice interrupting her thoughts, "she's not going to a meeting with Miles alone."

Olivia frowned. "It's not like any of you can walk in there with me, Sully. I have to go in alone."

As Sully opened his mouth to respond, Pelicia cut him off. "She's right. Until we know Zoe is safe, we can't risk having you all go rushing in there like a . . . well, like a pack of wolves," she finished a little lamely.

"An' it started out so well," Declan murmured with a grin.

"I know." Pelicia sighed. "I'm just not as clever with words as you lot."

"Well, you've zinged me more than a few times, sweetheart." Declan pressed a kiss to her temple. "Don't sell yourself short." He looked at Olivia. "An' just how are we to know that it's time to come in?"

She grimaced. "I hadn't quite worked that part out yet. As long as the place isn't soundproofed, you should be able to hear the conversation. I could use some sort of code word or something."

"This isn't a bloody spy movie," Sully muttered. When she looked at him with eyebrows raised at his tone, he had the grace to look chagrined. "Sorry. But sitting here doing nothing drives me 'round the bloody bend."

"I hear you on that one." Declan stood and stretched, then glanced at his wristwatch. "It's been nearly forty-five minutes since you talked to Miles. He'll be callin' soon."

"Speaking of calling . . ." Sully pulled his phone off the holder on his belt. "Give me your mobile number, love, so I can put it in my contacts."

Olivia did as he asked, feeling sad that all too soon he'd probably wipe that number out of his contact list.

The waiting became unbearable. She stood and began to pace, arms folded across her breasts.

Declan gave a low growl. "Come on, come on." He frowned. "Miles had best be callin' soon, or I may have to give him an extra kick up the arse for the inconvenience."

Olivia couldn't help but smile at the complete . . . Britishness of it all.

"What?" Taite idly swung one foot back and forth.

"Nothing. It's just . . . everyone here is so *British*. I'm not used to it."

"Bite your tongue, lass." Declan propped his hands on his hips. "Not everyone here is a Brit."

She pressed her lips together for a moment. "You're right," she agreed. She looked back at Taite and deliberately ignored that Declan had called attention to his own Irish heritage. "You're an American, too." When she glanced at Declan, she caught the roll of his eyes as he shook his head.

Taite only grinned.

"Back to the matter at hand," Pelicia said softly. "What happens once Olivia has Zoe?" She glanced at Olivia with concern shadowing her blue eyes. "From the way you've described this Eddy, I doubt very much he's going to let the two of you out of his sight."

"I'll try to at least get on the other side of the room from him." Olivia gripped her fingers tightly together. God, this had to work. It had to. "That will give me a few seconds, anyway, before he can reach us."

"What about the others? If one of them is close to you, would he try to attack you when we barge in, or will they all try to protect the pack leader?" Sully moved closer to her. His eyes reflected his readiness for the upcoming battle.

She considered that. "I really don't know. It depends on who it is, I guess. They'll take their lead from Eddy." She shook her head. "If you can keep him talking . . ." She huffed a sigh. "He loves the sound of his own voice."

"I remember that about him." Ryder grimaced. "Could that boy talk."

"And if he decides not to talk?" Sully asked.

Olivia clicked her tongue in thought. "Aaron might see the attack as a way to remove the pack leader and take his place. Calvin might see it as a way to finally get revenge on Eddy. The other two"—she paused, biting her lower lip—"will do whatever he tells them to. So if he wants to use Zoe as leverage, he'll tell them to grab her." She drew in a breath and stared at them, feeling the aggression of the wolf burn in her eyes. "I will kill anyone who tries to take her from me or die trying, I promise you that."

Her cell phone rang just then, and she nearly dropped it trying to tug it out of her pocket. She flipped it open and brought it to her ear. "Hello."

Everyone in the room fell completely silent and sat forward, listening intently.

"All right, we're here." Eddy sounded a little bored, which was never a good sign. "God, this place is . . . rustic. I don't know how people live like this."

Olivia bit her tongue to keep from demanding directions. He was toying with her, trying to make her do or say something for which he could punish her.

That punishment would be to withhold Zoe.

"Some people like rustic, I guess," she murmured, shooting a frustrated glance at Sully. He immediately went over and stood next to her. She reached down and took his hand, gripping his fingers as Eddy rattled on about the horrible service he'd received on the airplane, the long drive from the airport, and the run-down condition of the ranch his people had found. Finally, he said, "Although I am disappointed that you weren't the one who killed Sullivan, I do have a way for you to redeem yourself. We'll talk about it when you get here."

She took a breath. She knew he would tell her that he wanted her to kill one of the others—probably Declan, since Eddy seemed to want Ryder for himself. Thank God she'd made different alliances, even if they would most likely fall apart once the full truth came out. Her initial instincts about Eddy trying to turn her into a killer seemed to be on target.

Olivia reined in her impatience. "And where is here?" She freed her hand from Sully's and walked over to the table where the small notepad lay.

Eddy gave her directions, which she wrote down and then repeated back to him to make sure she'd gotten it right.

"How long will it take you to get here?" he asked.

She blinked. She didn't know anything about this town. She looked at Declan, who fisted his hand and then flashed his fingers three times.

Fifteen minutes. She'd fudge a little to give them time to scope the place out and get in position while she went in to get Zoe. "It should take about half an hour, I think. I'm not good with judging distance," she murmured, quite truthfully.

"City girl." There was enough genuine fondness in Eddy's voice to cause her momentary regret. Things could have been so much different if *he'd* been different. But she reminded herself that he was a monster, and whatever happened to him he'd brought upon himself.

It was a bitch when bad karma came back around to bite you in the ass.

"All right. I'll see you in half an hour." Eddy ended the call.

Olivia slowly closed her phone and eased it back into her pocket. She blew out a breath. "Okay. Here we go." She looked around at the group of people who had befriended her. "I think we should take two cars. You can park down the road from the ranch so they won't hear the engine and the car doors when you close them. Once I drive up, they won't be expecting anyone else." She crossed her fingers for luck.

Taite stood.

Ryder stood as well and looked at his wife. "Where do you think you're going?"

"With you."

"Ah . . . no. You're not."

She lifted her chin.

He cupped her cheek with one broad hand. "Darling, please. You're pregnant with our child. Something could go wrong, and it'd be like me handing you and the baby over to Miles on a silver platter. I couldn't . . ." He trailed off and cleared his throat. "I'd do anything for you, you know that. But don't ask me to put you in harm's way."

Taite glanced at Pelicia, clearly wanting to say something about her friend being able to go while she wasn't.

"I'm not pregnant," Pelicia said, holding up her hands in a surrender gesture. "And I'll be staying in the car."

"You're damn right you are." Declan planted a hard kiss on her mouth. "Let's go."

"Then I'm going, too." Taite waved a hand at Ryder's protest. "I'll take a gun. Pelicia needs someone to watch her back." She looked pleased at finding an excuse to go.

Ryder didn't buy it. "And who'll watch yours?" he asked. "Taite, please."

"We need somebody to stay here in case we need the cavalry." Declan raised his eyebrows at Taite's snort. "You're the one with the local contacts, darlin'. D'ya think if you picked up the phone right now, called the County Attorney, and told him you needed five squads of police he wouldn't send them without question?"

Taite's lips thinned. "Fine. Fine, I'll stay here. But none of you had better get . . . hurt." She'd clearly been about to say something else, something worse, and had cut off that thought.

Declan raised his index finger. "Hang on a sec." He left the room and came back a couple minutes later with a gun in each hand and a small box of ammunition under his arm. He gave one of the weapons to Taite and set the box on the end table by the sofa. "Had these made up when we first got back here. Cost me quite a bit, and earned me some strange looks from the gunsmith, but . . ." He shrugged.

"Silver bullets?" Taite raised her eyebrows.

He nodded. "Just in case." He handed the other gun to Pelicia, who took it reluctantly. "There's no trick to it, dar-lin'." He pointed to the safety. "Just thumb this off, point, and pull the trigger. Couldn't be easier."

She rolled her eyes and muttered, "Well, here's hoping I don't have to use it."

Ryder drew a deep breath and hugged his wife. "That makes me feel better." He pulled away and pressed his lips to her forehead. "All right, let's go. Everyone but you." He stared down at Taite. "If anyone tries to get in here, put one between the eyes."

Taite nodded. "Hey, I did it before. I can do it again." She brushed a kiss against his lips. "I'll be fine." She put a hand low on her belly. "*We'll* be fine."

Olivia couldn't stand it, the obvious love between both couples, a love she was very much afraid she'd never be able to realize with Sully. Muttering a quiet "Excuse me," she walked outside and got in her car. It would be dark soon. They had perhaps half an hour of daylight remaining.

Sully followed her and leaned in the open window of the car. "Don't take any chances you don't have to, sweet-heart. Just remember that you're not in this alone."

"I know." When he bent, she reached up and kissed him. "When this is done—"

"When this is done, you can introduce me to your daughter, and then we'll celebrate." He kissed her again.

The others came outside, and Declan walked over to the car. "Since I'm familiar with the area, I'll lead. I'll hit my turn signal when I reach the road you need to turn onto, but I'll go on ahead and double back, just in case." He stared at her a moment, as if asking if she was ready.

She gave him a small smile and a nod. He patted the door and went over to the SUV.

Sully stroked his fingers down her cheek. "Be safe," he murmured.

"You, too." She started the car and watched him join the others at the SUV. She noticed that Pelicia carried the bag of clothing the guys had put together so they'd have something to change into once the battle was over.

Olivia fastened her seatbelt, waiting until everyone except Taite piled into the big SUV and Declan drove out of the driveway. She put the car in drive and followed.

She tried to calm her racing heart. She was just minutes away from seeing Zoe, from seeing an end to the monster who'd made her life a living hell the last three years.

And from saying good-bye to the man she loved.

The desert sky was turning pink and blue with the setting sun, and the canyons were dark with shadows. The farther they drove the fewer houses they passed. The left turn signal on the SUV flashed briefly. She slowed and switched on her own turn indicator. As she began the turn onto the road for the ranch where Eddy was, her cell phone rang. She answered it before the second ring.

"Remember, we're going to come back around," Sully

said. "Declan says there's another road that hooks up with this one farther out, one that's not too well traveled." His voice lowered. "Just get to Zoe as soon as you can."

"No worries there." She paused. She had to say at least one more thing to him. There was a very real possibility one or both of them could be killed. Regardless of what she'd thought earlier, she knew she needed to tell him how she felt.

People deserved to know when they were loved.

Even so, knowing what she knew, it was the hardest thing she'd ever admitted. "Sully, I love you."

There was silence for a moment. "God, am I glad to hear you say that. I don't want to be the only one in this boat." His low chuckle was more a release of tension than an expression of humor. "I love you, too."

Her heart fluttered at his admission. It gave her a brief moment of hope followed by a plummeting sensation of loss. He didn't know the extent of her betrayal yet.

She knew that was how he'd see it. She'd turned him into a werewolf.

Betrayal number one.

Then compounded it by not telling him the truth.

Betrayal number two.

He must have taken her silence to mean she was scared about the upcoming confrontation, which she was, because he murmured, "It'll turn out all right, love. We won't let him hurt Zoe."

"I know. See you in a few." She murmured a good-bye and disconnected the call. Glancing around, she couldn't see anyone lurking behind any cacti, but if they were in their wolf forms, they could be hunkered down, blending in with the sand. She could easily overlook them, even with her enhanced vision.

She made another turn and drove down a winding dirt driveway, past empty corrals and stables, finally pulling to a stop in front of a ramshackle wood ranch house. It had clearly seen better days; the wood was bare in most places. Where it did have paint the paint was peeling. More than a few of the windows were broken, and an outbuilding to the left leaned to one side, looking as if the first stiff wind would knock it over.

An old well stood near the right corner of the house, along with a squat tub and pump handle. Beyond that was a corral with part of its railings lying on the ground.

It had been a long time since anyone had lived there.

Olivia shoved the gear lever into park and shut off the car. She sat there for a minute, studying the house and surrounding area. There were no other houses that she could see. Certainly she hadn't passed any on her way down the rough dirt road. It didn't surprise her that Eddy had managed to find such an isolated place.

The front door opened, and Calvin stood in the doorway. She caught movement from the corner of her eye and turned her head to see Walter approaching the car, his hulking body casting a large shadow behind him.

Let's get this show on the road. She drew in a breath and opened the car door. "Walter."

"Olivia."

Once she was out of the car, he took her elbow in one hand and escorted her into the house. She wasn't sure if it was out of courtesy or because he could sense her roiling emotions and wanted to try to keep her on a leash.

"Eddy's in here," he said with a wave toward a room on the right.

She walked into what appeared to be a den. A television rested on a small stand against one wall, VCR and DVD players stacked on top of it. A beige carpet, matted and stained with age, covered the floor. Eddy sat on a leather sofa, Zoe at his side looking at one of her picture books. As soon as she heard noise, the little girl looked up. Her face brightened. "Mommy!" She jumped off the sofa and ran to Olivia.

Olivia went down on her knees and enfolded Zoe in her arms. God, it felt so good to hold her, to feel the warmth of her body, smell that bubblegum and little girl scent once again. "I've missed you so much." She drew in a shuddering breath and fought back tears.

"I missed you, too." Zoe pulled back and touched her fingers to Olivia's cheek.

"Walter, I think you should take Zoe into another room while her mother and I talk." Eddy rose from the sofa.

"No!" Olivia and Zoe said at the same time. Olivia stood and clasped her daughter to her side. "I haven't seen her in almost a week, Eddy. You can at least give us a couple of minutes." As his eyes darkened, she added, "Please."

"Please," Zoe echoed.

He looked at the little girl, and his face softened. "Fine. Five minutes."

Olivia nodded. Five minutes should be plenty of time for the guys to make their way to the house. But she needed to get Zoe farther away from Eddy. "Let's go in here, okay?" She took Zoe's hand and walked into the large living room. Spotting a window seat by the large south-facing window, she sat down and pulled Zoe on her lap.

She noticed that Eddy and Walter both stood in the doorway of the den, watching her but giving her some space with her daughter. Not that they couldn't overhear what she said, but at least they were on the other side of the large room.

Anytime now. "How're you doing, baby?" She glanced out the window, at the same time straining her ears to pick up any sign that Sully, Declan, and Ryder were on their way.

As Zoe launched into a detailed account of what she'd been doing at Uncle Eddy's for the last several days, Olivia realized that she hadn't seen Peter and Aaron. Oh, dear God. Had Sully and the others had a run-in with those two? Had Peter and Aaron been patrolling the grounds and stopped the guys in the white hats?

When her daughter paused to take a breath, Olivia looked at Eddy and asked as nonchalantly as she could, "Where are Peter and Aaron?"

"Peter . . . had to go away," he said with a quick glance at Zoe. "Aaron's around."

Peter had to go away? She stared at Eddy. Walter made a quick slash across his throat, then coughed and scratched the side of his neck when Zoe looked his way.

So Peter was dead. That left it four against four. She'd say the odds had just gotten a lot worse for Eddy.

The sounds of a struggle came from the front of the house. As Eddy and Walter both whirled toward the sound, Olivia jumped to her feet. "Whatever happens, Zoe, don't you go to anyone but me, you understand? You stay away from Eddy, Walter, Aaron, and Calvin."

"Mommy?"

"What have you done, Livvie?" Eddy turned toward her.

"Promise me, baby." Olivia spared a second to meet her daughter's bewildered gaze. She saw that Zoe's face was in shadow and realized the sun was setting. From somewhere outside she heard a generator start up and a light outside flicked on. She said again, "Promise."

"I promise."

Olivia nodded. "Stay behind me." She broadened her stance, prepared to take on either werewolf—or both of them—if they started her way before Sully and the others could get inside.

Chapter 18

"Olivia, what have you done?" Eddy asked again. He looked at her, rage growing on his face. She saw his hands at his sides, the fingers growing longer and ending with sharp claws.

"I'm giving you that one thing you've wanted all these years." She paused and added, "Ryder. I mean, you do want to destroy him, don't you, *Miles*?"

At her use of his real name, understanding dawned. His eyes went tawny with rage, his face darkened, and his lips thinned. "You won't make it out of here alive." He looked down at Zoe, who was poking her head around Olivia's side. "Neither will she."

"That's where you're wrong." Sully strode into the room from the back. "You okay?" he asked with a quick glance her way.

"Yeah. Where are Ryder and Declan?" Olivia kept one hand out to her side, holding Zoe behind her.

"Declan's busy with some big blond guy." Sully stopped a few feet away, standing between her and Eddy, who looked at Sully with growing realization on his face.

"Son of a bitch," Eddy muttered.

"You got that right," Sully responded. "You just couldn't leave well enough alone, could you, Miles?"

Olivia tried to keep track of all the players. Declan was fighting with Aaron. That just left . . . "So Ryder's taking care of Calvin?"

Sully glanced at her. "No. There's no one else to fight except these two right here."

What did that mean? That Ryder had killed Calvin? Or that the other werewolf had run off? She supposed it didn't matter—As long as he was gone, he wasn't a threat.

Eddy stared at Sully and sniffed a few times. "Well, well."

She realized he smelled the wolf that was now part of Sully.

Eddy glanced at her with eyes flecked with amber. Then he looked back at Sully. "You look pretty good for a dead man."

"Reports of my death were greatly exaggerated."

"Not exaggerated. Merely premature." Eddy leaned to one side and looked at Olivia. "Someone's been busy, turning our Mr. Sullivan here into a werewolf."

Ryder walked into the room before she had to respond. "I see I'm in time." He stopped next to Sully and faced his cousin. From where she stood she could only see part of his face, but what she saw made her go cold. She was glad he was on her side, because Death stared at Eddy from that handsome, hard face. "Hullo, Miles."

A muscle twitched in Eddy's jaw. "Merrick." Eddy stared at Olivia over Sully's shoulder. A slight British inflection crept into Eddy's voice. "You'll pay for this, you little bitch."

"Don't you call my mommy names!" Zoe danced out from behind Olivia.

Ryder made an abbreviated move as if to grab the little

girl if she came too close, and Olivia sent him a look of thanks as she grabbed Zoe's arm and hauled her back. "Zoe Marie. Stay behind me." She appreciated her daughter's loyalty and admired her spunkiness, but now wasn't the time.

The little girl muttered a quiet, "Okay."

Eddy crossed his arms, his gaze going back to the two men standing in front of him. "So . . . what? You're going to talk me to death?"

Olivia said a silent prayer. Eddy seemed to want to talk. Otherwise he would have already given Walter the order to attack. She hoped Declan was doing all right with Aaron.

The back of Sully's neck turned red, but his words were even tempered as he said, "Make no mistake. You *will* die today. Not only for what you've put us through, but for what you've done to Olivia."

"Oh-ho." Eddy's gaze swung to Olivia. "Do you have an admirer, Livvie?"

She drew in a sharp breath. "Eddy—"

"So she got to you, did she, Sullivan?" Eddy stared at Sully with pursed lips. "I didn't think she had the guts to betray me, but I suppose once she got a taste of your blood it wasn't a matter of if, but when."

Sully frowned. He glanced at Olivia with confusion wrinkling his forehead.

Eddy's eyebrows rose. "Didn't she tell you?"

"Miles." Ryder's voice was full of warning. "Don't."

"Don't what?" He sent Ryder a look of innocence.

"I don't know what you're up to, except that it's no good. I've seen that look on your face before. Whatever little secret you're about to reveal, let it be."

Eddy lifted his chin. "Don't tell me what to do, *cousin.*"

Olivia recognized the stubborn look in his eyes, on his face. She shook her head. It was useless to plead with him. He was going to further ruin her life.

It didn't matter. She'd known it would happen sooner or later. She'd just hoped to be able to confess to Sully herself.

She had Zoe, and once the two of them were safely away, that's all that mattered.

"She didn't tell you, did she?" Eddy asked again.

"Tell me what?" Sully's confused expression turned to a scowl. "How you turned her three years ago and have used her daughter to keep her in line? How you've threatened to kill Zoe and tried to coerce Olivia into killing me?"

Eddy's delighted laugh chilled Olivia. *God, here it was.* The end of her hope for love.

"She has been a Chatty Cathy, hasn't she?" Eddy shook his head and clicked his tongue. He turned his gaze on Olivia, the dark glee in the depths of his eyes sending more ice through her veins. "Livvie, Livvie. How remiss of you." He looked again at Sully. "Obviously she told you the sad story of her life in order to get you to help her. Did she tell you she was there on St. Mary's? That she"—he paused, a slow smile curling his lips—"and I'm only guessing here, but it makes sense. Did she tell you that she's the one that turned you?"

Olivia briefly closed her eyes. Then she looked at Sully.

He turned his head and stared at her, disbelief on his face. "He's lying. Isn't he, Olivia?"

Miles laughed, the humor tinged with madness. "So she *didn't* tell you. How lovely." His affected New York accent completely fell by the wayside and his native British dialect colored his words. His upper lip lifted in a sneer.

"She was supposed to kill you then, but she failed. Instead she turned you into one of us, which she never told me."

"Olivia?"

She swallowed and drew in a shaky breath. She wished she could lie. Sully would believe her over Eddy any day of the week, but she couldn't do that to him. He deserved to know the truth.

But she couldn't bring herself to verbally confirm it. When his expression darkened, she knew her silence had condemned her.

"Son of a bitch." His lips firmed. A muscle began to twitch in his jaw. "It was *you*?"

She lifted her chin. She wasn't proud of the road she'd taken, but she had changed her mind, after all, and hadn't continued with the plan. "Yes."

His nostrils flared. Amber flecked the green of his irises, lighting them from within. His eyes narrowed. "You should've finished the job."

Vaguely aware of Eddy looking back and forth between the two of them, his smile growing ever wider, she fought back tears that sprung at Sully's words. "You can't mean that. Sully, you're still alive! How can you not want that?"

"How can I not want to be a monster?" He turned his back on her with a snarl. "Just . . . take Zoe and get out of here. Miles won't try to stop you." His next words were directed to Eddy. "Will you, Miles?"

Eddy slowly shook his head. "I can find her when I need to." He met Olivia's gaze. "She belongs to me, after all."

Sully's gut tightened. He didn't want to believe Olivia was the werewolf that had attacked him on St. Mary's. He wanted to believe that this cocky little bastard was lying.

But he'd seen the truth in her eyes. Now all those little twitches she'd given every time he'd talked about the bastard who'd turned him made sense.

Why hadn't she told him?

He glanced over his shoulder again and caught sight of her little girl. Zoe. That was why. Olivia had wanted to make sure she had help getting her daughter away from Miles.

He shouldn't blame her for that, but somehow he did.

She should have told him.

Sully looked back at Miles. "She doesn't belong to you."

"No? Well, she doesn't belong to you, either." Mike's face expressed the words that remained unspoken: *I've seen to that.*

"No, she doesn't." Sully had thought she had, but he'd clearly been wrong. He drew in a deep breath and squared his shoulders. Enough was enough. There was still an innocent life at stake. It was time to end this.

It seemed Miles was in agreement, because he motioned to the sandy-haired man at his side, who slowly began to move forward. Miles, for his part, started humming a song that took Sully a moment to place. *Ring around the rosie, pockets full of posies. Ashes, ashes, we all fall down.*

All the while, that bland face stayed expressionless. Sully turned his head but didn't take his gaze off the man he'd come to kill. "Olivia, take Zoe and get out of here. Now."

She didn't hesitate. She grabbed the little girl up into her arms. As she ran out of the room, he heard her whisper, "I'm sorry."

He saw Ryder shoot a sympathetic gaze his way, but his friend otherwise kept his focus on Miles.

Sully wouldn't be surprised if Olivia put Zoe in her car and took off, leaving them to survive or not, leaving Pelicia sitting in the SUV a quarter mile away wondering what was going on.

For his part, Miles didn't seem too concerned by her exit. The bastard was confident he'd win the fight and be able to track her down.

Sully clenched his fists and fought back the wolf that yowled to be set free to chase after Olivia and demand explanations. To exact retribution. He pushed aside thoughts of taking vengeance on the one directly responsible. He'd deal with her later.

For now, he had Miles to deal with.

Or not, as the big behemoth started toward him.

"*Bon appétit,* Walter," Miles murmured.

Sully backed away a few steps, putting some distance between him and the other combatants. He rolled his eyes. Walter. Sounded like the guy should be an accountant somewhere, not a madman's enforcer. "I guess Miles is all yours," Sully muttered to Ryder.

Keeping his attention on Walter, Sully saw the man's fingers morph into claws. Then his face changed, elongated, as he turned into something more than human and less than complete wolf.

Shit. How the hell was he supposed to fight the wolfman?

Sully focused and tried to do the same thing.

All he got for his effort was a slight headache and a tingling in his fingertips. "Fuck."

A broad smile crossed Walter's face. "Problem there, newbie?"

"For you, maybe." Sully wasn't going to let this giant see just how much trouble he was in. How could he fight against a guy who could easily flatten him? In the few seconds it would take for him to shift to his wolf form, Walter could pound him into the floor.

He saw Ryder launch himself at Miles, grappling with the other man. Harsh grunts came from both of them, then a low cry of pain as Miles raked across Ryder's chest with razor-sharp claws.

Damn it. Miles had morphed, too, into something not quite human but not yet wolf. From what he understood, Ryder *couldn't* transform that way. His type of lycanthropy precluded being able to be anything but either human or wolf. Nothing in between.

Sully dodged the clawed hand reaching for him and sent a hard-fisted punch to Walter's face. The man's head snapped back, but it didn't seem to faze him. He gave himself a little shake.

Shit.

He punched Walter again, and all it seemed to do was anger him. The wolfman snarled and rammed his fist forward, catching Sully in the jaw hard enough to jerk his head around.

Sully blinked his eyes, shaking his head to dispel the ringing in his ears. He ducked another blow and came up on the other side of the sofa in front of the large picture window.

Declan sauntered into the room. "Looks like I got here just in time."

Walter whirled to face the new threat, his head turning from Declan to Sully and back again, trying to keep his gaze on both of them.

With a lazy grin on his face, Declan held up his hands. Covered in blood, his fingers were thicker, longer, and ended with sharp claws. He laced his fingers together and then stretched his arms forward, turning his hands outward to crack his knuckles. "Let's play, laddies."

Ryder had one arm pressed against Miles' throat, holding him against the wall, and glanced at Declan. "When the fuck did you learn how to do that?"

Walter took advantage of the momentary distraction and reached for Sully again. Sully dodged out of the way. Sweat trickled between his shoulder blades, and he tried not to let the behemoth see how scared he was. If he couldn't shift to wolf, and soon, the fight would be over.

"I've been practicin'." Declan did a little boxer's dance, holding his hands in front of him in loose fists. "Come on, then, you bleedin' sods. Show me what you got."

Taking everyone by surprise, he launched himself at Walter, hitting him in the chest with both feet and knocking him to the floor. Declan bounded off him and went for Miles. "Now would be the time for the two of you to shift. Don't hold back on my account."

By the time Sully was able to quiet his mind enough to focus, Ryder had gone wolf. He dove for Walter's throat, but the big man was able to get his forearm up in time. Ryder latched on to his arm, worrying it like a dog with a toy.

Neither Walter nor Miles could take the time to finish their transformation into their full wolf forms. Sully only hoped that would be to the good guys' advantage.

He took deep, calming breaths and focused his attention inward, calling upon his wolf. As bones, muscles, tendons, and sinew shifted, he groaned and hunched over. Fur sprouted from his skin, his skull flattened and lengthened, his teeth elongated. The agony was just as bad as he remembered it, and just as short.

He drew in a quick breath and shook his head, chasing

away the lingering pain. Getting his bearings, he saw Declan had Miles in hand for the moment, so, paws scrabbling on the tile floor, he went to help Ryder.

Olivia reached the SUV and opened the passenger door. She glanced at Pelicia behind the wheel and set Zoe down on the seat. She took her little face in her hands. "Baby, I need you to go with Pelicia, all right? I have to go back and help the others."

Zoe's bottom lip trembled. "Why was Uncle Eddy so mean, Mommy? Did I do something to make him mad?"

Poor little sprite. She had such a tender heart, and loved Eddy like he was a real uncle. Olivia couldn't bring herself to destroy the illusion. Not yet. But she wouldn't let Zoe think any of this was her fault. "No, honey." She smoothed hair away from Zoe's face. "You didn't do anything except be your sweet self. If he's mad at anyone, it's me."

"But why?"

"I'll explain later, I promise." She pressed a kiss to her daughter's forehead. "But now I have to go back. You be a good girl and stay with my friend, okay?"

Zoe looked at Pelicia, and the woman gave her a warm smile. "Hullo, honey."

Apparently put somewhat at ease, Zoe turned back to Olivia. "Okay." Anxiety rasped in her voice, and Olivia's heart broke to see that, even as slight as it might be, Zoe had suffered from being apart from her. She pulled her daughter into a tight hug for several long seconds. "I love you, baby." She pulled back. "I'll see you again, real soon, I promise."

Zoe nodded. "I love you, too, Mommy."

Olivia bit her lip and looked over Zoe's head at Pelicia. "You should go back to your house now. Take care of her." Her voice came out husky from a throat tight with love and fear and remorse.

Pelicia's fine brows drew down. "But what about Declan and the others? They'll need a ride home."

Olivia glanced at Zoe. Pelicia was right, but Olivia didn't want her daughter to remain anywhere near Eddy.

"We'll be all right here." Pelicia gave her a reassuring smile and briefly showed her the gun she'd tucked in her waistband. "You go help the guys. And be careful."

Olivia nodded. With a last look at her daughter, she turned and ran back toward the ranch house. About halfway there she stopped at a pile of rocks and took off her clothes. She dropped them behind the rocks, careful not to disturb anything in case something venomous was hiding beneath them.

She went down on her hands and knees and called upon her wolf. While the power of the supernatural went to work, her back bowed, her fingers and toes digging into the sand as pain lanced through her body. A feeling of a final slide, her mind going slightly fuzzy, and the transition was complete.

She sprinted the rest of the way, much faster on four paws than on two feet. When she burst into the house, the sounds of fighting drew her back to the living room.

Declan was on the floor in human form, bleeding from several deep wounds. She skidded to a halt, sorrow clutching her until she saw his chest rise and fall. Still alive.

Good.

Walter lay over by the picture window. He was still part wolf, part man. His chest wasn't moving. Dead.

Better.

The fight had progressed from the living room into a sunroom. When she reached the doorway, she had to step over the body of a wolf. It wasn't one she recognized. She paused and looked at the two remaining werewolves who were fighting. One was fully wolf—Sully—and the other was in his man-wolf form.

Eddy.

He always felt superior being in a form between that of wolf and man. She knew it was because his cousin didn't have that ability, which meant she was standing over Ryder. She chuffed and nuzzled him, and he opened his eyes on a whine. He looked toward the fight as if telling her to help Sully. She gave Ryder a quick lick on his muzzle and then launched herself into the fight.

Her attack caught Eddy by surprise, flinging him off his feet and onto the floor. The fall made Sully skid across the tile. He banged up against the wall and slid to his belly, panting.

Eddy knocked her away before she could fasten her teeth around his throat. "Bitch!" He scrambled to his knees and grabbed her by the scruff.

He was bleeding from several wounds, some made by claws and some from teeth. Some deep and some superficial. None mortal.

Yet.

He brought one hand around, claws extended. She yipped and struggled in his hold. If he had a chance to rake those claws across her vulnerable throat, she was done for.

Sully charged to her rescue, teeth and claws bringing more blood as he latched on to one of Eddy's inner thighs.

Eddy screamed, a loud, shrill sound that echoed in the glass-encased room.

She saw blood spurt and knew that Sully had bitten into Eddy's femoral artery.

They just had to hold on for another few minutes. If she

could get at him, it would take even less time to finish him off.

Eddy kept one hand on Olivia's scruff, holding her at bay, while he pounded his fist on the top of Sully's head, trying to dislodge him.

Sully held on, growling low in his throat. Blood streamed over his muzzle, the coppery smell strong in the air. Eddy finally threw Olivia away from him, but not very far. He was fading fast.

She charged back at him, dodging his swipe at her, and fastened her teeth in his neck.

Hot blood filled her mouth. She bit down harder, locking her jaws, and began shaking her head back and forth. The bastard had done this to her, turned her into a monster. Made her afraid for her daughter's life every damn day over the last three years.

Made her witness things that would haunt her dreams until the day she died.

She and Zoe—and Sully and his friends—would never be safe until Eddy was dead. And she aimed to be the one to do it.

He'd wanted to turn her into a murderer, after all.

Be careful what you wish for.

Turn the tables.

Sweet justice.

She felt a blow to the side of her head, heavy enough to make her wince, but not strong enough to dislodge her. Another blow, and she snarled and violently shook her head. She pulled free a big chunk of his throat, spit it out, and went after him again.

Bastard. Enemy.

Die.

The blows against her head came more slowly, and were

much softer. After several seconds, they stopped altogether. Still she kept her teeth in his throat. He had to die.

Now.

Forever.

She vaguely became aware of Sully's voice, murmuring to her, soft over her own deep-throated growls.

"It's all right, Olivia. You can let go now."

When had he shifted back to human? She'd been so intent on finally stopping Eddy that she hadn't noticed. But what was he saying? She should let go?

Only when Eddy was dancing with the devil.

She growled again, tightening her jaws. He had to die. She wouldn't let go until he did.

Fingers stroked through the fur along her back. "Let him go, sweetheart. He's dead."

She paused and listened. Her heartbeat. Sully's heartbeat.

Nothing from Eddy.

Olivia slowly released her grip, realizing for the first time her jaws ached from being clenched so tightly. She ran her tongue along her muzzle, licking away sticky blood.

Eddy's eyes were open. Staring.

Dead.

She lifted her head and howled, closing her eyes as emotions roiled through her.

Sorrow.

Gladness.

Remorse.

Satisfaction.

Human.

Wolf.

She let the howl trail off and lowered her head to look at Sully. More sorrow.

Because he'd shifted back to his human form, most of his wounds had healed or nearly healed. He was naked, as they all would be after they shifted, which was why they'd packed extra clothing in the SUV.

The look on his face laid his emotions as bare as the rest of him—loathing, confusion, regret. Deep unhappiness.

She backed away from Eddy, never taking her gaze off Sully. He hated her and rightly so. She'd taken something from him that he'd never get back. And, seeing how much of a monster she was, he most likely held her in revulsion as well.

She took a few more steps away from him. She couldn't read his expression, and tried to put as much remorse in her wolfen gaze as she could. She couldn't bear to hear him tell her he hated her, that he'd been mistaken when he'd thought he loved her, so she turned away.

"Olivia."

She paused but didn't turn to face him. When he didn't say anything more, she glanced at him over one shoulder. When he still didn't say anything, she blinked slowly and then turned away. She stepped carefully over Ryder, who had transformed back to human.

Then she ran as if the hounds of hell were at her heels.

Upon reaching her rental car, she paused by the side of it and returned to her human form, suffering through the transformation silently. As in the early days after a shift, when she was fully human again tears streamed down her face. She opened the door and was about to get in when she heard her name being called.

She looked across the roof of the car and saw Calvin

standing on the other side of the vehicle. God, if he'd been on Eddy's side, she'd have been dead. She hadn't even heard him approach. She watched him warily.

"Is he dead?" he asked.

Olivia nodded. Deciding to go with her gut feeling— that Calvin hated Eddy and would have done what he could to ensure his demise—she said, "It's over, Cal. You can get your family and get the hell out of New York. Start over somewhere."

He gave an abrupt nod, hatred for Eddy seething in his eyes. "I saw you, you know. Drag Sullivan off into the desert after Peter ran him over." He drew in a breath. "I didn't tell Eddy because I figured you'd switched sides. Eddy talked about his cousin to me often enough. I knew about this obsession he had. So I took care of Peter. And once I heard Merrick was on his way, I figured the four of you were more than enough to handle Eddy, Walter, and Aaron."

"You were right." She rotated her head, trying to work out the kinks that the shift and tension had wrought. Her nudity in front of him didn't faze her; he'd seen her naked plenty of times after the pack had taken a run together. "Thank you."

He nodded again. "You can start over, too, you know."

"I plan to." She'd even thought about not returning to New York at all. She'd go get Zoe from Pelicia and head back to the hotel for the night. In the morning she'd call the landlord and tell him to sell whatever he could. She'd buy what they needed wherever they finally ended up.

"Have a good life, Liv."

She'd have a life. But without Sully, it wouldn't be good.

Chapter 19

Sully stayed where he was for a moment, swallowing back the bile that rose in his throat at the thick taste of blood. He wasn't feeling sick because of the taste or texture, but because he'd *enjoyed* it.

Damn Olivia. She'd done this to him. And then lied about it.

Well, technically she hadn't told a lie, but not telling the full truth was the same as a lie in his mind.

As anger surged, his eyes burned. Need, *want* tightened his gut. God. The damn wolf was always at the door, demanding to be set free.

A low mutter from Ryder drew his attention. Sully got up and walked over to where his friend still lay in the doorway between the two rooms. The room was in near darkness, the only light coming through the glass from an outside bulb several yards away. "You okay?"

"Do I look okay?" Blood smeared Ryder's right cheek from a cut perilously close to his eye, and several gashes across his chest had knit closed but still looked raw and pink. He struggled to sit up, his breath coming hard and fast from between pursed lips, and Sully reached down to help him. Ryder blew out a breath. "I'll be fine. Go see to Dec."

From what Sully could see, Ryder's wounds weren't too serious, so he straightened and went over to Declan. Squatting beside him, Sully reached down and patted his cheek. "Declan?"

Declan groaned but didn't move.

Sully perused his friend's body. He didn't see any obvious, serious wounds, though he supposed there could be some on Declan's back that he couldn't see. But, knowing Dec, he was just milking it for all it was worth to get sympathy wherever he could. "Come on." Sully made kissy noises with his lips. "Open your eyes and give us a kiss."

"Bugger off." Declan groaned again and rolled to his side, then to a sitting position. He drew in a deep breath and blew it out slowly. "Damn, but that bastard was big." He glanced around the room. "Where's Olivia?"

Sully pressed his lips together, then said, "She just took off. Probably gone to get Zoe and hightail it out of here." His voice rasped with anger.

Declan frowned. "That's what she was supposed to do, remember?" He stared at Sully. "What bee crawled up your ass?"

"Olivia's the one who attacked Sully back on St. Mary's." Ryder struggled to his feet and walked over to them, as unconcerned about his nudity as Declan seemed to be.

While sitting around a sauna or showering in a locker room with a bunch of naked men was fine with Sully, standing there starkers after all of them had just gone wolf was a bit too surreal for his puny little brain to process. He pushed it aside as best he could.

Also not wanting to discuss Olivia at the moment, he ignored Declan's shocked expression and looked at the dead bodies. Both Miles and Walter were still in that horrific state between man and wolf. "Are we sure they're really dead?"

"There's a surefire way to make sure." When Sully and Declan looked at Ryder, he shrugged. "I've had a previous encounter. Plus this has been in my family for generations, you know."

Sully grimaced and gave a nod of agreement. "What's your surefire way?"

"Decapitation."

Sully looked at Declan, who raised his eyebrows but didn't seem surprised. "Did a lot of reading," he mouthed.

Sully looked back at Ryder and repeated, "Decapitation? You must be joking."

Ryder heaved a sigh. "No, I'm afraid I'm very serious." He looked down at himself and shook his head. "This damn nudity is quite inconvenient at times."

"That's what I thought." Sully glanced down at himself and was surprised at the slight hard-on he saw. He'd just been in a fight to the death, had been wounded—not badly, but still!—and yet his randy cock didn't seem to care.

Shifting back from wolf made him ready for sex. Too bad there wasn't anyone there to help him with the problem.

His lips thinned. An hour ago he would have happily wandered off with Olivia to fuck like a couple of bunnies on Viagra. But not now.

"That happens, remember?" Declan gestured to his own semi-erection. "This is when you go hunt your woman down and have her share a shower with you." His face sobered into a faux serious expression. "For water conservation purposes, of course."

"Of course." Sully had a mind to hunt down a particular woman, but sharing a shower was not on the agenda. Getting answers was.

Declan pushed to his feet. He staggered a bit but soon righted himself by bracing a hand on the wall. "We need to take care of these two and the one I left out on the front porch." He peered through the big picture window. "There's an outbuilding there." He lifted one hand and pointed.

Sully glanced through the window into the darkness and saw the building, one corner of it illuminated by a light affixed near the roof. Other than that light, the area was in complete darkness.

Providing perfect cover for a few werewolves who wanted to hide some bodies.

He shook his head. If he weren't living it, he'd think it was all a dream.

A nightmare.

"I'll go see if there are any shovels so we can dig a couple graves. What we'll use for decapitation . . ." Declan shrugged and shot a look at Sully. "Then you can tell me more about Olivia bein' the one who turned you." He cocked an eyebrow and ambled out of the room.

Sully drew in a deep breath and released it slowly through pursed lips. He looked at Ryder. "We're supposed to take care of these guys while we're completely starkers?"

Ryder's eyes crinkled with his quick grin. "Well, it's bound to be messy and dirty, so I suppose it's best we don't ruin the clean clothes we brought." He sobered. "With any luck this is the last time we'll ever have to deal with something like this."

"Amen to that." Sully licked dry lips and scrubbed the

back of his neck with one hand. This was so out of his realm of experience. Every instinct he had as a cop was telling him to call in the authorities. But what the hell would they tell the cops? That the three dead men were really were-wolves who had tried to kill them? Oh, and to make sure the dead stayed dead they had to chop off their heads?

Or, no. Maybe it was some sort of birth defect that made them look so horrific. Sure, the cops would buy that ex-planation just as well.

Sully would never see British soil again. He'd be thrown into the American equivalent of Bedlam so fast his head would be spinning for years.

He *had* to listen to those other instincts, the dark ones that said they had to hide what had happened there and walk away when it was all done. That he could never tell anyone—ever—about it. Only those who were involved would know, and he was certain every one of his friends would take the secret to their graves.

But . . . what about Olivia? He couldn't help feeling be-trayed, but now that the adrenaline rush was fading, he could reflect on the circumstances that had brought him to that point in time.

Olivia had been turned into a werewolf unwillingly, just like him. She'd had a young daughter to protect as best she could, and when that little girl had been threatened, Olivia had done what any mother would. She'd responded to the threat.

He thought back to that critical day at Pelicia's, pushed his way past the shock of it, to reflect on the actual attack. The wolf had been on him so fast he'd not had a chance to do anything except lift his arms to try to protect himself. He remembered the pain of the bites, the sound of her snarling growls, the feral look in her eyes. She'd been determined, all right. From the moment she'd brought him to the floor, she'd planned to kill him.

But then she'd hesitated. At the time he'd thought it was because she'd heard Declan on the stairs, but now he realized the hesitation had come seconds before that. Even in his groggy, shocked state, he'd seen the indecision in her eyes.

Then Declan had started down the stairs and the decision had been taken away from her. She'd fled, and Sully's life had changed forever.

Had Olivia not turned him into a werewolf, he would never have survived that hit-and-run. Of course, he wouldn't have been walking along a road in Tucson to begin with if Olivia hadn't turned him. But that aside, any other attempt on his life by Miles or another of his minions would most likely have been successful—and there *would* have been another attempt. It was only because of the enhanced healing abilities that lycanthropy offered that he was standing there right now.

Regardless of what he had said to her earlier about finishing the job, he was damn glad to still be standing.

Declan walked back into the house carrying three shovels. He handed one to Sully and another to Ryder. "There's a nice spot behind the outbuildin' that will do for an impromptu cemetery," he said. "Grab a body and let's go." He turned back toward the front of the house. "I'll get the guy on the front porch."

Sully glanced toward Miles. "I'll let you have the honors," he said to Ryder.

Ryder gave a nod and walked over to his cousin's body. He stood there a moment, staring down at him. "It could have been so different," he murmured. "Why did he think he had to have it all and leave me with nothing?" His shoulders rose with his deep breath. "Why in the hell did he even want a life like this?"

"I guess we'll never know." Sully bent and lifted Walter over his shoulder, staggering a bit at the weight. He straightened, balancing the corpse with the hand that held the shovel, and started toward the door. "All I care about is that it's finally over."

"Is it?" Ryder lifted Miles and fell into step behind Sully. "What about Olivia?"

As they walked outside, Sully noticed that Olivia's car was gone. Cold rushed through him at the thought that she'd disappeared from his life, and then white-hot anger at remembering she was the reason for the life he now had.

He tightened his mouth. He was so goddamn confused, and that was her fault, too. He didn't know if he wanted to shake her for not being completely up front with him, or kiss her and try to take away all her pain. *Their* pain.

Christ. What a mess.

They headed toward the spot where Declan waited, and Ryder asked again, "What about Olivia?"

"I heard that," Declan called. "You wait until you get here. I've two cents to add to this conversation."

"Of course he does." Sully shook his head. When he reached Declan, he bent and laid Walter on the ground. He grimaced at the feel of blood sliding down his back. He glanced at the dead man and then at the shovel in his hand. Lifting his gaze to Ryder, he asked, "It's really not enough to just bury them?"

Ryder shook his head. "Listen. Declan and I can take care of this. You should go find Olivia. Talk to her."

"He's right," Declan added before Sully could respond. "So what if she's the one that turned you? Can you honestly say you're not the better for it? After what we've just been through?"

Sully grimaced. He wasn't sure he wanted to see Olivia again. Yet he was equally sure he did.

Anger still roiled beneath the surface. Yet the thought of never seeing her again caused his gut to twist.

He went with something he could deal with. "Just how am I supposed to function as a cop, Dec? What am I supposed to do if I'm still working when the full moon rises? Tell my team I need to have a private moment and duck around the corner so I can turn into a wolf? And then what?"

"Come work with me. As a private investigator," Declan clarified. At Sully's skeptical look, he said, "We'll talk about it more later, but I mean it. For now, get cleaned up an' go talk to Olivia."

He was right. He and Olivia needed to clear the air and see if, once everything was sorted out as to who'd done what and why, there was anything real between them. Sully nodded and started to turn toward the house when he saw a strange man heading toward them.

Ryder and Declan heard him, too, and their heads turned in his direction.

A faint, familiar scent of sage wafted to Sully—werewolf. He stiffened and held the shovel horizontal to his body like a weapon.

The man slowed and held up his hands. "I'm not here to fight with you. My name's Calvin."

He was the one Olivia had told them about—the one who'd lost his family to Miles' depravity.

"What do you want?" Sully asked, not loosening his grip on the shovel.

Calvin stopped a few feet away and tipped his chin toward the bodies. "I'll take care of them. And I'll clean up the blood inside." He gazed around at the dilapidated buildings. "This place was abandoned by the owners, who, as you can see, couldn't afford its upkeep. The bank foreclosed on it a few months ago, so no one should be coming around for a while." He looked back at them. "Long enough for me to scrub it clean, at any rate. So go on. Get out of here."

"And just how do we know you'll take care of 'em, boyo?" Declan leaned one arm on his shovel, looking nonchalant and relaxed, but Sully could sense the coiled tension in his friend. One wrong move from the other werewolf, and the Irishman would be on him in a flash.

Hell, he'd have three werewolves who weren't in particularly jovial moods on him before he could blink.

Calvin's eyes sparked with amber. "I hate him," he said, pointing to Miles. "He killed my family. Did Olivia tell you that? It was just me and them. I'd lost their mother years before that—cancer. When Eddy first turned me, the only thing I regretted is that it didn't happen while my wife was still alive. That way . . ." His voice broke, and he paused, clearly fighting to regain control of his emotions. He shook his head. "The way things turned out, I'm glad she didn't live to see what happened. Bastard took my children and . . ." His lips tightened. A lone tear slid down his cheek. Voice fierce, he said, "I'm glad he's dead. The only thing I'm sorry about is that I didn't get the chance to end him myself."

Sully glanced at Ryder and Declan, who both gave abrupt nods. Sully nodded, too, and held out the shovel.

Calvin came forward and took it, then walked past him. With his back toward them, he said, "Thanks."

"For what?" Sully asked.

Calvin motioned toward the men at his feet. "You haven't just set Olivia and Zoe free of this bastard. You just freed a hell of a lot of other people, including me and mine." He glanced at them briefly before raising the shovel over his head.

It came down with a sickening crunch. Miles' head rocked slightly, then rolled to the left a few inches.

It was done.

Sully exchanged looks with Declan and Ryder, and the three of them headed back toward the house. They primed the well pump and within a few minutes cold, clear water filled the small tub sitting beneath it. They washed away blood and dirt from their skin and hair. Sully rushed his bathing, wanting to get to Olivia. It was time for them to talk.

Fifteen minutes later the three of them piled into Miles' rental car and drove down to where Pelicia still waited in the darkened SUV.

Sully noticed she was alone, which he'd expected. Olivia had come and gone. He hoped one of them knew where she went.

He pulled to a stop at the back of the SUV. Ryder and Declan climbed out and went to the hatch, which popped open. The small overhead light turned on, illuminating the inside of the SUV and a little bit of the surrounding area.

Pelicia climbed down from the vehicle but waited on the side while the men took their clean clothes out of the sack.

"Are you guys all okay?" She crossed her arms. In the near darkness, Sully's wolf vision allowed him to see her almost as clearly as if it were broad daylight. Her eyes sparkled with tears, and she worried her bottom lip with her teeth.

"We're fine, darlin'." Declan handed Sully a pair of folded jeans.

Sully shook them out and slid his legs into them, watching as his friends did the same. He yanked the jeans up and fastened them, then took the T-shirt Ryder handed him and shrugged into it.

"Thank God." Pelicia's voice was soft, shaking. Declan tossed his shirt down onto the bed of the SUV, walked over to her, and dragged her into his arms.

Sully needed to do that to his woman, *after* he got some answers. He hopped up onto the floor of the cargo area and brushed the dirt off the bottom of his feet. He pulled on socks and shoes. "Please tell me you know where Olivia went."

"She mentioned something about a hotel. She didn't say which one," Pelicia added as she and Declan moved around to the back of the vehicle.

Ryder pulled his mobile out of the front pocket of his trousers and dialed a number. As soon as it was answered, he said, "Everyone's fine."

"Not everyone," Sully muttered. "Just the ones that count."

"Thank God." He heard Taite's voice almost as clearly as if he was holding the phone to his own ear. She took a few breaths, and he could tell she was trying not to cry.

He glanced at Pelicia to see she was pale but composed, her back straight and determination clear in her gaze. He was amazed at the strength of these two women.

And of Olivia. She'd been through hell in the last three years and still managed to raise a daughter that was as feisty as she was.

That said something.

"Let me talk to Taite for a minute." Sully held out his hand for the phone.

"Sweetheart? Sully wants to talk to you. Hold on a moment." Ryder handed the mobile over.

Sully wasted no time. "Listen. If I gave you a mobile number, do you think you have any friends at the local police department who could run a trace for you? I'm pretty sure the phone has a GPS."

Taite was just as no-nonsense. "Let me see what I can do. I'll call you back. Give me the number and yours."

Sully rattled off the numbers, then flipped the phone closed and handed it back to Ryder. Hopping down, he closed the SUV's hatch and headed toward the other vehicle. "You guys go on without me." He walked around to the driver's side and opened the car door.

Pelicia smiled. "You're going after Olivia?"

He sighed. "I think I have to. We have a lot to talk about."

"She's a good person, Sully. Faced with an impossible situation, she at first acted against her instincts. Which is why you were turned." Declan's gaze held his. "But then she followed her instincts in the end, which is why you're still alive. Otherwise, she probably could have killed you—*would* have killed you—back at Pel's two weeks ago."

Sully stared at him. God. It had been exactly two weeks to the day when he'd been attacked by the wolf—Olivia!—at Pelicia's bed and breakfast. A vicious assault that had been instigated by a man bent on vengeance, muted by an attack of conscience on Olivia's part.

He had to talk to her. Get all of it sorted out.

"She asked me to tell you that she's sorry." Pelicia's voice was soft with compassion. "Go to her. Listen to her. Let her explain. Let her tell you how she feels."

He bent his head and stared at the ground. "She told me she loves me."

"And you? How do you feel?"

That was the million-dollar question.

He hated her. He loved her. He wanted her with him. He never wanted to see her again.

"Hell if I know." He looked up in time to see Pelicia's quick smile.

"Well, I know from experience it'll sort itself out when you see her. Trust me. I was certain I never wanted to see Declan again, until I saw him again." She shook her head. "All the old hurts were still there, but the love was there as well." She put her hand on his where it rested on the open window of the door. "Give her a chance. Give yourself a chance."

He nodded. "I will." He waved his hand in the direction away from the scene of carnage. "Now get out of here."

"You go get your woman." Declan clasped Sully's hand, the other hand on his shoulder. Pelicia climbed behind the wheel of the SUV. Declan raised his eyebrows but didn't say anything as he walked around to get into the passenger side.

Ryder gave Sully a one-armed hug. "Call us if you need us." He opened the back door of the SUV and got in the vehicle.

"I will." Sully shook his head. "If she's stubborn, I may need you to come talk some sense into her like you have me."

Pelicia laughed and started the vehicle. "Good luck, Sully."

"Thanks. I'm sure I'll need it."

*   *   *

Olivia brushed Zoe's hair away from her face and smiled down at her. The little girl kept yawning but fought sleep with everything she had in her. It was early, but she was clearly tired and needed to rest.

"Go to sleep, baby." Olivia put her palm on top of Zoe's hands where they were clasped across her tummy.

Zoe shook her head, her curls dragging over the pillow. "I don't wanna go to sleep yet."

Olivia smiled in spite of the tears that threatened at the anxiety lingering in Zoe's voice. "I'll be right here when you wake up."

"Promise?" Sleepy eyes blinked at Olivia.

The uncertainty in Zoe's young voice brought Olivia closer to tears. "I promise." She bent over and kissed Zoe's forehead. "No one's ever going to keep us apart again. Ever."

"Good." The little girl's voice was already thickening with sleep. She sighed and wriggled a bit, then her breathing evened out, and Olivia knew she slept.

Olivia sat there for a few more minutes and watched her daughter sleep. Whispering a quick prayer of thanks, she pushed aside thoughts of Sully. She had her daughter, and she'd be happy with that.

She'd learned long ago that life wasn't always fair—wasn't usually fair. As long as Zoe was healthy and happy, that's all Olivia would ask for.

Chapter 20

Olivia heard the heavy tread of footsteps a few seconds before the knock came on the door. She jumped up from the edge of the bed and whirled toward the door, reflexively ready to do battle. Then she realized that anyone who meant to do harm to her or Zoe most likely wouldn't have knocked.

She checked to make sure Zoe still slept, then partially closed the bedroom door and walked through the living room of the hotel suite. She smelled him as soon as she neared the front of the room. Out of habit, when she reached the door she peered through the peephole. Her heart leaped into her throat at confirmation at what other senses had already told her.

Sully.

Even as she wondered how he'd found her—she hadn't told anyone where she was staying—she unlocked the door and opened it just enough to be able to see him. Feeling defensive, she took the offensive way, lifted her chin, and asked, "Have you come to take your revenge?"

Not that she would blame him if he did. But it wasn't in her to go down without a fight. She was done rolling over and showing her belly to someone who was physically stronger than her. If tonight had proven nothing else, it was that she was a survivor. She had to be, for Zoe.

He glanced over her shoulder toward the bedroom where her daughter lay sleeping. "What kind of man do you think I am?" he asked quietly. "Poor kid's been through enough, even if she doesn't quite realize it." He met her gaze again. "I came to talk."

She swung the door wide and stepped aside without a word. He had questions; she had answers. He deserved that much from her.

He walked into the room. Olivia closed the door and followed him, watching as Sully stood for a moment in the doorway to the bedroom, staring at her sleeping daughter. "She's beautiful." His raspy voice remained soft. He glanced at Olivia, his green eyes dark with a mixture of regret, anger and confusion. "She looks like you."

"All I see when I look at her is her father." Olivia moved closer and looked in at Zoe and then back at Sully. "She has his eyes, his nose, his mouth." She bit her lip and glanced away.

"I'm sorry." When she looked at him again, he added, "For the loss of your husband. It had to have been tough, with Zoe being so young."

Olivia nodded. "She was six months old." God, David had loved his little girl. His face lit up every time he saw her. Pushing away the memories of happier times that would never come again, she pulled the bedroom door mostly closed, leaving it open about an inch so she and Sully could talk without disturbing Zoe but ensuring that Olivia could hear her daughter if she wakened. Of course, with her werewolf senses she'd be able to hear her through a closed door, but habit died hard. It made her feel better to have that little bit of open space between her and her little girl. It meant she could get to her just that much faster.

Olivia squared her shoulders and walked over to a sofa beneath the front window of the room, ready to face the future. Whether it would be with Sully remained to be seen. He seemed ready to talk, but what he hated about himself couldn't be undone. And what he hated was what she'd done to him. Would he—*could* he—forgive her?

"You said you wanted to talk?" She sat down and crossed one leg over the other. She held her hands in her lap, fingers laced, and tried to stay calm when all she wanted to do was scream at the unfairness of it all. She'd never asked for any of it. Nor had Sully. Yet there they were.

Sully joined her, angling his body so he could watch her. "I understand why you tried to kill me. I do. I also understand why you couldn't. What I don't understand . . ." His dark brows dipped, and he shook his head. "What I don't understand is why you didn't tell me it was you." His tongue swept out over his lips. "How could you say you love me and not tell me you were the one who'd turned me?"

She twisted her fingers together. He sounded so . . . hurt. Confounded. "I was afraid." She drew in a breath and expelled it quickly. Unable to look at him, unwilling to see censure in his gaze, she stared down at her hands and poked at the cuticle of one thumb with the other. "I was afraid you'd refuse to help me if you knew."

"You think I'd let a child suffer because I was angry with you?" His voice went even raspier as anger built.

Olivia shot him a look. His face was hard, tight, the green of his eyes speckled with amber as his emotions rose.

"You weren't angry, Sully. You were *furious.*" She shook her head. "I knew even then that you were a good man, a decent man, but I couldn't take the chance that you'd let that fury cloud your thinking. Not with my daughter's life at stake." She drew in a deep breath. "Not once I had hope again that there was a way out of this without her getting killed. Without me getting killed and her then raised by that monster."

Sully studied her a moment. "You could always have tried to kill me again." On a purely intellectual level he understood that she couldn't have tried again—that once she'd made the decision it was the wrong thing to do she'd stick to her ethics. But he felt the need to prod her, to dispel the sorrow in her eyes. To get to her true feelings. He knew firsthand that in anger people spoke the truth they held the deepest. "I mean, why not? Since it was all about keeping your daughter safe, damn any consequences."

Her eyes flared with anger. "You . . . you bastard." She kept her voice low. "Just what was I supposed to do? You tell me that. It was just me, Sully. Me and Zoe. She had no one else." She bit her lip. "*I* had no one else. At first I tried to do what he demanded so I could protect her. If I wasn't there, Eddy would have kept her and raised her as his own, and then made her into a werewolf on her eighteenth birthday." Her fists clenched in her lap. "Then he told me to kill you or he'd kill Zoe. And I knew he'd do it." She spread her hands. "That's why I went after you to begin with. If I hadn't, he *would* have killed her. But . . ." She seemed to run out of steam and slumped back against the sofa. She wrapped her arms around herself, a heavy sigh leaving her.

"But?" he prompted. He needed to know her reasoning, needed to understand her.

"What kind of message would that have sent my daughter?" Her gaze was full of conflicting emotions. "Because I promise you Eddy would have made sure to tell her what a bad person her mother was and how lucky Zoe was to have him." Tears glistened in her eyes as she looked toward the bedroom. "The wrong thing done for the right reason is still the wrong thing," she whispered.

He saw the internal struggle she'd gone through, and admired her all the more for her ability to sort through all the crap and still come to the right decision.

She met his gaze and continued in a louder voice. "I kept trying to convince myself that I had to kill you, even though it felt *wrong* the whole time. But if it was between a stranger and my daughter . . ." She shrugged. "Then I fell in love with you, and I couldn't kill you. Not even to save Zoe." She bent over, covering her face with her hands.

He saw a shudder go through her and knew she was trying not to cry. He knew, too, that she'd probably not had a really good cry in nearly six years. There was a lot of grief and anger built up inside her. He wasn't making things any easier.

He reached out and put his hand on her shoulder.

She jerked away from him and stood, holding one hand out. "Don't." Her voice was strangled, her face wet with tears. "How can you be nice to me? I made you a monster." Fresh tears rolled down her cheeks. "I'm the one who took you away from the life you knew, took away your humanity."

At that moment Sully accepted the fact that his life was more complicated than he'd ever thought it could be, and recognized that he wouldn't have it any other way. He'd survived four attacks on his life—the initial one in the Isles of Scilly, Olivia's attack as a wolf in Tucson, the hit-and-run, and finally tonight's showdown. If it hadn't been for the initial assault that had made him what he was, he wouldn't have survived any of the others. He would never have been able to be there for his friends at the final battle with Miles.

He wouldn't have been able to play a part in saving an innocent little girl from a lifetime of horror and pain.

He had Olivia to thank for that. With her help and Declan's, he could learn to control his wolf so that it didn't interfere with his ability to make a living. To be the kind of man he should be.

The kind of man she needed him to be. The kind of man he *wanted* to be for her.

Still keeping his voice soft, he said, "Look at me." When Olivia shook her head and partly turned away, he repeated, "Look at me."

Her shoulders lifted with her deep breath and she turned to face him. But she didn't raise her eyes.

"Olivia, please look at me."

He saw her throat move with her hard swallow, and she finally lifted her gaze to his. Fear and despair warred in her eyes, and he hated that he had any part in making her feel either emotion. From now on, he wanted those eyes to only reflect love and happiness. He wasn't naïve enough to think that grief would never come their way again, but it wouldn't be because of anything he'd done.

Sully stood and moved closer to her, but didn't touch her. He didn't want her distracted by a touch she wasn't ready for. "I've been a werewolf for two weeks, so I hope you'll cut me some slack for my behavior," he said in an attempt at humor. A lame attempt, because neither of them laughed. "I didn't want this." She made a face and started to look away. "Don't," he said. "Don't look away. You didn't want this, either, Liv. Not for yourself. Not for your daughter." In a softer voice he added, "Not for me."

"No, I didn't," she agreed softly. Her blue eyes were round and pleading. "I didn't mean to . . . I just couldn't kill you. But then I told myself I had to, and Eddy gave me a deadline . . ." She trailed off and sighed. "I just didn't know what else to do."

"Yes, you did. You asked us for help." He went to her then and put his hands on her shoulders. "But the sticking point for me is that you didn't trust me enough to tell me the whole truth."

A tear rolled from the corner of one eye as she whispered, "I'm sorry."

He swiped the tear away with his thumb. "You were right."

She lifted her startled gaze. "What?"

"You were right." He frowned as he thought it through. "Not to think that I wouldn't still help, because I couldn't have lived with myself knowing I'd let an innocent child suffer. But my hatred of the person who did this to me overshadowed everything else I know about you, and that could have endangered us all."

Her gaze searched his, the slightest hint of hope in their depths. "What is it you know about me?" Her voice was a breath of sound, anticipation hovering in its depths. He hated that, too, that she was afraid to feel hope, afraid to think that there might just be a happily-ever-after in all of this for her.

"I know that you're a survivor. Like me. That you don't like asking for help. Like me." He couldn't stop stroking his thumb over the silken skin of her cheek. "That you love your daughter and will do everything you can to protect her."

"Not everything." She blinked and another tear dropped from her lower lashes.

In any other situation he might find it funny that she thought not killing him was a failure on her part. But it wasn't the time for humor, and certainly not gallows humor.

"I couldn't kill you."

"And for that I'm grateful." At her startled look he said, "Really."

"But you said—"

"I said a lot of nonsense, Olivia. For which I'm sorry." Unable to deny his feelings, he dipped his head and placed a gentle kiss on the corner of her mouth. It felt so good to be able to touch her again, to hold her. He couldn't imagine going on with his life without her by his side. "I can only hope that if I'd been placed in the same untenable position as you that I'd have acted as courageously."

She shook her head and pulled back. "I'm not brave, Sully." Her lower lip trembled, and she bit down on it. "I've been scared every single damn day of the last three years."

"Being brave doesn't mean not being scared." He cupped her face in his hands. "It means going ahead in spite of your fear." He glanced toward the bedroom. "It means pushing your fear aside and doing what you know is right, even if it's the hardest thing you've ever done in your life." He stared into Olivia's eyes. "I've met a lot of incredibly brave people in my life. I think you're the bravest person I've ever known."

Her face crumpled. She bit back a sob and leaned into him. Sully wrapped his arms around her and hugged her, letting her cry into his chest, and blinked back the moisture in his own eyes.

God, he wished Miles could die again. Sully'd be the first one to claim the honor of killing the bastard. But together, he and Olivia had destroyed the monster. He was satisfied that Olivia had been the one to make the killing bite. She deserved justice after all Miles had done to her. She needed to move past all of it so she could get on with healing.

Sully rubbed his hands up and down her back, glad she finally could let go, and sad that she had so much built-up grief and anxiety.

After several minutes, Olivia's tears subsided. She drew away, swiping at her cheeks with her hands. She sniffed, and Sully pulled a clean handkerchief out of his back pocket and handed it to her. She accepted it with a watery "Thanks" and wiped her face, then blew her nose.

She fiddled with the cloth a moment, not meeting his eyes. Then she looked up and held out the handkerchief.

"That's okay. You keep it." He smiled at her low chuckle. Clasping her elbows, he drew her close again. He stared down at her face, splotchy from tears, her eyes swollen and red. Even at her worst, she was the most beautiful thing to him. "Forgive me for my earlier less than charitable reaction to the news, Olivia. Let's start again." He held his breath as she seemed to consider it.

"There's nothing to forgive," she finally whispered. She looked up at him. "I hate it that you had to hear it from Eddy. I had planned to tell you when this was all over. I *should* have told you."

"We can't change what happened." He drew in a breath. "If you hadn't made me a werewolf, I would have died with your second attempt."

"My second attempt was here in Tucson. If you weren't a werewolf, you probably wouldn't even have been here."

She sniffed as if fighting back more tears. "Peter wouldn't have run you over, either."

He had thought of that. But Sully knew Miles wouldn't have given up. Ever. "Even if you'd quit after that first attempt, do you think Miles would have stopped trying?" He moved his hands to her shoulders and gave her a little shake. "Do you think he wouldn't have sent someone else after me? Someone like Walter, who wouldn't have had a second's hesitation about killing me?"

Olivia shook her head. "No." Her gaze skittered back to the bedroom door. "Both of us would be dead by now."

He knew her thoughts were once again on her daughter. "And where would that have left Zoe?" He put one hand under her chin and turned her head so he could look into her eyes. "You couldn't have left her to Miles' mercy without a fight, sweetheart. I don't blame you for that. She seems like a good kid—feisty like her mother. I'm looking forward to getting to know her." Thinking of what lay ahead, he smiled.

Her breath caught.

His keen hearing picked up her accelerated heart rate.

"Sully . . ."

"Give us a chance, love. Please." His own heartbeat picked up speed. He stared down at her, willing her to accept him. Accept them.

Accept herself. To believe—to *know*—that with all her flaws she was still a woman deserving of love.

She went up on tiptoe and placed her mouth on his, her hands cradling his face. Tongues met and intertwined, breaths mingled. When she drew away, they both breathed a bit heavier. "I love you, Rory Sullivan."

"And I love you, Olivia Felan. My little warrior wolf."

Whatever the future held—whatever difficulties being a werewolf presented—they would face them together.

The threat from Miles was over, and they had their entire lives to learn about each other and to raise Zoe. And any other children they might have together.

Whether that was in London or in Tucson. Wherever Olivia and Zoe were, that was home.

Epilogue

At Declan's a few days later, Olivia sat on a lounge chair outside and watched Zoe and Sully at the patio table, playing her daughter's favorite card game.

"Do you have any twos?" Sully asked, his voice deep and delightfully crisp. He sat sideways to the table, in a spot in the sun, his long legs stretched out in front of him. He wore only a pair of shorts. The sun glinted off his dark hair and glistened on his skin.

A week in the Tucson sun had given him the beginnings of a nice tan. It suited him. Not that he hadn't been extraordinary looking before, but his darker skin made his teeth seem even whiter, the green of his eyes more vivid.

"Go Fish!" her daughter cried out with glee. Zoe still wore her swimsuit, her feet in flip-flops swinging back and forth beneath the table.

Sully heaved an exaggerated sigh and picked up a card.

"Do you have any . . . sixes?"

He sighed again and handed over the card he'd just drawn. As Zoe giggled and took it, he gave her a suspicious stare. "Are you sure you didn't peek?"

"No!" She giggled again. "Do you have . . . any jacks?"

Sully smirked. "Ha! Go Fish."

Zoe rolled her eyes at what she clearly perceived to be his childish response but picked a card.

"She's really quite adorable." Pelicia sat in the lounger next to Olivia and set down a glass of iced tea on a low table between the two chairs.

"Yes, she is. Thanks," she added, picking up the glass and taking a sip.

"She's lucky to have you."

Olivia shook her head. "I'm the lucky one." She glanced from her daughter to Sully. "In a lot of ways."

Declan walked onto the patio, pausing in a spot of sunshine to close his eyes and tilt his face up with a long indrawn breath. He wore a pair of shorts and, like Sully, was shirtless.

"Did Ryder and Taite make it home all right?" Pelicia asked.

"Aye." He turned and walked toward them. Pelicia moved her legs, and he sat on the bottom of her lounge chair. "Your dad was happy to have them home."

"How is he?" She leaned forward and draped her arm over one of his brawny shoulders.

"He's good. Misses you." He turned his head and placed a kiss on her forearm. He reached up and twined his fingers through hers, holding her hand in a loose grip.

"I miss him, too. But I'll see him in another few weeks." She looked at Olivia. "Have you decided what you're going to do?"

Olivia settled back against the lounger and took another sip of tea. "Sully's going with us to New York. We'll stay long enough to gather some clothes, personal papers, and anything of sentimental value. I'm telling the super to sell everything else. Then we're heading to England to meet Sully's mom and brother."

"Well, I guarantee his mother will fall in love with little Zoe." Declan looked at Olivia with a grin. "She's been pesterin' Sully to settle down and give her grandchildren for years now."

Olivia felt some doubt. "But Zoe isn't her biological grandchild."

Declan shook his head. "Won't matter. Especially as soon as she sees how enamored Sully is of her. That'll make her happy." He looked at his friend. "He was beginnin' to be too much of a lone wolf to suit her. If she only knew."

"Very funny." Sully glanced toward them and then back at Zoe. "Go Fish," he said in response to her request for a three.

"What's funny?" the little girl asked as she reached for the deck of cards.

"Declan's funny. Just Declan." Sully shifted in his chair. "Give me all your sevens," he said in a raspy voice.

She grinned and handed over two cards.

"He is good with her, isn't he?" Olivia leaned her head against the lounger and closed her eyes. When the time came to tell Zoe what her mother was—what she and Sully both were—she was glad he'd be with her.

Her life had come full circle. Once again she and her daughter were safe, and they had a man they both loved who loved them in return.

All she'd had to do was follow her heart.

If you liked this book,
try Bianca D'Arc's
ONCE BITTEN, TWICE DEAD,
available now from Brava!

Somewhere near Stony Brook, Long Island, New York

"Unit twelve," the dispatcher's voice crackled over the radio. Sarah perked up. That was her. She listened as the report rolled over the radio. A disturbance in a vacant building out on Wheeler Road, near the big medical center. Probably kids, she thought, responding to dispatch and turning her patrol car around.

Since the budget cuts, she rolled alone. She hadn't had a partner in a long time, but she was good at her job and confident in her abilities. She could handle a couple of kids messing around in an empty building.

Sarah stepped into the gloomy concrete interior of the building. The metal door hung off its hinges and old boards covered the windows. Broken glass littered the floor and graffiti decorated the walls.

The latest decorators had been junkies and kids looking for a secret place to either get high or drink beer where no one could see. There didn't appear to be anyone home at the moment. They'd probably cleared out in a hurry when they'd seen Sarah's cruiser pull up outside. Still, she had to check the place.

Nightstick in one hand, flashlight in the other, Sarah made

her way into the gloom of the building. Electricity was a thing of the past in this place. Light fixtures dangled brokenly from the remnants of a dropped ceiling as Sarah advanced into the dark interior.

She heard a scurrying sound that could have been footsteps or could have been rodents. Either way, her heartbeat sped up.

"Police," she identified herself in a loud, firm voice. "Show yourself."

She directed the flashlight into the dark corners of the room as she crept inside. The place had a vast outer warehouse type area with halls and doors leading even farther inside the big structure. She didn't really want to go in there, but saw no alternative. She decided to advance slowly at first, then zip through the rest of the building, hoping no one got behind her to cut off her retreat.

She had her sidearm, but she'd rather not have to shoot anyone today. Especially not some kids out for a lark. They liked to test their limits and hers. She'd been up against more than one teenage bully who thought because she was a woman, she'd be a pushover. They'd learned the hard way not to mess with Sarah Petit.

She heard that sort of brushing sound again. Her heart raced as adrenaline surged. She'd learned to channel fear into something more useful. Fear became strength if you knew how to use it.

"This is the police," she repeated in a loud, carrying voice. "Step into the light and show yourself."

More shuffling. It sounded from down the corridor on the left. Sarah approached, her nightstick at the ready. The flashlight illuminated the corner of the opening, not showing her much. The sounds were growing louder. There was definitely someone—or something—there. Perhaps waiting to ambush her, down that dark hallway.

She wouldn't fall for that. Sarah approached from a good ten feet out, maneuvering so that her flashlight could penetrate farther down the black hall. With each step, more of the corridor became visible to her.

Squinting to see better, Sarah stepped fully in front of the opening to the long hallway. There. Near the end. There was a person standing.

"I'm a police officer. Come out of there immediately." Her voice was firm and as loud as she could project it. The figure at the end of the hallway didn't respond. She couldn't even tell if it was male or female.

It sort of swayed as it tried to move. Maybe a junkie so high they were completely out of it? Sarah wasn't sure. She edged closer.

"Are you all right?"

She heard a weird moaning sound. It didn't sound human, but the shape at the end of the long hall was definitely standing on two feet with two arms braced against the wall as if for balance. The inhuman moan came again. It was coming from that shadowy person.

Sarah stepped cautiously closer to the mouth of the hallway. It was about four feet across. Not a lot of room to maneuver.

She didn't like this setup, but she had to see if that person needed help. Sarah grabbed the radio mic clipped to her shoulder.

"This is Unit Twelve. I'm at the location. There appears to be a person in distress in the interior of the building."

"What kind of distress, Unit Twelve?"

"Uncertain. Subject seems unable to speak. I'm going to get closer to see if I can give you more information."

"Should we dispatch an ambulance?"

Sarah thought about it for a half a second. No matter what, this person would need a medical check. Worst-case scenario, it was a junkie in the throes of a really bad trip.

"Affirmative. Dispatch medical to this location. I'm going to see if I can get them to come out, but I may need some backup."

"Dispatching paramedics and another unit to your location. ETA ten minutes on the backup, fifteen on the paramedics."

"Roger that."

With backup and medical help on the way, Sarah felt a little better about taking the next step. She walked closer to the corridor's mouth. The person was still there, still mostly unrecognizable in the harsh light of the flashlight beam.

"Help is coming," she called to the figure. From its height, she thought it was probably a male. He moved a little closer. Wild hair hung in limp hanks around his face. It was longer than most men's, but junkies weren't best known for their grooming and personal hygiene.

"That's it," she coaxed as the man shuffled forward on unsteady feet. "Come on out of there. Help is on the way. No one's going to hurt you."

Sarah stepped into the corridor, just a few feet, hoping to coax the man forward. He was definitely out of it. He made small noises. Sort of grunting, moaning sounds that weren't intelligible. It gave her the creeps, as did the way the man moved. He shuffled like Frankenstein's assistant in those old horror movies, keeping his head down, and his clothes were in tatters.

This dude had to be on one hell of a bender. Sarah lowered the flashlight beam off his head as he moved closer, trying to get a better look at the rest of him. His clothes were shredded like he'd been in a fight with a bear—or something else with sharp claws. His shirt hung off him in strips of fabric and his pants weren't much better.

The dark brown of bloodstains could be seen all over his clothing. Sarah grew more concerned. He had to be in really bad shape from the look of the blood that had been spilled. She wondered if that was all his blood or if there was another victim lying around here somewhere in even worse shape.

His head was still down as he approached and Sarah backed up a step. His hair hung in what looked like greasy clumps. Only as he drew closer did he realize his hair wasn't matted with oil and dirt. It was stuck together by dried blood.

Then he looked up.

Sarah stifled a scream. Half his face was . . . gone. Just gone.

It looked like something had gnawed on his flesh. Blank eyes stared out at her from a ruined face. The tip of his nose was gone, as were his lips and the flesh of one side of his jaw and cheek.

Sarah gasped and turned to run, but something came up behind her and tripped her. She fell backward with a resounding thud, cracking her skull on the hard cement floor.

She fought against the hands that tried to grab her, but they were too strong, and her head spun from the concussion she'd no doubt just received. She felt sick to her stomach. The adrenaline of fear pushed her to keep going. Keep moving. Get away. Survive until her backup arrived.

Thank God she'd already called for backup.

Not one, but two men—if she could call them that—were holding her down. The one with the ruined face had her feet and the other had hold of her arms, even as she struggled against him.

She looked into the first one's eyes and saw . . . nothing. They were blank. No emotion. No feeling. No nothing.

Just hunger.

Fear clutched her heart in its icy grip. The second man looked wild in the dim light from her flashlight. It had rolled to the side, but was still on and lancing into the darkness of the building's interior nearby. Faint light shone on her two assailants.

They both looked like something out of a horror movie. The one from the hallway was, by far, the more gruesome of the two, but the one who wrestled with her arms was frightening too. His skin was cold to the touch and it looked almost gray, though she couldn't be sure in the uncertain light. Neither spoke, but both made those inhuman moaning sounds.

Even as she kicked and struggled, she felt teeth rip into her thigh. Sarah screamed for all she was worth as the first man broke through her skin and blood welled. The second man dove onto her prone form, knocking her flat and bashing her head on the concrete a second time. Stunned, she was still aware when his teeth sank into her shoulder.

She was going to die here. Eaten alive by these cannibals.

Something inside Sarah rebelled at the thought. No way in hell was she going down like this.

Help was on the way. All she had to do was hold on until her backup arrived. She could do that. She *had* to do that.

Channeling the adrenaline, Sarah ignored the pain and used every last bit of her strength to kick the man off her legs. She bucked like a crazy woman, dislodging the first man.

Once her legs were free, she used them to leverage her upper body at an angle, forcing the second man to move. The slight change in position freed one hand. She grasped around for anything on the floor next to her and came up with a hard, cylindrical object. Her nightstick.

Praise the Lord.

Putting all her remaining strength behind it, she aimed for the man's head, raining blows on him with the stick. When that didn't work, she changed targets, looking for anything that might hurt him. She whacked at his body with the hard wood of the stick. She heard a few of the bones in his hand crack at one point, but this guy was tough. Nothing seemed to faze him.

Finally, she used the pointy end of the stick to push at his neck. That seemed to get some results as he shifted away. He moved enough for her to use the rest of her body for leverage, crawling out from under him.

His friend was up and coming back as she crabwalked away on her hands and feet, toward the door and the sunshine beyond. Her backup was coming. She just had to hold on until they could find her.

The two men followed her, moving as if they had all the time in the world. Their pace was steady and measured as she crawled as fast as she could toward the door. It didn't make any sense. They could have easily overtaken her, but they kept to their slow, walking pace.

Sarah hit the door and practically threw herself over the threshold. She had to get out in the open where her backup would see her right away. She was losing blood fast and her vision was dancing, tunneling down to a single dim spot. She was going to pass out any second. She had to do all she could to save herself before that happened.

Backup was coming. That thought kept her going. They'd be here any second. She just had to hold on.

She crawled into the sunlight, near her cruiser. Leaning against the side of her car, she tried for her radio, but the mic was long gone—probably a victim of the struggle with those two men. They were coming for her. They had to be.

But when she looked up, she saw them hesitate at the doorway to the building. The second man stepped through, but the first stayed behind, cowering in the darkness. The second man's skin was gray in the outdoor light. He looked like some kind of walking corpse, with grisly brown stains of dried blood all around his mouth. Some of it was bright red. That was *her* blood. The sick bastard had bitten her.

The man walked calmly forward, under the trees that shaded the walkway to the old building. Sarah had parked on the street, out in open sun. She watched in dread as the man walked steadily toward her, death in his flat gaze.

Then something odd happened. He stopped where the tree cover ended. He seemed reluctant to step into the sun.

Sarah blinked, but there wasn't any other explanation she could think of. Then she heard the sound of an approaching vehicle. Her backup.

With salvation in sight, she finally passed out.

And try LEAVE ME BREATHLESS,
the latest from HelenKay Dimon,
in stores now . . .

"You call that a clinch?"

Whatever it was made Callie's head explode. "Sure."

"Tell me something."

No way was she agreeing to that without more information. Hand this man an opening and he'd steer a submarine through it.

He kept talking anyway. Looked pretty relaxed in his slouch as his smile inched up on his lips. "Do you have a boyfriend?"

If he wanted to shock her . . . well, he did. "How is that relevant?"

"Call me curious."

"Are you allowed to ask me about that?"

"You think there's a law against it?"

"There should be."

"So, you're not going to answer?"

Not until she knew where this was going. "What does the state of my love life have to do with anything?"

"You know all about me. Only seems fair I get some background on you."

"I need to know about your life in order to do my job." At least that was the excuse she used when she ventured outside the file Mark gave her. She'd lost her clearance when she walked away from her job at the FBI, but she still had friends of the computer hacker variety. In just a few hours she had all the paperwork that existed on Ben.

She had admit her little search mission turned out to be a huge disappointment. His background was so clean it squeaked. If he hadn't passed through screening committees and all sorts of interviews to get his current judicial position she would have thought someone manufactured his past. No arrests. No trouble. Great grades. Always within the law. For some reason she expected to find a smart guy with a bad-boy past. That sounded good in the fantasy she created in her head but looked as if it wasn't true.

"So, you're not poking around just because you're nosy?" he asked.

No way could he know about her travels through his personal history. She'd been careful and cleaned up behind her. "I don't poke."

"Tell me what you want to know."

She smelled a con. "Anything?"

"You get one question."

She thought about his decision to leave the military and about the scarce information on his parents. She skipped all of that and went with the issue at the front of her mind. "What's going on between you and Emma?"

"I've already answered that. We're friends."

Callie snorted just to let him know what she thought of his fake deals. "I don't climb all over my friends when the door shuts."

"Really? When do you climb on them then?"

"Huh?"

He closed in. One minute he shot her a lazy smile. The next he stood up straight and hovered over her with his cheek right next to hers. "What do you do with your friends?"

Heat thrummed off him, surrounding her and filling her with tingly sensation from shoulders to toes. "I don't—"

"Do you touch them?" Ben trailed the back of his hand down her cheek. Dragged his thumb across her lips.

"I . . ."

"Smell them?" He leaned down and nuzzled her ear. "Do they smell as good as you?"

His mouth traveled down her neck, nipping and kissing. Hot breath tickled her skin as his fingers caressed her waist. The double whammy of touching slammed her breath to a halt in her chest. Her body strained to get closer to him as her palms skimmed up his back.

Holy crap. "This isn't a good idea," she said.

"Probably not, but I've been wanting to do it all day."

"I thought you were mad at me."

"Be quiet for a second."

Then his mouth covered hers. His lips pressed deep and strong and his tongue brushed against hers. There was nothing teasing about this kiss. It shot through her hot and wet, electrifying every cell inside her. She fell into the sensation of being overpowered and claimed. Her stomach tumbled and her knees dipped. Muscles relaxed as her brain shifted into neutral.

"God, yes," he mumbled when their mouths lifted on gasps of harsh breaths.

He dove back in. His lips met hers over and over again in a kiss that had her winding her arms around his neck and pulling him close.

Him. Her. Touching. Nothing else mattered. Pleasure crashed over her, drowning out everything around them. Fingers searched and sculpted. Her hands swept into his hair while his pushed against her lower back, easing her closer to the junction between his thighs. She heard the grumbling moan in his chest and the deep breaths from her own.

She lifted her head in an attempt to get some air. "Ben . . . that . . ."

"You taste so good."

His mouth found that sensitive spot right at the slope of her chin. Her kryptonite. A few nibbling kisses and she wanted to strip that conservative shirt and tie right off him.

She dropped her head back to give him greater access. "Right there."

When his mouth found hers again, lights exploded in her brain. He kissed like he worked, with an intensity that sent her common sense screaming in wild defeat. The touch of his lips was all she dreamed about and everything she feared.

But her mind shouted out a red light warning through the sensual haze. She had a job and he had a girlfriend.

Callie pulled her mouth away, letting her forehead rest against his cheek as she struggled to breathe without wheezing. "We have to stop."

"God, why?" He mumbled the question against her hair.

"Emma." Callie now hated that name.

With the gentle touch of his palms, he lifted her head and stared down at her. The gaze from deep brown eyes searched her face. The rapid beating in his chest thumped against her as his eyes grew soft.

"I don't cheat," he said in a husky whisper. "If I were with Emma I wouldn't be kissing you."

Callie knew she should pull back, but she rubbed her hands up his back instead. "But, I saw—"

"Evidence of a lifelong friendship." He traced her cheekbones with his thumbs. "That's it."

"You're not—"

"No."

"Does Emma know that?"

His chuckle vibrated against her from everywhere their bodies touched. "Definitely."

Relief washed through Callie. She balanced her head on his chin as she tried to figure out what it all meant. "Now what?"

"You invite me to your house."

Don't miss INSTANT TEMPTATION,
the third in Jill Shalvis's Wilder Brothers series,
coming next month . . .

"I didn't invite you in, T.J.."

He just smiled.

He was built as solid as the mountains that had shaped his life, and frankly had the attitude to go with it, the one that said he could take on whoever and whatever, and you could kiss his perfect ass while he did so. She'd seen him do it too, back in his hell-raising, misspent youth.

Not that she was going there, to the time when he could have given her a single look and she'd have melted into a puddle at his feet.

Had melted into a puddle at his feet. Not going there . . .

Unfortunately for her senses, he smelled like the wild Sierras; pine and fresh air, and something even better, something so innately male that her nose twitched for more, seeking out the heat and raw male energy that surrounded him and always had. Since it made her want to lean into him, she shoved in another bite of ice cream instead.

He smiled. "I saw on Oprah once that women use ice cream as a substitute for sex."

She choked again, and he resumed gliding his big, warm hand up and down her back. "You watch Oprah?"

"No. Annie was, and I overheard her yelling at the TV that women should have plenty of both sex *and* ice cream."

That sounded exactly like his Aunt Annie. "Well, I don't need the substitute."

"No?" he murmured, looking amused at her again.

"No!"

He hadn't taken his hands off her, she couldn't help but notice. He still had one rubbing up and down her back, the other low on her belly, holding her upright, which was ridiculous, so she smacked it away, doing her best to ignore the fluttering he'd caused and the odd need she had to grab him by the shirt, haul him close, and have her merry way with him.

This was what happened to a woman whose last orgasm had come from a battery-operated device instead of a man, a fact she'd admit, oh *never.* "I was expecting your brother."

"Stone's working on Emma's 'honey do' list at the new medical clinic, so he sent me instead. Said to give you these." He pulled some maps from his back pocket, maps she needed for a field expedition for her research. When she took them out of his hands, he hooked his thumbs in the front pockets of his Levi's. He wore a T-shirt layered with an opened button-down that said *Wilder Adventures* on the pec. His jeans were faded nearly white in the stress spots, of which there were many, nicely encasing his long, powerful legs and lovingly cupping a rather impressive package that was emphasized by the way his fingers dangled on his thighs.

Not that she was looking.

Okay, she was looking, but she couldn't help it. The man oozed sexuality. Apparently some men were issued a handbook at birth on how to make a woman stupid with lust. And he'd had a lot of practice over the years.

She'd watched him do it.

Each of the three Wilder brothers had barely survived their youth, thanks in part to no mom and a mean, son-of-a-bitch father. But by some miracle, the three of them had come out of it alive and now channeled their energy into Wilder Adventures, where they guided clients on just about any outdoor adventure that could be imagined; heli-skiing, extreme mountain biking, kayaking, climbing, *anything*.

Though T.J. had matured and found success, he still gave off a don't-mess-with-me vibe. Even now, at four in the afternoon, he looked big and bad and tousled enough that he might have just gotten out of bed and wouldn't be averse to going back.

It irritated her. It confused her. And it turned her on, a fact that drove her bat-shit crazy because she was no longer interested in T.J. Wilder.

Nope.

It'd be suicide to still be interested. No one could sustain a crush for fifteen years.

No one.

Except, apparently, her. Because deep down, the unsettling truth was that if he so much as directed one of his sleepy, sexy looks her way, her clothes would fall right off.

Again.

And wasn't that just her problem, the fact that once upon a time, a very long time ago, at the tail end of T.J.'s out-of-control youth, the two of them had spent a single night together being just about as intimate as a man and woman could get. Her first night with a guy. Definitely not his first. Neither of them had been exactly legal at the time, and only she'd been sober.

Which meant only she remembered.